The Final Girl

WOL-VRIEY

Burning Bulb
PUBLISHING

The Final Girl

WOL-VRIEY

Burning Bulb
PUBLISHING

The Final Girl
By **Wol-vriey**

Burning Bulb Publishing
P.O. Box 4721
Bridgeport, WV 26330-4721
United States of America
www.BurningBulbPublishing.com

Cover photo by Alexander Krivitskiy from Pexels.
Back cover photo by Elijah O'Donnell from Pexels.
Author Photo: Lolade Akinsowon © 2014.

First Edition.

Paperback Edition ISBN: 978-1-948278-26-3

Printed in the United States of America

CHAPTER 1

Rita

"Okay, girls, first thing you need to know is that we're now underground. How far underground? Well that's for you to guess and us to know."

The speaker laughed, letting them know that she was joking. Her voice was warm, pure and oozed contentment. A rich woman's voice. The woman wasn't visible. Her voice appeared to emanate from the large tower in front of them.

"Wow, this is quite some setup they've got here," Rita Hillman told her stepdaughter Megan.

She and Megan were the same age—twenty-four. The pair of them were also dressed similarly, in denim pants, leather jackets and boots. Rita was a couple of inches taller than Megan. She had long black hair, while Megan was a brunette.

Megan Hillman was peering over their platform's breast-high chromium railing. Like she usually did when Rita said something, she merely grunted. However, her eyes were lit up with excitement. She was clearly impressed, but because doing this was Rita's idea, she was trying not to show how pleased she was.

Yeah, she's already caught the action bug, Rita thought coldly. *This'll be a new thrill for her; something to boast to the girls back home about. Though of course, no one will believe a word of what she says.*

"Wow, just wait till the girls back home hear about this," Megan said, confirming her thoughts.

Rita rolled her eyes. "Honey, you do know we signed that non-disclosure agreement, that means we've gotta keep out mouths shut?"

Megan gave Rita a look that asked if she was congenitally naïve. "Yeah and how are they ever gonna enforce that? Insert surveillance software in our tongues?"

"I'm just saying to watch your mouth when we leave here," Rita retorted in turn. "I've heard weird rumors about the guys who run this place: stuff about them being more technically advanced than the CIA."

Megan smirked. "Yeah, like that's even possible." Then she gave Rita another 'are you serious?' stare that made Rita feel like killing her, and turned back to staring at the play zone.

Rita also did the latter and quickly forgot about her stepdaughter as the play zone took up all her attention.

Underground are we? Yes, I can certainly believe that.

***

They were standing on a metal platform suspended halfway up a sheer rock wall, in an octagonal chamber that seemed to be about two hundred yards across. They were about thirty feet up, which afforded them a great view of the play zone. The chamber's perfect angles could be considered a work of art. Spread out below them was a small village—thirty-four houses, several roads between them, and lots of trees. On the enclosure's far side Rita made out a shimmering surface that might be a pond, but the tower obscured any clear view of it.

The tower. The building stood in the exact middle of the octagonal space. Six stories high, it rose to connect the 'valley' below with the stone ceiling. The tower was as much a support structure as a functional building. Only its lower five floors contained living spaces; its sixth level held in place groups of steel and concrete struts that fanned outward to connect to the underside of the play zone's stone ceiling, which itself slanted inward at a forty-five degree angle from about ten feet above Rita and Megan's heads, so that the ceiling was cone-shaped.

Beneath this immense structural adaptation however, was a glass building. Rita knew that it wasn't all glass; she understood that beneath that glittering black exterior surface lay metal and plastic and stone and wood and rooms and hallways and doors and furniture and maybe even people; but that was the impression one got while looking at it—of an immense block of black glass; a black gem exploding from the floor of this chamber hollowed out of rock.

The tower's entire surface was a huge monitor screen.

That's got to cost some serious money, Rita thought. Of course she'd seen giant monitors on the sides of buildings before. But nothing like this, where the screen was five stories high. She and Megan were too far from the tower to see if maybe the giant screen was really a composite of several smaller monitors merged into one.

But even then, considering that it extends around the entire building . . . someone sure sunk a whole lot of cash into this damn project!

The immense screen's uppermost area reflected the glow from the immense 'sun-screens' in the chamber ceiling that flooded everywhere with light; its lowest portion reflected the trees and ground.

At the moment the tower-screen was idling, its screensaver a bright red octopus that swam across its black vertical expanse in pursuit of a terrified mermaid, but never quite catching her; the CGI duo vanishing off to the right to continue their trip around the tower's other three faces.

An inset window at top/right of the screen displayed the countdown time: -15:23.

Quarter of an hour to showtime.

The idea was that regardless of where one was in the play zone, you could follow the action simply by looking up at the tower.

After a quick glance at her stepdaughter, who was still gaping in awe at everything—Rita looked left and right across the chamber. She quickly located the participant platforms on either side of her, each one at exactly the same height as she and Megan were. She knew that all the other six contestants—two women each to a platform—were currently watching the same time display, counting down to the beginning of the reality show.

She also noticed something else: that those further platforms hung along a set of vertical rails. Looking above her, she saw that she and Megan's platform was positioned on a similar vertical track. The metal door behind them was sealed shut.

I guess from here the only way is down.

Curling around the tower's left edge, the octopus and mermaid swum into view again.

Everyone's sharing those two, Rita thought.

Something about the mermaid gave Rita Hillman the creeps. She couldn't say what it was, but watching the fish-woman flee the red octopus filled Rita with an inexplicable dread.

Which is silly, because I should actually be scared of the hunter, not the prey. But instead, I feel a shiver down my spine each time I look at that mermaid; while the octopus leaves me unmoved. Why is that?

The glass tower also created unease in Rita, though she'd already been informed of its internal structure. She and the other contestants in this violent 'game' had been given brochures in which the tower's interior layout was explained. The building's top two floors contained offices. The three lower floors were part of the play zone.

Of course, the brochure had creepily left out what each floor contained. For instance, Rita supposed that the 'aviary' on the third floor housed birds, but she had no idea what species they were.

I for one don't want to stumble in on some buzzards tearing carrion apart. Because, from what I've heard about this reality show, that carrion might be human remains.

***

"This place is great," Megan said, beating on the platform's chrome rails. "I wish I had binoculars. There's so many trees down there that I can hardly see the houses. And cellphones weren't permitted either. I'd have *loved* to photograph all this."

Rita nodded and scratched an itch under her left breast. While replying her stepdaughter, she examined her right hand fingernails for imperfections in their red coating. "Yeah, I know what you mean. I think that's why we're so high up right now before game begins, so we can get a good look at the layout and commit it to memory."

Megan turned to look at her. The expression in her brown eyes was an unfamiliar one to Rita, who was used to Megan being bitchy and combative, determined to not get along; but now Megan seemed almost friendly.

"You sound very calm," Megan said. "Aren't you scared? We're here to fight, remember?"

Rita shrugged. "Not necessarily fight. We just need to find the money and we win the game."

Megan nodded. "Twenty-four million dollars is a hell of a lot of money. If we win, we'll be almost as rich as dad is." Her face took on something of its old belligerence towards Rita. "What you gonna do then, huh? Divorce my dad and marry a guy our age?"

Rita scowled. *Oh no, here we go again.* But she managed to remain calm. "No, honey, I'm not leaving your father for anything. I love Daniel Hillman dearly. And the sooner you accept that fact, the better for the three of us. If *we* win here, it just means our family will have more money."

Megan rolled her eyes. "Wow, and here I was thinking you were a gold-digger."

Rita didn't know how to take that. Was Megan being sarcastic? Was she joking? Or was she honestly surprised?

Has she had a rich-girl epiphany of some kind, and realized that the universe doesn't revolve around her . . . and that her father isn't her exclusive property? If so, there might still be some hope for us. If not, well, what will be will be.

Rita frowned. "Hey, if your dad ever finds out we did this there'll be hell to pay. You know how he is about me doing anything risky while I'm trying to get pregnant. So don't you dare tell him what we did tonight. I've made a point of keeping him in the dark."

Megan rolled her eyes. "Yeah, yeah, I ain't a kid. He'll never know." Then her facial expression turned puzzled. "But, Rita, even if we *can* explain how we've both been missing for over a day now without calling home, how are we ever gonna explain a twenty-four million dollar windfall?"

Rita was staring out at the play zone. Ten minutes left to get busy. Suddenly she felt impatient; dying to begin. "Leave that to me," she told her stepdaughter. "I'll come up with something plausible."

She returned her attention to studying the terrain below her; trying to commit as much of it as she could to memory.

CHAPTER 2

Karen

Memory: Gun in hand, she'd been hurrying down a dark corridor, in an abandoned Salt Lake City house where druggies congregated.

She'd pushed a dirty door open, heard some voices yelling, and then she was staring at Lexi Austin's drugged-up face. And then next thing there was a gun pointing at her, her perspective quickly narrowing to the black hole at the tip of its muzzle . . .

Bang!

A lightning flash. Something hit her in the head. For a fraction of time she felt intense pain as if her universe had exploded and then the world faded from around her. Faded completely to black.

Next thing it was hot, so intensely hot for a while that she felt as if she was baking . . . and she was screaming . . . and then even that terrifying heat faded.

And suddenly there was light again and she was here, standing on this artificial ledge, in this giant cave hollowed out of rock, staring at the giant black monitor tower in the middle of the area and trying to make sense of things.

Shit, I was dead. Yeah, I was dead for real. Lexi shot me in the head! She blew my brains out.

Salt Lake City cop Karen Rogers shook her head, trying to clear it and regain her memory. But there was nothing to find. She knew who she was; knew she was a police detective who'd been working a drug bust; but that was all there was.

No, there was a little more: *I'd gotten a late-night tip that Lexi's boyfriend, Johnny Walker had just gotten in a big shipment from his connection in Ohio. But the Chief had just suspended my partner Rick for some reason, so I set out alone and . . . Oh heck! I wish I could recall more than this!*

The memories hurt. *It's like Lexi's bullet blew my personality out of the back of my head, not my brains. I can't even remember if I had a family—husband or kids or whatever.*

And no, Karen Rogers hadn't really just woken up out here on this platform. It just seemed that way because trying to recall the past had completely disoriented her.

She'd been awake for several days now, but groggy . . . first lying in a hospital bed in a room with a red octopus painted on its ceiling, while lots of doctors examined her; asking for a laptop or phone to contact the outside world and being told "Not yet," and later sitting in another room with seven other women, listening to explanations as to why she was here; explanations that still made little sense.

I'm a contestant in a reality show? Me? What the hell?

She had seen the repair work the doctors had done on her head. Her brown hair had since grown back, but when she'd first woken up her scalp had been shaven, and the surgeons had held up a pair of mirrors so she could see both the front and rear of her skull. She had two souvenir scars: a small stitched puncture on her left temple and a larger patch (the skin graft was about the size of a beer coaster) at the back. Both wounds were already healed.

She'd wondered then what she wondered now: *Why am I not dead?*

Being a cop meant Karen Rogers was no stranger to gunshot wounds. The way her head had looked . . .

Like this bitch beside me blew my brains out that night. I was dead—I'm certain I died . . . and that hot place? Was that Hell? And if I died and went to Hell, how the hell am I alive again, standing up here on this wall with the woman who shot me handcuffed to me? Why is Lexi here with me?

That was the final part of the puzzle. Karen's partner in this crazy game was none other than the murderous Lexi Austin.

Lexi had been staring out over the game chamber. She seemed to feel Karen's gaze on her and turned to stare at her. "You got all your wits about you yet?"

Karen nodded. "Yeah, sort of." She was too confused to muster up any rage against the woman. Instead she concentrated on Lexi; hoping that staring at her would trigger some fresh memories.

No success. All she remembered was that the redheaded Lexi Austin was a prostitute. She looked to be about 25-years-old. Karen figured the young woman was a cocaine addict too—because her boyfriend Johnny Walker sold coke—but she seemed clearheaded

7

enough now. In contrast to Karen, who was wearing jeans and a tee shirt, Lexi had on a sheer pink halter top, black hot pants, red pantyhose and red high heels. She had large breasts and was conspicuously not wearing a bra, her nipples poking the gauzy pink fabric of her top as if she was sexually aroused. A garish red purse completed her outfit. Her makeup was thick and unflattering, the centerpiece of which was a pouting red mouth that seemed to primed to suck penis.

Once a hooker, always a hooker, Karen thought with distaste, looking the woman down and then back up again. *Like there's anyone here to sell herself to.*

Her blue eyes met Lexi's green ones and the girl flinched.

"Yeah, girl, I shot ya in the head," Lexi said. "And the way you look right now? You look like you need me to do it again."

Karen felt some anger. "What? You dare say that again and I'll throw you over the side of this platform." To make her point, she gestured out into space, towards the tower, where that cute hungry octopus was busy chasing the creepy mermaid in circles around the black building-screens. Didn't the silly thing realize that the mermaid was dangerous and was merely teasing it, luring it to its death?

Lexi looked scared for a moment, her green eyes widening in fright. "Hey, I didn't mean it like that—of course, I ain't gonna shoot ya again. I'm just making a point here." Then she frowned. "And you can't throw me over even if you wanted to."

Karen was about to retort angrily to that, when Lexi added with a nervous smile, lifting her right wrist, which was cuffed to Karen's left one, "Hey, I think that's why we're chained together? The organizers of this reality show assumed one of us might want to hurt the other, but they don't think we're suicidal?"

Karen nodded. She saw sense in that. "Yeah, you're right. Just don't make any crappy jokes about shooting me again. You already did enough damage once. At the moment I can't remember either poop or the toilet I'm supposed to crap in."

Lexi nodded nervously and smoothed her top. "Listen, I know this sounds crappy after I did it anyway, but I'm sorry about shooting you. Honest. I didn't mean to. I was just coked up to the gills that night and scared and Johnny was yelling and . . . and the gun just went off in my hand."

Karen waved her apology off. "Yeah, whatever, girl. That's what you cop-killers all say—you never meant to shoot us law-enforcement officers."

"Listen, it's true," Lexi protested. "I didn't mean to shoot you. I've never shot anyone before in my life. I don't even own a gun!"

Karen rolled her eyes. "Yeah, yeah. Okay, I forgive you. You didn't kill me, though I sure thought you had." She stopped when she saw the strange look on Lexi's face. "What's it now? You're having a change of heart about not succeeding?"

The prostitute quickly shook her head. No, it isn't that. It's just what you said about me not killing you. 'Cos I sure as hell thought I had. When I shot you, I mean. Your brains all blew out the back of your head like wet popcorn. I know, 'cos see, jacked up on coke like I was? I went over and had a look and even poked my hand around in the hole—it was so big my entire fist fit in there. I was giggling at all the blood squirting out. And it sure was a damn lot and your brains were all over the floor? I was sure you'd bought the farm, but . . . seeing you here now like nothing happened? Well, that don't make no sense."

While talking, Lexi had been fiddling around inside her purse for something. She pulled it out now—a small jar full of white powder. Cuffed to Karen as she was though, using the cocaine initially proved difficult; as there was no way she could simultaneously uncap the jar and dip into it with just her left hand free.

Finally, after shrugging apologetically at Karen, she lifted their linked wrists up onto the brass rail around their platform, and then after transferring the coke jar to her right hand, uncapped it with her left hand.

Karen smirked as Lexi dug a long red fingernail into the cocaine, and raised it to her nose. *Girl, hasn't that narcotic caused you enough grief already?*

"Ah, that feels much better," Lexi said with approval. She offered the coke to Karen. "Want some? The organizers gave it to me; the highest grade blow I've ever had. Really helps clear the head."

"Put that shit away before I take it from you and shove it up your pussy. You should know better than trying to corrupt a cop."

Lexi nodded and quickly put her cocaine back into her purse. But what she'd just said about clearing her head had made Karen realize something.

Hey, my mind is perfectly clear—as clear as the sparkling water in that pond over there, so long as I don't try to remember anything that happened before this cokehead slut shot me. She tapped her foot and frowned. *But I've still got more questions than answers. For instance, I've no idea where I am now—or even how I got here. Who were those doctors who fixed me? The hospital walls were decorated with images of red octopuses just like the one floating on the tower. And why, after fixing me, wasn't I returned to police duty in Salt Lake City, or at least sent home to properly recuperate? Where do I live anyway? How old am I? Do I have a husband? Boyfriend? Kids? Parents? Or a girlfriend? Am I gay or straight even?*

Lexi wasn't saying anything more, so Karen forgot her for a while and instead stared out at the black tower that dominated the landscape ahead, and around which the octopus still pursued the mermaid. The onscreen time was -9:13. Then she looked down at the houses and routes spread below them in the play zone. She tried to recall what she could of the game they were supposed to be playing down here:

The Final Girl? The prize is twenty-four million dollars, if we can find it. She sneaked a quick glance over at Lexi. *Unfortunately, only one of us can win the money, so I'm sure Lexi is planning on shooting me in the head again once she has a chance. So much for apologies.*

What else had she heard during those shadowy briefing sessions? Despite the fact that she could think clearly, short-term memory required some effort.

Yeah, there's supposedly monsters down there in the play zone and boogeymen too. Yeah, right. Like this is some kid's nightmare. Pull the other one, guys. And there's weapons down there too; deadly weapons. Guns and whatnot. Tonight is apparently time for some serious violence.

Karen Rogers didn't consider not competing in the game. In fact, now that she was out here on this platform staring down at the 'play zone,' she felt impatient to get started. She intended to win. She felt the desire to locate and hold on to the money down in the zone as an intense compulsion.

Yes, that prize money is all mine. Though I'm not even sure why I want it so bad. But those other girls in this? The creepy twins and the mother and daughter? It's a goddamned joke if they honestly think they stand a chance against me.

But, oh, the past tantalized her with its secrets.

However, there was something that she *could* find out.

"Hey, Lexi. How did you get here?"

This time Lexi didn't turn to look at her. Her attention was instead taken up by a drone that was flying past them.

Oh yeah, that's the other thing, the REALLY CREEPY THING about this. According to what the games-mistress Miriam told us, this is being beamed out live on the Dark Web for a select group of wealthy viewers to enjoy and bet on. Everything we do down there in the play zone will be seen and rated. This is entertainment. We are entertainment.

-7:31, the clock on the tower read.

She tapped Lexi's shoulder. "Hey, slut, I asked you a question: How did you wind up here?"

Still staring at the video drone, which was hovering five yards away from them as if filming close-ups, Lexi said: "That's the other weird thing that happened. See, when the cops found your body—hey, they said you were dead too—I was arrested and charged with murder. At first, no one even knew who'd shot you, but then one of the crackheads had a fight with Johnny because he wouldn't sell any stuff to him on credit—I mean, the S.O.B already owed Johnny a grand— and he ratted us out to the pigs. So like, I got arrested at the nail salon, and the Salt Lake City cops were still looking for Johnny to arrest him too as an accomplice . . ." Her voice turned confused. "But then all the charges against me were suddenly dropped. Which I thought was odd, 'cos even if you weren't dead like Johnny's flashy new lawyer told me, shouldn't I have been prosecuted for at least *attempted* murder? I mean, I did shoot ya, even if I didn't mean to do it."

"Yeah, that's weird," Karen agreed. The drone had flown off now, zipping down towards a clump of trees that lay beside the road directly below them. Karen gave a sudden start. She'd seen something pale and unnatural-looking scuttle along a branch as the drone flew past it, something that a sent a chill down her spine and also brought the idea of monsters afresh to her mind.

"So well, then this rich lawyer dude gives me a ride home in his swanky limo—girl, I mean that car was the shit. I ain't never been in a limo before, not even to suck dick—and so I'm sitting in the back there, living it up, drinking fancy champagne, and suddenly I smell gas . . . well, you know the rest of the story."

The redhead hooker then stood up on tiptoes and peered down, bending so far forward over the railing that Karen got prepared to grab her in case the cocaine in her system had her thinking she could now fly. "Oh, and then they—Miriam and Aaron Heller and the

ROC—they offered me a chance to win twenty-four million bucks. Now, who the hell's gonna be crazy enough to say no to that? Well, not me anyway. I've been poor and downtrodden all my life; so damn poor that for me, hooking up with Johnny Walker and getting into the drug-dealing life was like going to Heaven while still alive. So, no way was I ever gonna say no to playing this game here. But then, I saw you again. I don't mind telling you, girl, seeing you that first time? Now that was frigging scary."

Lexi had been speaking while practically hanging in midair, her feet hovering off the floor like she was exercising in a gym. Now she settled back down onto the platform. Karen found herself heaving a sigh of relief.

Five minutes more. Okay, what I've gotta do now is ensure Lexi doesn't snort any more coke until the show begins and we're safely down in the play zone.

She stood quietly, digesting what Lexi had just told her, waiting for the game to begin.

And still that CGI mermaid swimming across the black tower opposite them bothered her. *What is wrong with that thing? Why do I find it so creepy?*

CHAPTER 3

Berry/Cherry

"Hey, I've worked it out,"

"Worked what out?"

Cherry Poole pointed. "Why that cartoon mermaid on the tower looks so damn creepy."

Berry Poole nodded. "Yeah, she really is a creep. So why?"

"It's 'cos she's really human."

"Huh? Sis, make sense!"

Cherry did her best to explain: "You know, I know—everyone knows that mermaids are half people and half fish, right?"

"Yeah, so?"

"Well, that one isn't. She's all 'people.' Take a good look at her body. What she's got below her waist isn't scaly. It's skin like you and I have."

"For real? Hey, you're right! Yeah, I see it now. She doesn't have any scales."

"I see scars on her tail. Do you see scars, sis?"

"Yeah, I do too! Long scars—"

"—like someone sewed her legs together to make a tail. Oh my God, that's so creepy. Sis, maybe we shouldn't have—"

"—come here after all. Daddy Poole's really gonna miss us if anything goes wrong."

"Calm down, calm down," Cherry said, hugging her twin sister tightly like they always did to each other. "We'll be fine. We're gonna win this thing."

Berry smiled. "You really think we will?"

"Of course we will."

"I agree with you. We'll win! We'll win." And on that optimistic note the twins returned their attention to the giant tower screen, where the creepy mermaid had once again reappeared. The pursuing crimson cephalopod's tentacles would almost encircle the green-haired girl's tail but always just miss it. Oh, the twins now found the tail gross. It really did look like someone had sewn the girl's legs together to make a tail: the big fin at its end looked like flattened feet with very long froglike webbed toes.

"Ugh, that's grotesque."

"Yeah, for real, it is. Who the hell—"

"—could've done that to her?"

"She's just a cartoon animation. Look at her—"

"—her tail's flapping about like a fish's body does. She doesn't have legs down there—"

"—except someone's broken them. Ugh, you're right. But what if—"

"—someone *did* break 'em? Sis, they didn't. She looks too normal to have broken legs in her tail."

"Are you sure? 'Cos there's a pond down here right in front of us—"

"—and I can see weird pale things swimming in it. But still, let's not get—"

"—all dramatic now. Those are just the reflections of the bright lights overhead. Hey, that rich witch Miriam said there'll be monsters after us. And boogeymen. Maybe the mermaid is one of the monsters. Ugh!"

"You know, I don't think the rich witch likes us."

More sibling hugging ensued. Then, breaking apart again, they returned their eager stares towards the black tower.

"But we're gonna win—"

"—the damn prize. Right!"

"Damn right we are!"

Doing things together (often in perfect synch) was always the case with the Poole twins. The girls were 23-years-old (with Berry the older by fifteen minutes), both five foot five inches tall and completely identical. (Their longsuffering parents had given up on working out which one was which by the time they were six. At that age Cherry and Berry had had the epiphany that looking at one another was the same as staring in the mirror, and that simply by pretending to be each other and answering one another's names and wearing one another's clothes they could get away with catastrophic levels of mischief.)

The only way to tell them apart was by their hair. At the moment Cherry had red hair and Berry had blue hair—or was it the other way around? Truth be told, the girls themselves often weren't certain which one of them was which on any particular day.

In the seventeen years between their 6-year-old epiphany and the present day, the twins had become completely enmeshed. Each was now completely unable to function normally without her sister being nearby; if not in the same room, then within vocal-summoning distance. Most times they had to be doing exactly the same thing at the same time, or else they got anxious and began trembling.

Berry and Cherry Poole had essentially become the same person, with a shared personality that each could tap into as she wished.

It generally made no difference which of them made a comment, as they tended to agreed with themselves about everything. And when the girls were on a psychic roll like right now? Then they even finished one another's sentences, continuing a conversation or train of thought in one long unbroken stretch of words that disoriented and sometimes even unnerved the listener.

Now the girls stood there staring at the black tower. Both were dressed exactly alike—black sneakers, white skirts, black leather jackets over white tee-shirts.

It was quite hot here in the play zone, hot enough to grow palm trees apparently, because there was a clump of the plants around the pond, in which Berry (or was it Cherry?) still thought she could make out something long and white sliding along the rocks down at the bottom of the water, though this time she didn't mention it to her sister.

"I think we're somewhere hot, maybe in Florida."

"Texas. New Mexico." She waved at a drone as it floated below their platform, its video camera tilted up towards them. "Sucks that they gassed us out cold before transporting us here. So now we've no idea where—"

"—the hell we are. Yeah, I know. The palms say we're in—"

"—sunny California. Maybe Hollywood even, 'cos they're filming us. So remember, sis—"

"—no masturbating. Yeah, I know. There's cameras watching us."

"Like that ever stopped us before. Remember our—"

"—webcam show '*Two for the Price of Fun?*'"

"Yeah, that was really hot and really cool; we were raking in the dough. But Daddy Poole found out and—"

"—that was that. He was right though. We didn't need the money, so why—"

"—prostitute ourselves? But we do need the money now."

Cherry (or Berry) grinned. "Yeah, we do. It'll suck to be poor after being well off. So we'll do our absolute best to win this damn game." She leaned over the railing and yelled down at the pond surface. "Hey, monsters, we're—"

"—coming ta git ya! Whoopee! We're gonna—"

"—win this contest even if it kills you to do so! Yeah we—"

"—are, bitches! Whoopee!"

***

Cheryl 'Cherry' and Beryl 'Berry' Poole were from Columbia, South Carolina. Their parents were Marilyn and Darryl Poole (the twins called their father 'Daddy Poole' because they thought it was cute). Marilyn and Darryl had initially wanted two more children, but once their twin daughters had begun acting like one person all the time they'd given up on sex-for-reproduction and switched to sex-for-relaxation-and-pleasure instead. Thank God for contraceptive implants.

Anyhow, Darryl Poole had run a successful business until he'd suddenly gone bankrupt overnight.

If Darryl's loving wife Marilyn had been distraught at the penny-pinching changes this would mean to their lifestyle, his two daughters had been devastated. For one thing 'Daddy Poole' had promised them a brand new Ferrari Portofino for their 24th birthday—November 27—and now they wouldn't be getting it. And that was just the tip of the iceberg of the cash-strapped changes to come.

The twins weren't having it. The solution to their problem was obvious. They had to earn money.

But how do you earn money when you're completely enmeshed with someone else? Previously they'd worked for their father, which meant they could usually be in the same room at the same time. Few businesses outside of the porno industry hired twins just for the sake of it, and the girls weren't into whoring themselves.

Berry and Cherry had worked for others once before. After an argument with their father three years ago, Cherry had somehow wrangled a job at a cake shop and Berry had simultaneously gotten employed at the bookshop directly across the road from it. They'd chosen these two jobs because both places of employment had wide storefront windows through which they expected to be able to see each other.

It hadn't worked out though. Although Berry was at the cash register in the bookshop's front room, Cherry had unfortunately been banished to the cake shop's back rooms.

Their employment didn't last long. Both of them got fired for continually phoning the other to ask how she was doing, or hurrying across the road to check on her.

The girls' only gripe on being fired after just two weeks of employment was that although they'd lost their jobs on the same day, they'd not been fired at exactly the same time. (Cherry had lost her job fifteen minutes later than Berry had; though neither twin had realized or questioned the significance of this.)

But wherever there's a will, there always tends to be a way to achieve one's goals in life. Fortunately for the Poole girls there were people with money who didn't mind spending it on frivolities. Unscrupulous folks with LOTS of money, and who desired strange and twisted entertainment.

Enter the Dark Web. And the Red Octopus Corporation a.k.a the ROC. And the reality show called *The Final Girl*.

"How the hell are we gonna earn some dough?" Cherry (or Berry) had asked one night. The identity confusion between them that night was a regular one. That afternoon they'd both dyed their hair at the salon—naturally, the twins were blondes—and now, despite previous agreement on who would have which hair color (at that time peach or orange because they'd been on a fruit kick), they couldn't remember which of them was which. The normal cure for this was to use their cellphones' fingerprint ID scanners. But they'd switched their identities around so much now that even if their identical white Samsungs identified one of them as 'Cherry' and the other as 'Berry,' it really meant nothing: they had no way of remembering what their names had been when they'd purchased the phones, or even which phone actually belonged to whom.

To their credit, the Poole twins were both gorgeous—with movie star looks—and weren't geeky, which made them quite popular and also helped people overlook their many character quirks.

They always ate together; always eating and drinking exactly the same things and exactly the same amount, so they'd continue to weigh the same thing. For the Poole twins a difference in weight between them of even 1 kg was a tragedy; one to be tackled with vigorous exercise and dietary restrictions.

So, "How the hell are we gonna earn some dough?" Cherry (or Berry) asked.

"Hey, I think I know," Berry (or Cherry) replied. "Remember that reality show that Chill told us about—"

"—when he was stoned? I think it's still on."

"Yeah, let's have a look!"

'Chill' Bill Wachowski was their cousin, a rapper. It was generally agreed by all and sundry (including Chill's own parents) that the guy had zero talent. And yet someone kept pushing his songs on the radio and spending exorbitant amounts of money producing killer hip-hop videos for him. Almost as if he'd made a deal with the Devil.

Berry shook her head. "Hey, forget Chill. I remember now that—"

"—we asked him about it the next day and he denied it all. But you know, sis—"

"—yeah, I'm sure the dude was lying—I saw it in his eyes. He was acting scared; like he imagined—"

"—his rap crew were gonna gut him for snitching to us."

"Or maybe like El Diablo will come—"

"—to collect his soul if he told us. Girl, sometimes Chill acts creepy as hell. And that stripper girlfriend of his—"

"—I mean, Cancer Dancer? I'd swear that girl is a bonafide witch. I can honestly imagine Cancer—"

"—riding a broom and looking for babies to eat."

"Yeah, me too. Chill's cool, but he does—"

"—way too many drugs. You know rappers and weed and coke and shit. But let's—"

"—not get distracted. You're right, sis. I know he mentioned a website. Dark Web stuff. But I don't—"

"—remember it."

"I do. Finalgirl.roc.org. I memorized it. Chill said there—"

"—was a lot of prize money involved. Millions of bucks."

"Yeah, imagine if we won that. Just imagine it. We'll be—"

"—real rich bitches. Ha ha, yeah—"

"—sis, we'd be wealthy again."

And that had led to the here and now.

By the time Cherry and Berry Poole had applied to join *The Final Girl*, the show's roster had already been finalized. But once the underground show's producers had seen how gorgeous the twins were, there had been no question of not inviting them to participate. And so the original six contestants had become eight.

***

The digital clock on the tower now read -6:13.

Cherry yawned. "This had better start soon. I'm getting bored."

Berry yawned too. "Me too. But let's keep studying—"

"—the layout of this place so we don't get lost—"

"—once we're down on the ground. Yeah—"

"—we need an advantage in the game."

One of the twins pointed at the tower. "The play zone is octagonal. There's eight of us competing. That girl—"

"—and her stepmom—I don't recall her name—"

"It's Megan, but I don't recall—"

"—her stepmom's name either. Weird though that they're both like exactly the same age."

"Yeah, I bet her dad's a dirty old man. Okay so, well—"

"—Megan is right opposite us. Directly behind the tower. Hey, I wish that mermaid display would change to something nicer."

"Me too. Then going left, or anticlockwise, next are that redhead hooker—"

"—and the other girl who looks out of her mind—the one with the scar on her forehead."

"Lexi and Karen."

"Then there's us over here."

"Correct, sis."

Cherry pointed right, to about seventy-five yards away, where, above a tropical explosion of foliage, the final contestants waited on their own suspended platform, halfway up another of the octagon's sheer vertical walls. "And over there are that Arab girl Fatima, and the nurse—"

"—yeah, I think she's a nurse—what's her name again?"

Berry pouted and thought for a minute. "Emily. Emily Ford. I don't think—"

"—that she likes us. It's 'cos she knows we're gonna give this crazy game whatever it takes to win it. And I don't think that—"

"—Muslim girl Fatima likes us either. Each time she looked at us during the briefing I could read—"

"—the judgment in her eyes, like she considered us decadent western sluts."

"No problem there—we are decadent sluts! Well, yeah, Cherry—"

"—we're *sort of* sluts, when we have a boyfriend to share. But what I'm saying is—"

"—we gotta watch out for Fatima. She might try to kill us early in the game. But there's—"

"—zero chance of that happening. Hey look, the screen is—"

"—coming alive. Thank God the creepy mermaid's gone."

"Hey, Cherry, it's Miriam Heller."

"I'm Berry, Cherry. Don't get us confused again. We need to keep—"

"—a clear head for this."

"Sorry. Okay, I've got blue hair—"

"—so I'm Cherry. You, Berry, have got blue hair."

"That's right. I'll let you know when you can be me again, and we'll switch then, right?"

"Cool, let's hear what Miriam has to say."

***

The entire face of the tower opposite them had altered to show the games-mistress, meaning the twins (and those staring at the tower's other three faces) were looking at a thirty-foot-high image of Miriam Heller. The games-mistress was wearing a blue pantsuit over a pink blouse.

The woman was a cold-faced brunette, and showed all the signs of being immensely rich; for instance both her wristwatch and her earrings sparkled with large diamonds. She and her husband, the always-smiling Aaron Heller, had been very nice to the twins during their series of meetings.

Cherry and Berry Poole greatly approved of Miriam, and desired to be like her: wealthy and powerful.

"Welcome again to the show, ladies," Miriam Heller said, gesturing with a giant hand at the digital clock which still remained at the top/right of the screen. "In exactly five minutes, the platforms you're standing on will lower you to the ground and you'll step into the play zone. The game starts once you're all down on the ground." She laughed, a beautiful if cold sound that, like her voice, seemed to come from the air around them. "This is your last chance to ask me any questions you might have before then. Each of your platforms has a powerful microphone built into its protective railing. The microphone is activated by covering that little octopus-shaped hole in the top of the rail with your hand. So go ahead and speak, I'll hear whatever you say."

The twins had both ignored the octopus-hole in the chrome railing, thinking it was merely a design thing. Similarly, neither of them initially noticed the pair of drones that now floated into filming range twenty feet away from them; the one on the right focusing on Cherry (Berry?), the other angling its lens to capture images of her sister.

"I wanna ask her something," Cherry said and moved her hand to cover the octopus-shaped hole. But before she could do so, an inset window flickered into view on the tower face beside Miriam and Fatima's face appeared in it.

"Yes, Fatima, what is your question?" Miriam asked pleasantly.

"That chick is really starting to really annoy me," Cherry Poole said.

"Me too," her twin agreed with a vigorous nod. "She just stole our face space."

"And I can't help but feel jealous of her. She's so damn—"

"—hot-looking. It should be illegal for a non-American woman to be that pretty."

"Yeah, too bad we're gonna have to kill her, right? It's a shame—"

"—a total waste of beauty."

"Shit happens, Cherry, even beauty salons have toilets. The game is the game and we're in it—"

"—to win it. Yeah, so we might as well listen to—"

"—what Fatima wants to know?"

CHAPTER 4

Fatima

"Well, Mrs. Heller," Fatima Noori said, "I just want to make sure I completely understand the rules here."

"There are no rules," Miriam promptly replied, her voice loud, regal, and powerful in the void above the play zone. "None whatsoever. What you have here is an objective . . . and that objective is to find the sum of twenty-four million dollars which the Red Octopus Corporation has nicely hidden down there in the play zone for you pretty ladies . . . and once you've located that money, you hold onto it—taking on all comers—until we determine you to be the winner of the show."

Fatima felt uncomfortable. She knew it was silly, but she couldn't shake the impression that the giant female image on the tower was staring directly at her and maybe even reading her mind. This impression was reinforced by the two drones now hovering in front of her. The one on the left was clearly the one projecting her image on the tower beside Miriam. The other drone would be filming Emily, who was standing on her right.

Fatima kept her hand pressed over the hole that activated the microphone; she didn't want anyone interrupting till she'd had her say—the clock above the digital games-mistress showed that there were just four minutes left to showtime and she needed to clarify some things. "Well, when you say—no rules—do you mean that literally?"

Miriam looked thoughtful and then shrugged. "Well, work this out, Fatima"— she made a sweeping gesture with her arm—"hey, and that goes for the rest of you girls too . . . this reality show is called the *Final Girl*. Final . . . meaning only *one* of you can win. We've grouped you in pairs not because we want you to work together, but because due to time constraints and shipping problems we've not yet built the remaining four platforms. So, down there in the zone there's twenty-four million bucks waiting to be found and kept, but . . . to keep it, you'll have to do whatever it takes . . . by any means necessary. Do you all get it now?"

Fatima Noori imagined a series of nervous nods from the other women suspended above the 'play zone.' She was about to ask for even more clarification, but Miriam spared her the hassle of the question, pacing left and right across the giant screen and counting off points on her fingers:

"So, let's get this straight, so you all understand me clearly before I send you down there to fight it out. Once more, there are no rules at all on this show. You're permitted to kill, maim, mutilate—to do whatever it takes for you to win. So, despite the fact that three of you pairs are very familiar with each other, I expect double-crossing and good old-fashioned backstabbing to soon be the order of the day." She paused for a moment with her hands held in a prayer-like pose before her face, which let them all see her perfectly manicured fingernails. "And that's just concerning you contestants. Remember there are also the boogeymen and monsters to contend with. Ignore those at your peril. The monsters will just eat you. The boogeymen might mutilate, kill, maim . . . or even rape you."

Miriam seemed to remember something then, because she laughed coldly. Fatima once more had the impression that the giant female image was staring directly at her. She wished she could shoo away the drone that was filming her.

"Oh, and Fatima?"

"Yes, Mrs. Heller?"

Miriam laughed. "This show has one great plus for you—unlike on my other game show, losing your virginity here doesn't automatically disqualify you. If you get raped by any of the boogeymen you're still in the show. So you don't need to die to protect your hymen. Just try not to die, period."

That comment made Fatima blush and step back, involuntarily breaking her contact with the octopus-hole. She leapt forward to cover the hole again, but another face had already replaced hers on the inset screen; that of the policewoman Karen, the one who said she'd couldn't remember the past.

"Wow, that must've been embarrassing for you. Letting everyone know you're still a virgin at your ripe age."

Fatima turned to stare at her companion. Emily Ford seemed to be about her own age, about twenty three. But there the similarities ended. Where Fatima Noori was tall and athletic, with long black hair and piercing dark eyes, Emily Ford was petite and busty, with short brown hair and blue eyes. However, they were similarly dressed, in jeans, sneakers and tee shirts. All of the women on the show were lookers, and Emily was no exception; she looked very sexy and Fatima knew the show's male watchers would kill to have her in their beds.

Emily was also deceptively fast; which Fatima knew she had to watch out for once the show got under way. Because, as Miriam had just implied, unlike she and Emily Ford, who hardly knew each other, the three other pairs—the mother and stepdaughter, the cop and the hooker, and those twins—all had some history together and shouldn't get around to backstabbing one another for a while.

Fatima wrinkled her brow in disgust. Ugh, those twins were just . . . ugh! So creepy, acting like they couldn't do anything if separated from each other. Fatima knew there was a word—a psychiatric term—for the way Cherry and Berry Poole behaved, but she couldn't remember it. *No, I don't think 'codependency' is quite the right term to describe their behavior—this seems way more serious than that.* And without her cellphone she'd had no way to look it up online.

Once they'd realized that Fatima was a devout Muslim, both Poole girls had made a point of proclaiming themselves 'sexually and socially liberated' whenever she was nearby.

Damn sluts, the pair of them. She had no idea if they were harassing her simply because they were racist bigots, or if they were doing so to unsettle her before the competition started, so as to reduce her chances of winning. Either way, she really disliked those twins.

Fatima Noori was herself an identical twin, and she and her spitting-image sister Khadija were nothing like the Poole girls. *We're Persian-American women with dignity. We're not tramps handing out our precious bodies to just anyone who comes knocking on our door.*

"Where I come from, being a virgin at my age is a thing of pride and joy, and not a disgrace," she finally replied Emily. A joke really, because she was actually from the Bronx in New York. But she was referring both to her Iranian heritage and her faith in Islam's holy prophet.

Emily laughed and shrugged. "Well, each to her own, I guess. But consider this, honey—what if you die here tonight, without ever having known the sweetness of a man's caresses? Won't you regret that?"

"Let's pay attention to what the cop is asking," Fatima retorted. "We might learn something of interest that could keep us alive in the play zone."

"Oh, someone's feeling touchy," Emily said with a giggle.

"Oh, I don't mean to be nasty," Fatima quickly apologized. "It's just that I think we're missing vital info by talking to each other instead of listening." But really, Emily's statement had struck a raw nerve in her. Questioning her faith—or more accurately her father's ultra-strict version of it—was the key reason why she was here competing on the *Final Girl.*

And yes, it will be absolutely horrible to get killed tonight without ever having kissed a boy before.

She and Emily both returned their attention to the giant screen. The policewoman had finished speaking now. They'd missed Karen's question, but Miriam's answer quickly cued them in:

"Yes, there *are* monsters here. And boogeymen."

"But how is that possible?" came Karen's follow-up question, her inset face crinkling in confusion. "In the real world there are no such things as monsters."

Miriam laughed. "The play zone is an upgrade of the real world. Believe me, sister, here there be monsters . . . because we made them."

The policewoman's expression grew even more confused. "What? How can you make monsters?"

Miriam shrugged and looked at her diamond-studded watch. "Well, the live feed for the audience should begin in two minutes, but maybe I can spare a few minutes more to explain this, so that you're not so paralyzed with wonder when you encounter our creations that you lie down and die on first sighting."

The sound faded for a moment, while Miriam's giant image spoke to someone off-screen.

"This had better be good," she told Emily.

"Oh, it will be," Emily replied in amusement. "You won't believe some of the things they've got waiting for us down there."

"Huh?" Her comment made Fatima look at her questioningly. She was about asking Emily if she'd been on the show before, but then remembered that this was its maiden edition. Maybe the info had been in the brochure for the show, and she'd missed it. The brochure had been packed with technical stuff that she hadn't felt like reading, and she'd mostly skimmed through it.

The sound returned then anyway, so Fatima boxed her thoughts. She noticed that five minutes had been added to the digital display, and then concentrated on what the giant woman on the tower was saying:

"Like I was explaining, there are monsters and boogeymen down in the play zone, because we made them."

Karen's face was still inset on Miriam's right. "Please go on."

Miriam nodded. "The question you asked, Karen, is of course a valid one: how can we 'create' monsters? The answer is however simple and less than magical. We made the monsters by bioengineering them. Same goes for the boogeymen. But enough talk, I'll show you girls a couple of examples." She looked off-screen and this time the audio stayed on. "Pluto, come here."

A hulking form in a black hoodie strode into view, with Miriam's own image shrinking a little so that the man could fit beside her on the giant screen.

Fatima gasped at the man's size. Side-by-side, the new arrival was at least a foot taller than Miriam, who was about Fatima's own height of five feet seven inches.

Even before the giant removed his hood, Fatima realized she'd sorely misunderstood what would be expected of her on this show.

"Strip for the ladies, Pluto," Miriam instructed the giant.

When he did strip naked, Fatima imagined she heard the collective gasps of shock and horror from the six women on the other three distant platforms. Emily though was silent.

What on earth . . . ?

"This is a boogeyman," Miriam said in quiet amusement. "You must agree that Pluto here looks very impressive."

But Fatima was no longer listening to her. She was gaping in fright at the unrobed and unhooded man—no, man-creature.

For a start, the 'boogeyman' had three huge eyes, the third one right in the middle of his forehead. The creature was also completely bald and his mouth contained just four or five giant interlocking teeth.

The boogeyman's craziest disfigurement, however, were the two giant crab-like or lobster-like pincers that he had in place of his hands. With a start, Fatima realized that the pincers were exactly the same color as the man's pale skin.

"Those aren't prosthetics," Emily said, like she was reading her thoughts. "They're actually part of his body. If you look at his elbows, you'll notice the surgical scars where they were attached to him."

Fatima looked where her companion had indicated and indeed saw the scars; the sutures were healed and faded but still clearly visible as darker lines on the monster's skin.

He looks like a djinn, something out of a fairytale. No, out of a nightmare!

The rest of the boogeyman's body was normal, though he was very impressively muscled, more muscled in fact, than any normal man should be. But he was also covered in stitch-scars, as if some of his muscles hadn't originally been part of his body. Keeping in proportion with the giant's size, his penis was large, but flaccid.

"Do they honestly think it's fair to set us against something that hideous?" Fatima asked Emily. "We're just girls, for Allah's sake— that thing will make mincemeat out of any of us. Just look at how little Miriam looks beside it!" She gazed left towards Karen's suspended platform, wishing and willing the policewoman to take her damn hand off the octopus-hole on her railing, so she could question Miriam herself. Oh, she had quite a few questions for the games-mistress now.

"We're gonna be armed," Emily pointed out. When Fatima turned to look at her, she saw that Emily was grinning.

"That isn't the point," Fatima pointed out in turn. "Miriam said 'boogeymen' not 'boogeyman,' meaning there's gonna be more than one of those"—she pointed at the tower without looking at it— "things . . . after us."

Emily shrugged. "So what? They're still flesh and blood. We'll have guns. A bullet to the head will stop even a bull in its tracks."

Fatima felt frustrated. She didn't think killing that giant would be that easy. She turned back to the tower.

Miriam was smiling coldly. She'd stepped close to the hulking figure, and now stroked first his muscular chest, and then his right arm, letting her fingers slowly trail down to the heavy pincer at its end. "Pluto here is just one of several boogeymen we have down in the play zone waiting to play with you. How many of them are there, you ask? That's for us to know and for you to dread finding out."

"Oh, the bitch is toying with us!" Fatima said angrily.

"It's her money," Emily said. "Remember the rules."

"She said there are no rules."

Emily laughed. "There's just one—the golden rule: she who has the money, makes the rules. Miriam Heller is paying the winner of this game show twenty-four million dollars. She can have as much fun with our lives as she pleases."

Fatima didn't bother replying.

"But enough fun," Miriam said and waved her hand at the nude giant. "Leave me, Pluto. I'm talking to the girls."

The boogeyman meekly picked up his clothes and shambled off. As he departed, Fatima noticed a line of sutures at the rear of his head, as if he'd recently had brain surgery. She shivered.

Fatima stared at the tower. She expected Karen to ask Miriam a question; any question at all to halt the horrified thoughts now flooding through her mind, thoughts that she must have been crazy to have come here. But Karen's inset face said it all: she was as horrified by what she'd seen as Fatima was. Karen's mouth hung open like she'd forgotten it was there.

"So, alright, ladies, you've now seen one example of our boogeymen. Time to meet one of our monsters." Miriam was already gesturing off-screen again. "Yes, come over here, darling."

"Aw shit!" Fatima groaned as the creature Miriam had just summoned shambled into view. She never used profanity, but right now polite terms just didn't cut it. "What the hell is that fucking thing?"

"This is a human centipede," Miriam explained as if she'd heard the far-off question. The creature was too long to entirely fit into the screen, and Miriam strode along its grotesque length while continuing to address them. "As you can clearly see, 'Centi' here is composed of the torsos and arms of"—she paused as if she was counting something off-screen—"about twenty people. We didn't need either their heads or asses and legs." Miriam gazed directly into the camera and Fatima thought she read intense malice on her face. "Now do you understand?"

Fatima was trying hard to make sense of what she was seeing. Being told that an absurd thing is logical is one thing; making that ridiculous thing fit in with an accepted system of logic is another thing entirely.

The 'human centipede' that Miriam Heller had called onscreen *was* clearly built from human torsos, five of which were visible onscreen and which were seamlessly attached end-to-end. The monster stood on the torso's arms as if they were legs, and now, as it turned to face the video camera, it lifted its first 'segment' completely off the floor and waved its 'hands' as if greeting them.

Seeing its face felt to Fatima like being sucker-punched in the gut. The monster's head was human, but (using Miriam as a reference point) about four times the normal human size. Also, in a parody of a true insect's eyes, this human centipede had six or eight eyes on each side of its face, the eyes being lumped together in a circular shape. The 'centipede' had no nose and its ears were large and elfin. It had more teeth than the boogeyman; its giant mouth was filled with jagged interlocking teeth.

Fatima felt Emily's touch on her shoulder. "I know what you're thinking," the other young woman said. "Seeing that thing makes me want to flee screaming too, and I'd be shitting myself all the while I was running away."

Fatima nodded but didn't look at her. She however noted that Emily Ford no longer sounded as smug and self-assured as previously. The monster was still waving at the camera, its pale face happy and inquisitive and Fatima noticed that it had claws and not fingers on its hands. A quick glance along what was visible of its extended body revealed that all its 'feet' were the same—claws, not fingers.

That is one deadly beast they've created, she thought, her gaze now plummeting down to stare at the expanse of forest and houses and routes and water spread out below her. *More of these things and others like them are down there waiting to kill and eat us. But . . . but things like that—* she was forced to look back up at the human centipede, on which Miriam was now blithely sitting as if it was a couch—*things like that can't exist. They simply can't exist.*

Fatima realized she'd been so locked in her thoughts that she'd missed a few things. Most obviously, Karen no longer had the inset focus. The inset window on the tower screen was now occupied by Megan Hillman, who seemed too confused to even remember what question she'd meant to ask. Then the inset window was taken over by Megan's young stepmother Rita, who also looked like she had a question concerning the new origins of the human universe, but couldn't find adequate words to express herself either. Fatima sighed in deep empathy with both of them; viewing that human centipede thing would do that to you.

She regretted getting lost in her worries; she needed that inset window to herself. She really, really, really, wanted to demand some explanations from the games-mistress.

But maybe Megan had already asked her question, because Miriam was explaining something anyway:

"If you've knowledge of basic science, some things should be immediately obvious to you," Miriam was saying as she lounged luxuriously atop the human centipede and stroked its bald head, while the pieced-together monstrosity snarled at the cameras as if her actions were merely priming it up to kill them all. "For instance, that any part of a human body can be grafted to any other part of that body. The fact that it hasn't been done more often is simply because the human race lacks imagination; but maybe we should be grateful for that. Secondly, ladies—okay, yes, I know this takes lots of technical know-how—but once you have sufficient control over the human genetic code, additional body parts not in God's original human blueprint can be grown to specifications and attached as desired. Also, you can clone people and use body parts from those duplicates to repair or augment the original person's body. Now, this show's sponsors, the Red Octopus Corporation—the ROC—the ROC have this knowledge and have put it to use in creating a transhuman menagerie, as you'll all discover when you encounter their deadly creations. And . . ." she added with a saccharine smile, standing up from the segmented creature's back and grinning cruelly at them, "this is something I must make very clear to you all. 'Centi' here knows *me* as a friend. He and those of his kind down in the play zone will recognize you contestants purely as *food*; he and they will all attempt to eat you, maybe even while you're still alive and kicking and screaming." She shrugged. "Just like some of the boogeymen will try to kill or rape you on sight. Others—like Pluto whom you've just met, will kill you first and rape you afterwards."

"Rape? Kill? Kill and then rape? But that's crazy!" Rita Hillman managed to spit out.

Miriam nodded in agreement. "If you're observant, you'd have noticed the scars on the back of Pluto's head? The boogeymen have all been lobotomized to some degree. Not one of them is what a psychiatrist would define as even borderline sane. Get this point clear in your minds: all of the boogeymen are sickos and psychos. They hate all you ladies intensely without having ever met you; they want to maim and torture and mutilate and destroy you all. Think Ed Gein, Ted Bundy, John Wayne Gacy—that level of brutality and mental illness is what I'm talking about here. So watch your backs, everyone. Whatever gets done to you in the play zone, gets done, period. You've no one to blame for what happens to you down there but yourselves."

"No one to blame but ourselves?" Megan Hillman had regained control of the microphone from her stepmother. "But . . . but . . . !" she sputtered in rage.

Miriam smirked. "This is adult entertainment, sister. The contract you signed contains a 'no-holds-barred' clause, which I know our lawyers insisted you read before affixing your signature to the document."

Rita Hillman gulped and fell silent. Fatima knew why. Miriam Heller wasn't lying. A 'no-holds-barred' clause *had* been in the contract she'd signed. She'd almost skimmed over it herself, figuring that clause was just there so the ROC could escape liability if she broke an arm or leg on the show; but the lawyer, in her case an old man named Ellsworth—had insisted that she read and understand fully what she was getting herself into. He'd said Mrs. Heller had insisted that all the lawyers insist on the contestants reading through that segment and understanding what 'no-holds-barred' meant.

And yet, we really had no idea what that simple phrase meant; and looking at that human centipede creature I still think we don't.

"Miriam's right," she said quietly to herself. " 'No holds barred' means exactly that—anything goes down there."

"And we're on our way down right now," Emily said.

Fatima at first thought that Emily was replying her statement, but then realized that Emily was referring to their platform, which had just begun its slow descent to the play zone. She looked left and right across the octagonal chamber. The two other visible platforms were also lowering to the ground.

She felt a moment's intense panic, turning and stretching her hand towards the steel entrance door in the chamber wall as it rose up and away from her, and she also began willing and praying for the platform to malfunction and cease its descent. But then she got a grip on her fear and instead stared at the tower, at the giant image of Miriam Heller, who was waving at them.

"Bye for now, ladies," Miriam said with a wink at the camera. "Try to stay live. And remember, there's twenty-four million dollars hiding from you somewhere in the play zone. All you have to do is find the money and hold on to it." She clapped her hands. "And now our worldwide internet audience expect the performance of a lifetime from you all. I suggest you give it to them. You'll be dead meat if you don't."

Heart-in-mouth, Fatima Noori watched the ground come closer and closer.

Well now, it's do or die time, she thought grimly. *I asked for this, and now that I've gotten it, I'm gonna give this madness everything thing I've got. For me it's win or die trying.*

CHAPTER 5

Rita

"Hey, you don't think that mermaid that was swimming all over the tower display was actually real?" Megan asked in a worried voice as she and her stepmother hurried down the steps from their platform.

"I've no idea," Rita distractedly replied. The steps led to a short stonewalled tunnel that ejected them onto a single-lane street. Viewed from above, the street led directly to the black tower, but here on the ground it curved like a snake in motion and quickly became lost in the tangle of trees. The face of the tower now glittered bright black, waiting for some violent, disgusting, sexy or gory action to display.

The previously brilliant overhead lights were now considerably dimmed, creating the impression of twilight or dawn in the play zone. With the only bright lights in the play zone now those streaming from the windows of the houses, everywhere was filled with long shadows, shadows which might or might not be alive.

Rita noticed two video cameras attached to trees, and also a drone perched on a nearby rooftop, its camera swiveled to faced them.

Megan had also noticed the drone. "It's sick that anyone would pay to watch this," she said in her usual annoying voice.

"It's sick that anyone would *participate* in this," Rita replied. "And yet here the both of us are, doing exactly that. Give it a rest, girl."

Megan tugged her to a halt and glared at her. "Hey, hey, you know what I mean. Neither of us knew the show was gonna be like this. Or did you?" She looked over at the tower and then back at her stepmother. "Tell me, Rita, did you know about the damn boogeymen and the monsters? That gross human centipede—Ugh, just remembering that thing makes me wanna puke! How could anyone do that to someone else?"

Rita sighed at her. "No, no, I didn't know, alright? We both signed the same contract, didn't we? On the same day, in the same room in Frisco. You saw the wording 'boogeymen' and 'monsters' just like I did. We even discussed them. We both thought it meant dress-up, with people playing at being serial killers and maybe a wolf or mountain lion or two, maybe a crocodile in a pool that we had to wade through or cross somehow. And besides, they'd made it clear that we were gonna be armed and could shoot them." Rita grimaced. "Never in a million years did I imagine they meant real boogeymen and real monsters; because we both knew those things didn't exist."

Megan nodded. Rita figured she was satisfied that her stepmom was also upset.

"So answer my first question again," Megan asked. "Do you think the mermaid was real?"

Rita managed a smile. "Honey, just stay away from the water."

Thankfully, Megan let it go at that and changed the subject. "We need to find some weapons, and quick," she said.

Rita nodded. She was studying the layout of the area, not wishing to commit herself to entering the woods on either side of the road until she was sure what she'd find in them. Here on the ground the visual perspective was very different from that overhead and she was attempting to reconcile both. Which side would be better? The brochure had explained that the play zone contained thirty-five buildings. Twenty-two of those were bungalows, twelve were story buildings; and then there was the tower. Rita felt certain the money was hidden somewhere inside the tower.

But of course, it's gonna be a bitch to find out where.

Rita stood on the sidewalk staring at the trees everywhere. The trees seemed to have been purposely planted to confuse her. Trying to get a clear view of anything in the distance was impossible—there was always a tree trunk (sometimes two or three) in the way. An example of this was the route to the tower. Of course the black tower loomed up ahead, lurking over the play zone like a god, but because the street twisted off to the right about twenty yards ahead of Rita and her stepdaughter, the foot of the giant building was invisible from where they stood and they were faced with about eighty yards of possibly monster-infested woods to walk through to reach it if they proceeded in a straight line.

"Hey, this way," Megan finally said, yanking Rita off the street when she seemed unable to commit to a direction, and dragging her under a clump of trees. "We need to get under cover. Everyone and their stepmother can see us out there."

Rita followed without protest. "Like you said, we need guns," she agreed.

"And knives and whatever else is available," Megan said while leading the way towards one of the nearer bungalows. "Searching the buildings is the smart thing to do. It'd be silly to think they'd leave the weapons lying around in the open. Once we're armed we can plan our own assault."

"I'm more worried about what might be hiding up in the trees," Rita said, peeking worriedly up through the overhead branches as the sound of rustling leaves startled her. "You're right though, we'd better start searching the houses."

While Megan strode off ahead of her, she froze and stared at a low hedge of leaves and branches to their right. She'd seen the hedge shake violently; she was certain of it. She waited. The hedge didn't rustle again, but now she saw a pale and hairless arm lift off the forest floor near its base. A moment later, a second arm 'walked' into view.

Rita didn't need any further urging to get a move on. Something was clearly watching them as they made their leisurely way towards their chosen bungalow. And maybe that watching creature was very long and had segments made from human torsos. Rita hurried past Megan and dragged the protesting girl after her to the bungalow's back door, which was its nearest entrance. The house's lights were all on, but that wasn't a sign of danger. All of the houses' lights were permanently on because of the hidden video cameras set up in them.

"I've got a good feeling about this house," Megan said as Rita pulled the door open and dashed inside. "Seeing as it's so close to the platform, it's a logical place to hide stuff. I'm sure we'll find some weapons inside here."

"Just get inside," Rita pulled her stepdaughter inside the house. Then she slammed the door shut and bolted it.

"What's the matter?" Megan asked, seeing the fright on her face.

"I think that damn human centipede thing, or one just like it, is following us."

"Oh, I didn't hear anything."

Rita nodded. "Well I did. And it's too early in the contest to take any chances with our lives." She stood there, hands on her hips, and stared levelly at Megan. "How the hell am I gonna explain it to your dad if something happens to you?"

Megan rolled her eyes. "Rita, I can look after myself. Just in case you haven't noticed—we're the same age, meaning I'm not your baby!" She spun on her heel and stalked angrily down the short hallway to the living room. "I'm gonna start looking for the weapons in here. You search the bedrooms."

By now Rita was used to her stepdaughter's temper tantrums. Still, she watched her go with regret.

She wasn't regretting the lack of bonding between them. Rather, she was wondering why she'd just let her emotions get the better of her; wondering why she'd insisted Megan hurry into the house to save herself.

Wow, I definitely messed that one up. How silly can I get? All I needed to do was lock the little bitch outside and let the centipede freak eat her. But no—call it misplaced maternal instinct or whatever . . . dammit, now I have to kill her myself!

This murderous thought of hers wasn't some spur-of-the-moment decision, or something caused by Rita's greed and desire to have all of the prize money for herself.

No, the reason why Rita Hillman had suggested to Megan that they both compete on *The Final Girl* show was so she'd have a legal way to murder her.

Megan was screwing up her life.

***

22-year-old Rita Mitchell had been tending the cash register at a convenience store in Yuba City, California, when Daniel Hillman had driven in to fill up. And after buying gas for his Land Cruiser he'd walked into the store to buy a Diet-Coke and a sandwich and wound up flirting with Rita instead.

Dan Hillman was forty-five years old and a successful Sacramento realtor.

Rita hadn't initially been interested in the flirtation; because obviously, a man that old and that rich had to be married, right? But then she'd noticed he wasn't wearing a wedding band.

"How come you aren't wearing a wedding ring?" she'd joked. "Is it just to pick up innocent girls like me?"

He'd laughed and explained that his wife had died ten years ago, and that since then he'd just not met the right woman to take her place.

Greatly encouraged by this revelation, Rita had agreed to go out on a date with Daniel.

Things had progressed rapidly from there. Within two months, Rita had quit her job at the convenience store and moved into Daniel's luxurious Sacramento house. They'd begun planning their wedding.

And then trouble arrived. Daniel's daughter Megan, a junior manager for the Cashstretch supermarket chain, had been living a condo on the other side of town. But when a storm crashed a tree through the wall of her living room, she moved in with her father until repairs on her own place were completed.

This arrangement should have been temporary, but once Megan Hillman began living with her father again, she immediately seemed to develop an intense dislike to the woman who would be taking her mother's place. Rita had done all she could to be conciliatory, but Megan wasn't having it. Fortunately she'd arrived too late to halt the wedding, which went ahead as planned.

But once the wedding was over, Megan simply refused to leave home again, even though her condo was back in livable condition. Her father threatened her, pleaded with her, and finally tried to bribe her to move back into her own place—all to no avail. Megan stayed put.

"I'm the custodian of my late mother's memories," she told Daniel Hillman. I don't want her exorcised out of her own house." This argument defeated her father, who secretly felt guilty over his wife's passing, though she'd died of breast cancer.

And so life continued in the Hillman house for a year and a half.

Megan was civil enough with Rita. She was more of a hovering storm on Rita's horizon that an emotional tornado laying waste everything in its path.

But there was a problem.

See, Rita wanted to get pregnant. And soon at that. And the problem was that Daniel had pleaded, really pleaded with her to not take in until he'd found a way to exorcise Megan from their house.

Daniel Hillman *knew*, he just *knew* the way parents sometimes do, that Megan was certain to go ballistic the moment she realized she had a sibling on the way.

Rita had of course agreed with her new husband's request. Though her grown stepdaughter assumed otherwise, she truly loved Daniel and wanted to be the best wife to him that she possibly could. So they put off having children for at least two years.

In the meantime, Daniel continued trying to bribe Megan to leave home.

But something had gone wrong. Two months ago, Rita had discovered she was pregnant. She had no idea how it had happened. She and Daniel always used condoms while making love. Maybe one of them had burst; or had they forgotten one night, maybe on her last birthday? They'd both gotten really drunk that night and so anything could have happened then.

Anyway, what mattered now was that Rita Hillman was pregnant, and now had four problems:

1) She didn't dare tell her husband what had happened.

2) She wasn't about having an abortion for any reason; and certainly not because Megan wouldn't approve of her pregnancy.

3) She wasn't about giving birth to her child while Megan still lived with them. She'd never feel safe with Megan nearby. And who knew what kind of tragic 'accident' her stepdaughter might arrange for her new sister or brother.

4) She needed to find a workable solution before Daniel noticed she was growing fat around the middle, which was certain to happen in a month or two. He was already curious about her morning sickness, but she'd managed to convince him that she was just reacting to her new sleep medication.

So, of course, Megan had to go. And since the bitch was unwilling to leave home willingly . . .

But how exactly do you kill someone, make the corpse disappear for good, and also ensure no one suspects you of being involved?

And that's where *The Final Girl* came in.

Rita had stumbled on the show purely by accident—while researching 'baby girl names' on Bing. Afterwards, she was certain she'd blanked out for a few seconds and typed 'final girl names' instead or something like that, because suddenly her browser was at *https.finalgirl.roc.org* and she had no idea of how she'd arrived there.

But she quickly realized it was fortuitous that she had. The ROC—the Red Octopus Corporation—was recruiting beautiful young women for their violent contest, and even being modest, Rita was aware that she and Megan more than fit the 'beautiful' description.

Convincing Megan to come along was easier done than said. With her boyfriend Ricky working up north in Montana for two months, Megan was dying of boredom, and was game to do anything that wasn't sitting around doing nothing.

"Only, thing is—you don't tell your dad that we're doing this."

"Oh, I ain't gonna tell him anything," Megan readily agreed. "If I sit in this house one day longer than necessary I'll start raving at the walls."

And so one Saturday morning they'd sneaked out of the house and driven along I-80 to San Francisco to meet with Miriam and Aaron Heller. The interview had gone well and Rita had felt optimistic about their chances of being accepted on the show. The fact that on their arrival at the Heller's temporary office, they'd met two ravishingly beautiful girls departing, and that there had been another pair of supermodel-grade beauties arriving as they were leaving hadn't fazed Rita a bit. She'd been certain she and Megan would be accepted; they had that special 'something' she knew TV viewers liked to root for.

And she'd been right. A week ago, Miriam Heller had contacted her again, asking she and Megan to come back to San Francisco two days ago to compete on *The Final Girl*.

By then Rita Hillman was more than prepared for what she had to do. She'd spent the intervening time between their interview and their getting the call-up figuring out the most satisfactory way to murder her stepdaughter.

***

As she stepped through the bedroom door on her right, Rita reviewed 'arrangements' in her mind. Following the instructions they'd been given, she and Megan had driven to a Burger King on San Francisco's Mission Street. They'd entered the eatery, had lunch, and on walking out again, had seemingly been accosted by two men in black suits and dark glasses.

"Misses and Miss Hillman?" one of the men had asked them.

After confirming their identity, they'd followed the men from the Burger King to a white limousine parked down the road with a uniformed chauffeur at the wheel, had gotten in and been driven away. Another man had driven their own car behind them.

"We're taking you to Mr. Heller's private airstrip outside of town," the men explained.

Somewhere along the way Rita and Megan had been gassed. Rita had no idea why the gas she'd smelt hadn't affected either their escorts or the chauffeur, but next thing, she and Megan had woken up in a luxury suite. Their cellphones had been taken away from them while they slept, but the clock on the wall revealed that it was now the morning of the next day.

The entrance door to their suite had been locked, which had really scared both young women—with all sorts of horrible thoughts of trickery racing through Rita's mind—but then a screen on the living room wall had come alive and Miriam Heller had welcomed them to the show.

"Make yourselves at home," she'd told them. "We'll let you out in a little while; once all the other contestants are awake."

***

That had been yesterday. Now, Rita Hillman searched the small bedroom for either a case or a bag of weapons.

The bedroom was nicely furnished and although no personal belongings were in evidence, it smelt as if people actually slept in it.

Maybe the ROC staff sleep down here in the play zone—all these houses must be used for something when they're not hosting crazy reality shows.

After finding nothing useful in either the closet or nightstands, Rita knelt to peek under the bed. But right as she was dipping her head down to look, she saw something pale and large flash by the bedroom window.

She instantly abandoned searching under the bed and hurried out to the living room. "The human centipede followed us here!" she exclaimed to Megan.

Megan was bent over a large case she'd opened up on the coffee table. "And not a second too soon," she quipped with little interest. She turned and grinned at Rita. "This is what we were looking for. It was hidden in plain view, tucked under the TV."

Rita forced a smile, though the segmented shadow she'd seen through the bedroom window still had her spooked. And now she was also aware of a heavy smell in the air; stink like a bucketload of stale sweat. "Great," she said, surveying the array of knives and pistols in the case, an arsenal which also included two pump-action shotguns. "Wow, they weren't jerking us around when they said we'd be armed."

Megan noticed the smell too. She paused from examining the revolver in her hand, sniffed the air and said, "Well, I guess with as many armpits as that thing has, it can't be helped. The ROC could at least have invested in some deodorant."

Rita laughed at the joke. Then she bent down, picked up a shotgun and chambered a round; all the guns had been pre-loaded for the show and there were lots of spare boxes of ammo; you simply had to match the caliber of round to the firearms. "I'd like to see one of those creepy boogeymen try to rape me now," she growled. "In my humble opinion, ain't nothing cures mental disease better than a shotgun blast to the head."

Now it was Megan's turn to laugh. "You're really turning badass, aren't you? Soon you're gonna be wanting a cowgirl hat too." She picked up the other shotgun, cocked it, and grinned. "Alright, so what are we gonna do about Mr. Long out there?"

"We're gonna give it heavy metal food for thought," Rita replied. "I imagine it's still lurking around the back door, 'cos that's the way we came in here and it's following our scent. So, we'll act like we're going out that way too. I'll open the door and you shoot it. Try to either hit it between the eyes so you pulp its brain, or in one of the eyes—it'll be less of a threat if it's half-blind."

"Yeah, gotcha!" Megan said. Her eyes glittered with excitement, which surprised Rita, because she mostly felt afraid. And her fears increased when suddenly she heard a rustling sound at the windows.

"Hey, over here," Megan said, hurrying over to the nearer of the living room windows and pulling the curtains back. "Dammit, how long is this thing anyway?"

It was out there, now curled around the front of the house too. Rita couldn't see the human centipede's tail.

"We're still good to go," she told her stepdaughter. "Its head is still over by the back door."

Megan frowned. "Rita, how can you be certain of that? It could have turned itself around and have its head out by the front porch now."

Rita shook her head, and pointed outside and down towards the ground. "No, you're wrong. We're looking at the rear part of the creature. Look, all of its leg-arms are facing towards the left, meaning that that's the direction of its head"—she gestured across the living room towards the rear hallway—"and so I'm willing to bet that the centipede's head is still out back where I left it."

Megan nodded. "Yeah, that makes sense. But what's this bit doing back here then?"

"The nasty thing is trying to block off our other exits by wrapping itself around the house. You know, like how you catch rabbits or hares? They usually have bolt-holes, so you've got to find and block those up before you dig the rabbit out, or it'll escape."

The monster did look like a living fence out there, with those muscular and hairy leg-arms like skin-covered pickets, those pale segments that twitched like a dog's sides and which also heaved occasionally as if each individual human torso was breathing. The latter was particularly creepy to look at: the way the torsos all seemed to be breathing independently of each other. And then there was the monster's intense sweaty-armpit smell to consider too.

"Ugh," Megan said. "This thing is so damn gross we'll be doing everyone a favor by killing it."

"Except that there's likely several more out there hunting the other contestants. Listen, let's stick to the plan. It doesn't have brains or eyes in its ass. Once you blow its brains out or blind it, it'll be helpless to stop us fleeing to a safer place."

Rita was worried that Megan would protest this and ask her to handle the shooting instead. That approach wouldn't fit in with what she had in mind.

But Megan was too caught up in the thrill of the experience to want to switch places with Rita. Her face was flushed and she was breathing fast. The young woman was clearly riding an adrenaline rush, and was too excited to suspect that her stepmother harbored any bad intentions towards her.

"Yeah, let's do this," she said. Without waiting for Rita, she turned away from the window, and crossed the living room to the hallway entrance, where she paused and waved her shotgun at Rita.

"Hey, you coming or do I have to do this on my own?"

"I'm right behind you," Rita replied, waving back with her own shotgun.

When she looked up, Megan had already vanished into the hallway, like it was a dark mouth that had swallowed her up.

Great, Rita thought, picking up the long and sharp survival knife she'd had her eyes on since first sighting it in the case. She slipped the knife into her belt.

For a moment, she remembered the video cameras watching and recording all the action. From what Miriam and Aaron Heller had told them during their briefing yesterday, each building here had at least forty video camera inside it and about ten outside it. There were also microphones listening in, but because of problems with feedback, those were less in number than the video cameras.

She spared a moment to look around. No, she couldn't see even one camera, even though they were surely tracking her every motion.

"Hey, are you coming, or do I have time to take a nap while you get your courage up!?" Megan yelled from the back door.

"Be right with you!" Rita yelled back. Feeling a pleasant resurgence of her dislike for the girl, she walked out of the living room to join her by the back door.

Megan was waiting there and smirking. "I almost thought you'd lost your nerve," she said. "Be just like you."

"I'm a changed woman, honey; knowing you has given me a totally new perspective on life," Rita replied sweetly, trying not to let either her anger or her fright show; because now, she couldn't just *smell* the human centipede, she could *hear* it too. Loud and clear out there. It was scratching at the back door in frustration and snorting at each failed attempt to break in and reach them.

"I dunno," she told Megan, "maybe we should just shoot it through the door."

Megan shook her head. "No, that sounds like the old wimpy you. We stick to the original plan."

Rita nodded and set her shotgun down on the floor, and then unlocked the rear door. "Okay, you ready?"

Megan stepped back, planted her feet firmly on the floor and aimed the shotgun at the door. "Yeah, mom, open the damn door. Let's get this over with."

Rita pulled the door open and ducked behind Megan.

The door yawned open and suddenly they were staring at the monster, while its sweaty smell poured in over them. Up close, it was even more horrible than Rita remembered from the giant screen; hairy and pale fatty flesh apparently stitched together in the Devil's surgery lab and somehow kept alive. Its head was massive, much larger than a lion's, and the arms on its first and second segments were as muscled as if the creature had been lifting weights.

The human centipede had just reared up to batter at the door again. Maybe that was why Megan didn't immediately fire at it—she was waiting for it to lower its head again, so she could get a clear shot at its 'bunch-of-grapes' eyes or its brain.

"Easy, easy, now," she said coolly as the centipede, confused by the door's abrupt opening, slowly lowered its front end to the ground. "I've got something nice and painful waiting for you, you— Ahhhhurrggghlll!"

Rita was impressed by her stepdaughter's calm. But not impressed enough to refrain from stabbing her in the back with the survival knife. She felt an unfamiliar pleasure as Megan's blood exploded out over her hands. She dug the knife in as deeply as she could, trying to sever as many crucial blood vessels and damage as many vital organs as she could, and twisted the knife around.

Megan seemed to be rendered speechless by agony. With her mouth gaping open in shock, she immediately dropped her shotgun and reached behind her, but Rita countered this by yanking the knife out of her back and stabbing her in the belly instead, ripping the knife downwards and sideways.

Rita was sure she'd done a good job. She didn't see Megan recovering from the wounds she'd given her—the girl was leaking redness like a bombed blood bank. But still, partly to be certain, but mostly simply to vent more of her pent-up rage on the girl, she stabbed Megan several more times in the lower back, each puncture producing a bloody gurgle from Megan, who was clutching at the door and trying to turn around to look at her.

Then Rita shoved Megan out to the human centipede.

The thing must've had some intelligence, because it hadn't moved to attack them yet. It seemed to understand that Rita was doing its killing for it. As Megan stumbled through the doorway, it rose up and embraced the bleeding girl and its face came towards hers as if to kiss her.

Rita watched the human centipede rip off Megan's head and toss it away and then she slammed the door shut and locked it.

Okay, time for me to get away while it's still occupied with her.

Though horrified, she felt no regret, only relief. She'd accomplished her aim on the show. Megan was out of the picture for good, and now she could return home and be happy with her husband and be pregnant and have her baby in peace. She already had her alibi story worked out: she and Megan had been kidnapped outside the Burger King on Mission Street in San Francisco. Just in case there was CCTV footage to contradict this story, she'd say the kidnappers told her they'd taken her husband Daniel captive and would harm him if she didn't come along quietly. Then they'd gassed she and Megan—which was at least true—and taken them 'somewhere,' she didn't know where (also true), and then, after they'd raped and murdered Megan, she'd been gassed again (which she expected to happen anyway once the show was over) and had found herself back in San Francisco.

All good, she thought with a chill. Beyond the door, she could hear the centipede feasting on Megan; the noise was sickening, and made her feel like wetting herself. The noise made her realize she'd be wise to make her escape while she had the creature distracted.

I'd better get out of here before it's done with her and remembers me!

She hurried down the hallway to the bathroom and washed her bloody hands and arms clean. Then she cleaned Megan's blood off her knife and stuck it back in her belt. After toweling her arms dry, she hurried back out to the hallway, picked up her shotgun and returned to the living room.

Rita's plan now was to pretend to compete on the show. But really all she intended to do was stay out of danger until the show was over. She didn't need the prize money; her husband had more than enough. And now that they didn't have to share it with Megan, that gave them even more to spend on themselves.

Time to go!

She didn't think she had too much time before the monster was done with Megan's corpse. She grabbed a spare box of shotgun shells, hurried to the front door and pulled it open, and stepped outside.

Warm air and the creature's raunchy smell greeted her. That was fine. The monster was still blocking the way, its body jerking and twitching as its head ate Megan. It stood about three feet off the floor and really did look like a fat whitewashed fence, or a garden hedge that someone had dusted with talcum powder. Its tail end was curled out of sight around the right wall of the house.

Rita considered whether to go over or under the creature. Finally she decided on climbing over it: if she tried to go between its leg-arms, the 'rear' pair might kick her or tear into her, and those claws were razor-sharp; with a shudder she recalled the way Megan's skin had burst like a balloon when the centipede had grabbed her before tearing her head off.

So, no way, Jose!

She took two steps towards the human centipede and then, remembering how Miriam had used the one in her studio as a couch, sat on its back, intending to carefully pull her legs up over its top.

But suddenly it heaved up and spilled her to the floor again.

She landed on her ass, but on the other side of the creature, where she'd wanted to go anyway. She wasn't hurt, just a bit dazed, but her head was right next to one of the human centipede's hairy armpits and she felt like she was drowning in its sweaty reek.

Relieved that she'd fallen over the monster, Rita sat up and began collecting her things. The shotgun had dropped near her feet, so she left it where it was for the moment and looked around for the box of shells. She located the box a few yards away and went to pick it up.

And while picking it up, she heard a rustling noise behind her.

She spun around in alarm, thinking that maybe one of the show's boogeymen had found her. If that was the case, she might still be able to reach her shotgun and shoot the boogeyman and flee.

But what was waiting for her was much, much worse.

Oh my God! It has two heads!?

The human centipede's front head was still occupied with eating Megan. But this second 'rear' head was just as terrifying as the other. It was just as big, just as full of eyes and teeth, and was apparently just as hungry for human flesh as its twin.

With a shriek of terror, Rita Hillman saw that the set of hands below this rear head were reaching out to grab her. She backpedalled fast, but not seeing where she was heading, soon backed into a tree trunk.

The creature attacked her before she worked out what was blocking off her retreat, its teeth agonizingly sinking into her skull and biting her face off.

Even though Rita now had no face and her brain was exposed to the air, she wasn't dead yet. While she shrieked out agonizing noises and two drones flew in to record everything, the human centipede's rear head began ripping open her belly.

Maybe the monster had sensed the new life growing in her, because one of the first things it ate was Rita's womb.

Rita expired shortly after that, cursing the day she met Daniel Hillman.

CHAPTER 6

Karen

Rita and Megan's deaths were displayed in gory HD color on the tower's surfaces. They were displayed split screen, with Rita in the lower picture.

Karen Rogers had a sinking feeling in her stomach as she watched the human centipede tear into both young women's abdomens; its teeth and claws shredding their flesh like knives. It fed with inhuman savagery, as if the brains of several starving lions had been crammed into its giant skull and it viewed the world through their multitude of eyes; those eyes packed on its face like bunches of grapes.

Not letting us know it had heads at both ends was quite a dirty trick, Karen thought, surprised at how little emotion she felt. She felt as if there was a glass panel between herself and her feelings. She was aware of how she felt; but somehow couldn't connect directly to her outrage.

Seemingly not as emotionally insulated as herself, Lexi Austin was bent over next to her and was busy retching. They were standing off the road, amidst a grove of olive trees and Lexi's vomit had formed a neat little mess on the well-manicured lawn of the house they'd been heading for when the screen had come alive with the nauseating display.

Not wanting to be splattered with puke, Karen had stepped as far from her companion as the handcuffs joining them allowed, which wasn't very far. While Lexi kept dry heaving, Karen studied the monster feeding on the tower screen, trying to determine its weaknesses. Whenever the human centipede raised its heads for air, it looked like a true nightmare—blood dripping from its chins and scraps of skin and lengths of intestine swinging from its interlocking teeth.

A bullet to the brain, or failing that, into the chest of its first segment should put it to sleep.

One thing that was glaringly missing from the tower display now was a clock. As Miriam had explained yesterday: "The game is played till it ends—no time limits. You'll have no watches or clocks—no way to keep track of time. Time is unimportant—play the game as if every second might be your last—remember, the world is watching you."

Lexi finished throwing up. The prostitute straightened up, wiped her mouth clean with a tissue from her garish red purse and threw Karen a horrified look. She made a point of not looking at the tower, which was easy, since they weren't actually headed towards it and the images it displayed were silent.

"Well, now we know the show's organizers mean business," Karen told Lexi. "We're really gonna have to earn that twenty-four mil." She laughed coldly. "And on the bright side of things—"

"There's a bright side to this!?" Lexi practically shrieked this at her.

"Calm down, someone might hear you," Karen whispered. "Remember there's boogeymen out here too."

The threat of boogeymen immediately calmed Lexi. "You said there's a *bright side* to . . . this?"

Karen nodded. "Sure there is. Now there's only six of us left to compete for the prize money. That automatically increases the odds in our favor."

"Okay, okay, you've got a point there," Lexi grudgingly agreed. "But let's just get into the house. After seeing that, I feel completely exposed standing out here in the open."

Karen nodded and they set off up the short gravel driveway to the bungalow. "Yes, let's. I need to find the keys to these handcuffs ASAP; before someone thinks I'm a hooker too."

Lexi scowled. "Ha ha. Bitch, I'll have you know it's a good life, working on your back. Comfortable as fuck."

"Whatever. It's your pussy, not mine. But I'm certain your feminine charms won't do you any good tonight. You've noticed that the boogeymen have been lobotomized, haven't you?"

Lexi laughed cynically. "Men have *two* brains, darling, and it's the one in the lower head that I'm interested in. Crazy or not—men are still men. I think I'll have little trouble taming the savage beast."

The woman sounded serious. Karen shrugged and pulled her up the steps of the bungalow's front porch and through the screen door.

"Hey, stop dragging me along like this!" Lexi protested. "You're hurting my damn wrist."

Karen paused for a moment and smirked back at her. "Don't blame me, blame these cuffs linking us together. Me, I'll happily leave you outside for the monsters to get. Then there'll only be five of us left in the competition. Not to add that the good housewives of Salt Lake City will be delighted to see the last of you."

With a look of fright on her face, Lexi hurried past Karen and through the front door. The lights were all on.

Once inside the house, Karen's cop instincts asserted themselves.

"Hey, not so fast," she cautioned Lexi, who seemed set to drag her across the living room and into the kitchen simply for the hell of it. "We don't know if anyone else is in here with us." Her wrist ached too. These handcuffs were really a problem. Being chained to this airhead prostitute wasn't how Karen Rogers wanted to spend the rest of the night.

Lexi halted and frowned. "What's the matter?"

Karen rolled her eyes. "Don't you have any self-preservation instincts?"

"I just wanted to see if there's some beer in the fridge."

"Now you're thirsty?"

"Nah, I just wanna wash the taste of vomit out of my mouth."

Karen nodded. "Later. Let's first search this house for some guns and stuff. Then we'll be able to defend ourselves if someone breaks in while you're having your beer."

"C'mon, Karen, find a heart somewhere. My mouth stinks like someone just pooped in it?"

Karen laughed. "Lexi, how d'you know what a mouth filled with poop smells like? No, I don't wanna know the answer to that. And no, we're gonna search the house first. For weapons and the keys to these damn handcuffs. If I spend much longer chained to you, I might kill you just to get free."

"Kill me?"

"Lexi, you're a walking annoyance. And despite just throwing up out there, you don't seem to fully realize the gravity of our current situation. We're inside a house that might also contain some monsters and you're only concerned about how your mouth smells. So no, I don't intend on dying just because you suddenly feel you need to douche so your pussy smells like roses when one of Miriam Heller's freak boogeymen finds us." Karen realized that she too had thrown caution to the winds by raising her voice. But she didn't care. Lexi Austin was just too annoying to live. She frowned at the prostitute. "So, if I strangle you, that's at least one worry less for me."

Lexi scowled at Karen. "Hey, no need for that. I got the key to the handcuffs right here with me."

Karen gaped at her. "You've what?"

Lexi nodded. "Yeah, you heard me right. The key to the handcuffs is here in my handbag." She smirked at Karen. "When the ROC told me they were gonna pair us up, I told them I wasn't having it unless they did something to stop you from tossing me over the platform railing. So they cuffed us together and gave me the key?"

Karen got over her shock. "And why didn't you say so earlier?"

Lexi didn't reply. She just fished in her handbag, produced the key and unlocked the cuff around her own wrist. Then she handed the key to Karen. "Free yourself, cop girl. Me? I'm off to get myself a beer."

Karen felt like decking her. But she didn't. "Listen," she said reasonably, "the beer can wait; let's look for some guns first."

Lexi shook her head. "I can drink and search the house at the same time." She turned and hurried off through the dining area to the kitchen.

Karen shrugged. "Yeah, whatever." She unlocked the handcuff around her wrist, placed cuffs and key on a chair, and began rubbing some circulation back into her wrist.

At least I'm free from her now and—

"Yeah!"

Lexi's yelp of joy was so loud that Karen felt like she'd been shocked with an electric current. *What the hell is wrong with that girl? Or has she found the money? That would be an insane stroke of good fortune.*

"Yes, yes," Lexi was saying from the kitchen. "Hey, Karen, I've found the guns!"

She's found the guns? Karen walked into the kitchen. True enough, Lexi had a case of handguns opened up on the kitchen counter. There were some knives in there too.

"Where did you find them?" Karen asked in surprise.

Lexi grinned and popped the tab on a can of Budweiser. "They were in the fridge with the beer." She gestured behind her. "There's a shotgun in there too."

51

Karen peered behind Lexi and saw the shotgun propped up in the fridge. The fridge's crisper and lower shelves had been removed to make space for the gun case. Only the top two shelves remained. The lower one held sandwiches, the upper one more beers.

Karen looked back at the case of weapons and grinned. "Pass me a beer too," she told Lexi. "Maybe you aren't so useless after all."

Lexi grinned back and slid a Budweiser to Karen along the counter. Once Lexi had finished gargling and rinsing out her mouth at the kitchen sink, they carried their drinks and the weapons case and shotgun out into the living room.

***

The beer tasted odd to Karen. Not like it was poisoned or anything like that; but like another memory she couldn't properly connect with. Or maybe it was more than that:

It's like I don't know how beer is supposed to taste. I asked for a beer, but I'm not even sure if I like beer. I must have a favorite drink, but if I do then I don't remember what it is.

"Hey, what do you remember about me?" she asked Lexi.

Lexi had balanced her beer on the left arm of her armchair and was examining a Glock handgun. Karen was at first surprised by how efficiently Lexi popped out the gun's magazine, studied its bullets and then replaced it; but then she remembered that Lexi's boyfriend was a drug dealer.

And she shot me in the head, so she does know how to handle guns. She lifted a hand and felt the back of her scalp, where, according to Lexi there had been a gaping exit wound. She felt nothing out of the ordinary there now. The Red Octopus Corporation truly were surgical wizards.

"Huh?" Lexi asked, setting down the Glock and picking up a revolver. Karen had already decided she'd just take the shotgun and a knife. No point in complicating things. But Lexi seemed to like pistols.

Yeah, 'cos they'll fit in her purse and not mess up her sexiness.

"I asked what you know about me," she told Lexi now that she had her attention. "What do you know about my life before you shot me? Not personally, but there must've been some stuff in the papers. My mind is a total blank . . . but did I have a boyfriend? Or a girlfriend even—was I a dyke? Was I married with kids? Husband, family, parents? Did you hear anything like that from the cops who arrested you?"

Lexi thought a bit. "Well, I do remember something about a boyfriend. Yeah, a guy named Jake. Dude was on the news with tears in his eyes. So he must've really loved you. But no, there wasn't any mention of any kids you'd had together." She grinned. "Hey, pull up your shirt and see if you've got stretch marks."

"Huh?"

"Stretch marks from pregnancy."

"Oh. No, there's none of those." In fact Karen had a six-pack, like she'd often worked out in the gym. She was in as good physical shape as her companion; better even, because she was sure she didn't foul up her system with narcotics like Lexi was doing now, shoveling cocaine up her nose, using the key to the handcuffs as a spoon.

Karen sipped her beer, shut her eyes and smiled to herself. She'd been loved; someone actually cared about her. *I have a boyfriend named Jake who really loves me. And he'll be delighted to see me again once I sur—*

"Hey! Hey, cop girl!"

Karen opened her eyes and instantly cursed herself for getting sentimental and letting her emotions take her out of the game.

Lexi was pointing both of her handguns at her. Karen felt a moment of total déjà vu: yes, she damned well had been in this situation before, with Lexi about to shoot her.

The prostitute's eyes were drug-wide, bright and intense, her nostrils flaring. There was white powder on her upper lip and her red hair seemed to float around her head. Her mouth was a crimson smirk. Karen looked from Lexi's doped-up face to her two guns; the revolver in her right hand, the Glock in her left; at those two black holes in their tips which, any moment now, would discharge fire at her.

"I just wanted to say goodbye . . . again," Lexi said with excitement in her eyes. "I don't know how you survived the last time, but this time I've got *two* guns. More firepower, ya know."

Karen flung herself sideways to the left the moment Lexi began firing at her. She felt a burning pain in her left forearm and then hit the ground. She glanced back at Lexi.

"Damn, I missed the bitch," Lexi was saying. She swung the pistols towards Karen and fired again, but now Karen flung herself into the corner of the living room and the shots destroyed the television instead. Next Karen rolled behind the couch she'd been sitting on.

She lay low back there, pressed flat against the rug while Lexi kept shooting at her through the couch, filling the air with fluff.

"Hey, cop girl, no hard feelings, you hear me? I'm just increasing the odds in my favor."

"You damn bitch!" she shouted back. "I should've known you were going to double-cross me first chance you got!"

"Hey, don't blame me! I'm like, greedy, ya know? I had a deprived upbringing. What more can I say?"

Lexi kept firing, but possibly because of the cocaine in her system, she kept aiming high, not down toward the floor. A bullet lightly grazed Karen's buttocks but that was all. Thankfully there were no ricochets. Lexi's other shots all floated harmlessly over Karen, though after ripping their way through the couch they shattered the wall and sprayed her with shards of plasterboard.

Karen remained pressed to the floor back there until she heard both of Lexi's guns click empty.

Alright, time to move.

She surged to her feet and leapt over the back of the couch. Lexi had been standing and grinning at her handwork, admiring the new holes in the couch's leather upholstery. But when she saw Karen coming, she shrieked in fright, dropped both of her guns and fled, with her high heels clopping like a horse's hooves.

She was gone out the front door even before Karen had picked up the shotgun and aimed it. The only thing the following shotgun blast accomplished was to slam the door shut behind her.

"You damn skanky murdering whore," Karen cussed at the new hole in the door. "You just wait till I catch you again."

Then she dropped the shotgun on the couch and examined her injured left forearm. The bullet had chipped away a patch of skin and some flesh, but it had missed both forearm bones. Surprisingly, she wasn't bleeding much and wasn't really in pain.

"Kudos again to the ROC's surgeons," Karen said aloud. "I'll survive." She got up and walked towards the kitchen. "And while I'm still alive I think I'll have another beer."

CHAPTER 7

Fatima

Even though they were both safely inside a house before the tower screens displayed Rita and Megan's gory deaths, Fatima Noori and Emily Ford watched it anyway. There was nothing between their refuge and the tower except the pond, and so they essentially had ringside seats to the double slaughter, staring through parted drapes at the glossy high-definition images.

While watching Rita murder her stepdaughter, Fatima felt like she imagined the spectators in the Roman coliseum did in ancient days. The gore both thrilled and disgusted her. It also terrified her.

"That could be us in just a little while if we don't watch each other's backs," Emily said, giving Fatima a meaningful glance and then turning away from her and striding purposefully across the living room towards the hallway.

"Well, I'm not about to stab you in the back like that," Fatima said, hurrying after her. "I'm not that kind of person."

Emily turned to stare at her. "No, you actually don't look like a killer. So why are you here? What are you doing on this game show where everybody wants to murder you?"

Fatima laughed at the question. "I'm wondering about that too myself now. I had no frigging idea it was going to be like this."

"And we're just getting started," Emily added.

Fatima couldn't tell if the other young woman was scared or delighted at the prospect of the bloody violence to come. Sometimes it seemed like it was both.

"Come on," she said. "Let's check the bedrooms and the bathrooms for weapons. There clearly aren't any here in the living room. And I doubt that the show's hosts would be so obvious as to hide knives in the kitchen."

She led the way and Emily followed. It wasn't that Fatima was in a hurry to get involved in the killing herself, it was rather that being busy meant she didn't have to think too much about the deaths she'd just witnessed.

"You search on the left while I take the right," she instructed her shorter companion, relieved that they weren't having arguments over who was in charge here.

She watched Emily Ford enter a storeroom and then stepped into the bedroom on her right.

This bedroom both smelt of male cologne and was in a male-inspired mess, as if its previous inhabitants had left in a hurry. The bed was unmade, with three pillows scattered across its surface like stepping stones in a lake.

Fatima, who was a fastidious girl, hoped she wouldn't find used condoms floating in the toilet bowl.

Thankfully, such was not the case. She did however find two hunting knives and a small axe hidden in the bathroom cabinet, along with a baggie of white powder, which, being from New York, she was street-smart enough to recognize as cocaine.

With a shudder of revulsion Fatima flushed the cocaine down the toilet. Even though she'd never done drugs herself, she was quite familiar with their effects.

In her everyday life Fatima Noori had a degree in Education and was an elementary school teacher. It was one of the few jobs which her father and twin sister didn't consider demeaning and corrupting for an unmarried young Muslim woman.

After flushing away the cocaine, she went to find Emily and show her what she'd found.

CHAPTER 8

Flashback: Iran–USA–Brazil

In the last years of the last decade of the last century, Fatima's father Saeed Noori had fled Iran as a young student, after publishing a pamphlet supporting the rights of his country's womenfolk. An uncle of his had caught wind of a police raid to arrest Saeed and his fellow student 'troublemakers' and had smuggled the protesting young man out of the country in the hold of a Kuwait-bound airplane with a cargo of fruit and vegetables.

From Kuwait the young would-be revolutionary had been flown out to his Uncle Hassan in the USA.

On arriving in late 1990's America however, Saeed, a simple young man who had merely wanted to improve the political lot of the women in his country, had discovered that rather than American women not having enough rights, they seemed to have too many.

Uncle Hassan, his mother's older brother, lived in the Bronx in New York, that melting pot of planetary culture. Coming from a place as conservative as Iran, Saeed Noori was practically traumatized by the sight of (in his opinion) 'almost naked' women prancing about. This devout young Muslim man imagined he'd fallen into Hell itself with all these temptations everywhere.

But finally he'd adapted. He'd settled down and taken over running Uncle Hassan's halal butcher shop. The old man wanted to return home to Iran, to—in his own words—"die and be buried in the soil of my birth." Uncle Hassan had no children of his own, and as such no one to inherit his business. He had long ago named Saeed as his heir, but until Saeed's brush with the Iranian government, his nephew's father had been unwilling to let the boy travel to 'decadent' America.

After his uncle's departure for home, Saeed began thinking about getting married. However, one thing was certain: even though he had adapted very well to his new country, and was now mostly 'doing as the Romans do while in Rome,' he had no desire to chain himself to one of America's decadent 'Jezebels' for life.

Saeed finally opted to marry Jamila Sattari, the pretty younger sister of the Iranian immigrant who owned the newsstand down the road from his halal butcher shop.

Jamila Sattari had apparently also been in love with Saeed for quite a while, because she quickly accepted his proposal. The pair got married on a rainy Saturday in April.

And things were great between them until the year after their twin daughters were born.

One morning Saeed left to attend to some business at the post office. On his return, he found his little girls crying in their playroom and a 'goodbye' note taped to the television.

In her goodbye note, Jamila explained that she just wasn't cut out to be a poor butcher's wife. She added that, educated and cultured as she was, she saw no point in hanging around Saeed any longer. He was to give her love to the girls and she would try to send him some money from time to time to help raise them.

Saeed was understandably devastated. Here he was, after having done his absolute best to avoid marrying an American 'Jezebel,' discovering that he'd been living with an Iranian one.

Carrying both of his daughters, he walked down the street to his brother-in-law's newsstand and showed him Jamila's letter. Muhammad Sattari was even more confused than Saeed. The last time he'd spoken to his sister, she'd professed her delight with her husband and said she wanted them to try for a third baby, and had even joked that she hoped she wouldn't have twins again.

***

With Jamila apparently gone for good, the heartbroken Saeed returned home and began raising Fatima and Khadija as a single parent.

Muhammad Sattari had been telling the truth about not knowing his sister's whereabouts. However, he soon found out where she was.

A week after leaving home, Jamila Noori phoned him and told him she was now living in a swank penthouse with her new boyfriend, a Brazilian named Roberto Silva whom Muhammad knew both by sight and reputation to be one of the Bronx's most dangerous drug dealers.

Once given the information Muhammad did the sensible thing and kept quiet, not breathing a word about his sister's whereabouts to her heartbroken husband. Telling Saeed where Jamila was would certainly result in him going over there to try to win her back and this would most likely result in Saeed's untimely death.

And besides, Jamila had also told Muhammad that she'd be leaving for Europe with Roberto Silva in a week. Muhammad kept his mouth shut and Jamila departed for France with her new lover.

And so the years passed.

True to her word, Jamila did send money back home to help take care of her daughters. She sent the money through Muhammad.

But the very first time that Muhammad tried to give the money to Saeed, Saeed furiously rejected it.

"Don't you dare give me that prostitute's earnings," he raged at his brother-in-law.

Muhammad was taken aback by this refusal. Not so much that Saeed hadn't accepted Jamila's offering, but that Saeed had found out that his ex-wife was now working as a high-paid call girl in Paris.

Muhammad now found himself with two thousand dollars in cash and no one to give it to. Being an honest and devout Muslim himself, one who definitely didn't approve of his sister turning herself into an object of commerce, there was no way Muhammad Sattari was going to spend the money. And since Jamila's husband wasn't about to accept the cash from him for exactly the same reason, Muhammad's only other option seemed to be to return the money to his sister.

But just as Muhammad was about to call long distance to France, he spotted a blind young woman being helped across the road by a guide dog.

Muhammad then decided to put Jamila's money to good use. He did some research and finally found an NGO down in Brazil that focused on providing eye surgery to underprivileged children. He sent them Jamila's money in her name. He considered it both ironic and fitting that the proceeds of her whoredom were being used to improve lives in her original seducer's country.

Muhammad never told Jamila what he was doing. She sent him money on a quarterly basis and he sent it all down to Brazil.

And this was why Jamila imagined all was well, well as well as could be under the circumstances, between herself and Saeed.

***

Three years later, Jamila came to see her twin daughters.

Even though she was barely five years old at the time, Fatima remembered that day vividly, just like it was yesterday. It was a Sunday morning. Her mother had arrived at the halal butcher shop (the twins and their father lived in the apartment right above the shop) in a flashy white chauffeur-driven limousine.

Jamila had gotten out alone and Fatima could still recall how beautiful she was, how proud and aloof and different from everybody else out on the street that Sunday morning, glossy and glittering and painted like a bird of paradise. She seemed ethereal, like a creature from Heaven. Whenever Fatima and Khadija asked their father about their mother, he had always referred to her as an 'agent of Shaitan,' but now, seeing Jamila Noori in person for what was really the first time, Fatima was surprised that the 'agent of Shaitan' could be so lovely.

"Papa, mama is here!" she yelled joyously as her mother bent to pick her up, an act that Jamila never completed because right in the nick of time she noticed the cleaver blade cutting through the air towards her head.

Jamila leapt back to safety, and because Fatima was blocking Saeed's way, she was able to get outside to the sidewalk unharmed.

Outside, Jamila instinctively forgot the limo she'd arrived in and took off running down the sidewalk, with Saeed in hot pursuit, waving the cleaver at her like a serial killer. After about twenty yards Jamila paused, kicked off her high heels, and resumed running.

"You won't corrupt my daughters, you dirty whore!" Saeed screamed as he chased her, with frightened Sunday morning shoppers scattering left and right to let them through. Meanwhile Jamila's chauffeur had gotten over his own surprise and was tailing his mistress with the limo, trying to get her to get in the car, but she was too panicked to listen to him.

What saved Jamila's life that morning was the appearance of her brother Muhammad at the door of his newsstand. In an ironic twist of fate, Jamila hadn't stopped by her brother's house before visiting her ex-husband. If she had, he would have warned her not to go to the butcher shop. Indeed, what Muhammad had had in mind was to bring the girls to the newsstand under some pretext and let Jamila meet them there.

But now, while arranging magazines on a rack, Muhammad was alerted to a commotion in the street. He looked up just in time to see Jamila run past him, as fleet-footed as a gazelle, and with Saeed hot in pursuit.

Quickly working out what was going on, Muhammad figured that if Saeed killed Jamila (which he wasn't entirely adverse to, as it would keep her from sullying the family name further) and went for jail for it, it would leave his two daughters parentless. So, acting fast, Muhammad stuck out his foot and tripped Saeed up.

Saeed went flying one way, his meat cleaver went flying the other way, and while Jamila safety crossed the intersection and finally climbed into her limousine, which instantly zoomed off, Saeed fell and hit his head on the curb, knocking himself unconscious.

This of course marked the end of the pursuit.

However, since then Jamila had gotten the loud and clear message to stay away from Saeed and his daughters.

Jamila was middle-aged now, and married to a rich rancher in Brazil.

And in this too there was another twist, the final irony as it were; because Jamila's current husband was the man who had set up the NGO for the blind that her brother had been sending the money intended for her children to for all these years.

Jamila had continued sending the girls money even after her almost fatal visit, because in the light of what had happened that day, Muhammad hadn't had the heart to tell her what he'd really been doing with the cash she was supposedly sending home.

***

After Jamila's visit, Saeed had become very strict with his daughters.

His explanation to his brother-in-law Muhammad was that he was raising his daughters to be "devout and God-fearing young women and not prostitutes like their wayward mother."

And so the years passed, with Fatima and Khadija Noori both growing up into gorgeous young women, a fact that gave their father endless cause for concern (and peptic ulcers) once they entered high school, and made his parenting regime even more strict.

Because, see, both girls were much more beautiful than their mother had ever been.

But Saeed needn't have worried. Neither Fatima nor Khadija had any intention of straying from the straight-and-narrow. Whenever the liberal-minded Fatima seemed about to take a wrong step as dictated by the Muslim faith, her more conservative sister Khadija always reined in her wayward impulses.

And so both of Saeed Noori's gorgeous daughters made it through high school in NYC without either smoking marijuana, getting drunk, or even kissing a boy, talk less of being deflowered. And this state of affairs, this state of virginal purity in both of them, had continued through their college years until the present day.

In college, Fatima studied Education, while Khadija majored in Social Work. Both of them completely ignored all of their mother's attempts to reconnect with them through social media. As far as Saeed Noori's daughters were concerned, they had no mother.

But now that they were out of college and in the adult world, their father's influence in their lives had begun waning somewhat.

Fatima in particular, had begun questioning all she'd been taught over the years. She didn't question Islam itself, or the Holy Prophet either, but rather her father's interpretation of their faith, which in the years since their mother's desertion had become more and more draconian, until each time she thought about him she couldn't help likening him to Ayatollah Khomeini.

Khadija, however, who was socially-minded and worked at a homeless shelter, was perfectly okay with the situation at home. If anything, in her own divergence from their father's teachings she had become more right-wing, radical and evangelical.

An example of the differences between the two sisters, was the disagreement they'd had while watching a documentary on the use of fashionable face masks in China and Japan.

Fatima saw no difference between a face mask and the Muslim veil. All she saw was that both covered the face. She'd mentioned this to her older sister (by eight minutes) but Khadija had gotten so angry at the suggestion that face masks and veils were the same that Fatima had quickly backpedaled and apologized profusely. Khadija had looked angry enough to stab her with the pair of scissors she was holding.

Sometimes Fatima's own sister scared her.

She wondered what all the fuss was about the hijab and veil anyway. And her father had taken Khadija's side in the argument, going so far as to suggest that she and her sister adopt that ultra-conservative dress style now that they were of marriageable age. Khadija already wore a hijab on a regular basis but Fatima had so far resisted doing so.

That argument with her sister had been the final straw that broke Fatima's camel's back.

She'd felt that her father was now really taking things to extremes. None of her Arab-American girlfriends felt compelled to attire themselves as if they still lived in the desert, and all the black Muslim girls she knew dressed like the other young negresses in the concrete jungle that was NYC.

So yes, Fatima had had enough. She was getting out of her controlling family situation no matter what her father or sister thought.

Her memory blurred by the intervening years, Fatima had also recently begun sympathizing with her estranged mother Jamila. Not having been old enough at the time to remember the truth firsthand, she now wrongly assumed that her father had always been this strict and that he was most likely responsible for driving her mother away from home in the first place.

She began to resent him, and for the first time to desire freedom, personal freedom to be the young woman she felt she could be.

But she would do it with honor. No matter what her hyper-religious twin thought, she wasn't a slut.

And this was where Miriam Heller's *The Virgin* game show had seemed just perfect for Fatima Noori to achieve her twin goals of becoming rich and leaving home.

The Virgin was an underground reality show where young women in a state of 'sexual purity' competed to keep their hymens intact. Fatima had applied and had quickly been accepted.

Fatima had had no fears about competing. An athletic and strong girl, she'd been certain she would win *The Virgin* game show, thus retaining her purity and becoming rich into the bargain.

But two days before *The Virgin* was to be held, Fatima had caught a bad dose of the flu and had been unable to compete.

She'd been very depressed afterwards, because *The Virgin* reality show was only held once a year, and she honestly didn't see herself surviving another year of her current family situation without losing her mind.

But then help had come from an unexpected source. Miriam Heller (who had been impressed both by Fatima's courage and her beauty), had phoned and asked her if she'd be interested in competing on another underground reality show—*The Final Girl.*

"But you need to consider this very carefully," Miriam had warned her. "Because, if anything, this new game show will be more dangerous than *The Virgin*. A lot more dangerous. But on the plus side of things, this time the prize money is twenty-four million dollars, more than double the ten million you stood to win on *The Virgin*."

"Oh, you're a total lifesaver," Fatima had gushed to Miriam over the phone. "Yes, yes, please sign me up. I'll do it. I'll definitely do it."

After that, all that had remained for Fatima to do was to play the dutiful and loyal daughter and sister, so as not to arouse either her father's or Khadija's suspicions.

And she'd done just that. And so here she was now.

And now all I have to do is win and I'll be set for life, she'd told herself on her arrival.

CHAPTER 9

Fatima/Emily

Fatima found Emily sitting on the living room floor, with an attaché case full of guns and ammo open in front of her.

"Like I suspected, the case was in the storeroom," Emily said with a wild gleam in her eyes. "Right out in the open. I didn't even need to search."

Fatima waved her knives and axe at Emily. "These were in the bathroom cabinet." She set them down on a chair.

The TV was on, but was idling like the big tower screens outside, with a red ROC logo bouncing across the black screen as a screensaver.

Fatima returned her attention to Emily and the guns. Now she saw that there were also knives in the case. Very sharp-looking knives.

The sight of the weapons impressed the seriousness of this so-called 'game' on Fatima.

She'd taken a few steps towards Emily, but now froze because Emily was pointing a pistol at her.

"Oh no," Fatima said, instantly raising her hands in a show of harmlessness, "I thought we weren't going to backstab each other yet."

But then Emily laughed, reversed her hold on the gun and handed it to Fatima grip-first. "Oh, I'm sorry if I scared you. I didn't mean to."

Fatima had never handled a gun before. It was heavier than she'd expected considering its size. But holding it gave her a strange feeling of confidence, made her feel that now she was really up to the task ahead.

She curled her index finger around the trigger. She glanced down at Emily, realizing that now she had the other woman in her power and could kill her if she so desired.

Emily seemed to sense this conflict in her because she looked frightened. But then Fatima lowered the gun and slipped it into her waistband at the rear of her jeans, just like she'd seen done in movies.

Emily heaved a sigh of relief and leaned back against a couch. But then she began laughing.

Fatima smiled. "Hey, what's so funny?"

"Well, I guess I can trust *you*," Emily said, handing Fatima a short metal container.

"What's this?" Fatima asked, before turning it around and realizing that it contained bullets.

"Just the magazine for the pistol I gave you," Emily explained. "I wasn't about taking a chance on you murdering me."

Fatima felt confused. "But we already agreed on that, didn't we?"

Emily nodded. "Sure we did. But while you were searching in the house, I turned the TV on and saw that hooker—the redhead who's paired with the cop—shooting at her and then running off."

"Did she kill her?" Fatima asked breathlessly. This violence was both stimulating and frightening.

"No, the cop survived. She has lightning-fast reflexes." Then Emily frowned. "But still, now there's just six of us girls left on the show and none of us have encountered the boogeymen yet."

Fatima pulled the gun out of her waistband and fiddled with it and its magazine for a while, finally working out how to slide the clip properly into place. Then she pulled back the slide like she'd seen done on TV, and replaced the gun in her waistband again. After completing this she returned her full attention to her companion.

"Hey, I've been meaning to ask you about *that* for a while now," she said. "Is there something you know that I don't? Because, Emily, you didn't seem particularly surprised to see either the boogeyman or that monster when Miriam showed them to us."

Emily handed Fatima another gun and a survival knife in a sheath. Then she got up from the floor and instead sat on the couch she'd been leaning her back against, resting the gun case on her lap.

Then she laughed. "Oh, I wasn't surprised because I work here. And I'd seen those surgical freaks before, just not a big human centipede like that one. The ones I'd previously seen had just three or four segments, and they had just one head too." She laughed again, a cold and very harsh sound. "I guess the bosses didn't want me having an unfair advantage against you other contestants on the show."

Fatima sat next to Emily on the couch. It was taking her some time to digest her companion's words.

"You . . . you work here? You're a member of the ROC? You're a member of the Red Octopus Corporation?"

Emily nodded. "Yes, medical division—I'm sure you already know that I'm a nurse. but I'm low-ranking, not very high up the corporation ladder. But still, I know a few things. For instance, I assisted the doctors who created some of the boogeymen."

"So if you're ROC, how come you're on the show then? Is this punishment? Did you commit an offence or what?"

Emily laughed and stuck a pair of large guns into her waistband. "A chance to become rich as punishment? Hell no. The guys being punished are the ones who were used to make the human centipedes."

"So, how come then?" Fatima was really curious now.

Emily shrugged. "Oh, I just wanted to be on the show. I've always liked action and adventure and just couldn't pass up a chance to compete in something like this. And besides, I'm not stinking rich, like many of our other members are—I've got a son and a mortgage and two cats. I can really use that twenty-four million dollars prize money."

Fatima nodded and glanced at the idling television. She wondered if there were cameras built into the television, watching them as they watched it. Because, for certain, they were under surveillance right now, even though she had seen no sign of video cameras or microphones since they had entered this house.

She shrugged. She figured that if anything crucial was happening, the TV would be sure to show it. Which meant she could question Emily a bit more before they left the house.

"Hey, how is it even possible to create freaks like the boogeymen?"

Emily shrugged again. "It's just advanced biological technology. I'm assuming that at least you have some background knowledge about human DNA?

Fatima nodded. "Yeah, but just a smattering. I just know what everyone else does: that DNA contains the blueprint for human life and that everyone's DNA is unique." She laughed and added, "Oh yeah, and that for us girls, it's great for paternity tests when you're unsure who your babydaddy is."

Emily laughed at the joke, then explained:

"Well, if like the ROC, you have the ability to perfectly clone human tissue, to grow flesh in vats, then you can graft those muscles—and other organs—wherever you like in a human body. So long as the DNA code is the same, the host body will always accept the new organs, misinterpreting them as an original part of itself. And if—again like the ROC—you know how to connect up the nerves—how to rewire them to that individual's brain—you can make those grafted muscles work normally in their new body. Hence, you can easily create a person with six fully functional arms or legs, or with five or six heads." She frowned. "I'm actually oversimplifying this—it's the only way you'll understand. The Red Octopus Corporation actually have the ability to graft tissue from *different persons* together, without any tissue rejection occurring. That's how they made the human centipedes—like I earlier implied, those were men and women scheduled for drastic punishment, for example ROC members who had betrayed the organization. Or foolish journalists who had tried to infiltrate and expose us."

"But . . but that's impossible," Fatima sputtered. What Emily was saying sounded too much like science fiction to be true.

"All it takes is the know-how," Emily went on. "And I assure you, they . . . I should actually say 'we' . . . do know how. The ROC doctors can also graft or connect living tissue from different species together. For instance, they can give a person a dog's head, or vice versa. The same applies to birds and fish, even to bugs and worms."

"C'mon, that's science fiction."

"Here it's science fact. We just aren't gonna share our discoveries with the world."

"But why not? Think about it: by sharing such incredible technological advances you'd be saving millions of lives."

"Help people?" Emily laughed. "Darling, we're not into that goody-goody stuff. The ROC is an *evil* organization. We're out to establish worldwide evil and chaos." She gestured behind them, at the giant tower visible through the open windows. "That technological marvel and everything else out there, and us being here in the game, is merely entertainment, recreation for ROC members. It's to remind us that we're privileged . . . superior. So don't get it into your pretty head that we're gonna help anyone live forever except ourselves."

Fatima didn't understand how eternal life had gotten entwined in their conversation but she let it go.

Emily Ford shook her head. "And anyway, I'm sworn to silence. We all are. I couldn't tell you any deep ROC secrets even if you tortured and killed me." She laughed. " 'Cos, think about it yourself, which fate would you rather prefer: to be dead, or to be a segment in a human centipede?"

"Me, be part of a human centipede? Ugh!" Simply remembering the creature made Fatima shudder. "Hell no, I'd rather die!"

"My choice and point exactly," Emily Ford agreed in a painfully sober voice. "And you don't even know the half of it. A doctor friend of mine recently told me that the centipede segments aren't exactly mindless . . ."

"They're not?"

Emily sadly shook her head. "No, they're not. What this guy said was that because the ROC want the offenders to really suffer, the surgeons keep those portions of each person's brain that houses our human consciousness, along with the parts that sense pain and torment. Everything else is discarded, but those saved bits are nurtured and stored in each person's torso near their heart; so that in essence, in each segment of a human centipede you have the living mind of someone who is in a sense still alive, but who is also suffering eternal torment, complete agony for as long as they're a part of the centipede . . . and who is utterly powerless to do anything to save themselves."

Fatima's eyes widened at the revelation. "But that's utterly terrible—hellish!"

Emily laughed. "Oh, Hell isn't a strong enough word to describe the ROC. Trust me on this, sister—you're much better off not knowing anything about us other than that we're putting on this insane and lucrative show."

Emily fell silent then and looked rather subdued. Fatima felt intense pity for her. Because, if there was one thing that she'd learnt from this short discussion of theirs, it was that the ROC—the Red Octopus Corporation—was a VERY evil organization; one which no sane person should want anything to do with. And Emily Ford currently gave off the vibe of someone who wanted out of a personal hell that she'd somehow fallen into.

Oh wow, girl, Fatima thought in empathy, *I can definitely relate to that.*

Then Emily smiled at her, her old brash personality restored. "Come on, bitch, let's go find that money!" she said.

Fatima nodded and managed to grin. Emily shifted the gun case off of her lap and onto the couch and both young women got to their feet and departed the house together.

"Hey, what do you imagine those creepy twins are up to right now?" Fatima asked Emily as they set off through the surrounding woods.

Emily sniggered. "Those two psycho bitches? Girl, your guess is as bad as mine. That pair are so clueless, they're most likely counting floaters in the toilet."

CHAPTER 10

Berry/Cherry

"Sis, how do you conjugate the verb 'to poo?' "

"I pooed, you pooed, he pooped, she pooped."

"Dad and mom pooped. Mr. and Mrs. President pooped. The US Senate—"

"— pooped. Everyone in the world poops all the time. All the men—"

"—all the women, all the little boys and girls. Yeah and—"

"—it really stinks too! And especially the babies—"

"—never forget the little babies. Babies poop all the time."

"All the aliens, both legals, illegals and E.T's pooped! Which is why Mr. President—"

"—refused them green cards and gave them toilet roll instead!"

"But don't you dare forget—we're the Poole twins, not the Poop twins!"

"Even though we too poop all the time. Even though Cherry—"

"—is pooping right now!"

"Hey, sis, I'm *Berry*, you are Cherry."

"My bad. I forgot I have red hair now."

So far the Poole twins had had no luck whatsoever with finding a weapons cache. The house they had entered, one of the play zone's two-story buildings, had seemed promising. But that had been ten minutes ago. They'd since checked through both floors but found nothing.

The girls were about to leave the house when Berry suddenly realized that she needed to use the toilet.

As was usual for this totally enmeshed duo, Cherry had accompanied her sister to the toilet and stood beside its open door watching Berry relieve herself.

Which was how they had begun 'conjugating' the 'verb' 'to poop.'

It was one of the great tragedies of the Poole twins' life that they couldn't perfectly synchronize their bodily functions. True, they could eat and drink at the same time, but they couldn't always urinate and defecate at the same time.

Even more frustrating was when they used to masturbate together. That hadn't worked at all. No matter what she did, how much she tried to hold back from climaxing, Cherry always came faster than her sister, who was a slow burner. Most times Cherry would reach orgasm in four minutes flat; while it generally took Berry at least seven minutes to come. The difference remained even when they had a boyfriend, and was usually the factor that drove those young men away, seeing as it was hard to concentrate on sex when the twin sister of the lady you were making love to was timing you with a stopwatch and either urging you to go faster or slower, depending on which of them currently had the timepiece.

Even the benefits and joys of having 'two for the price of one' had its limits.

Berry finished, wiped herself clean, and then discovered that she couldn't flush the toilet.

"The damn thing is broken," she told Cherry.

Cherry stepped up to the water cistern and depressed the flush button. "You're right!" she exclaimed. "It is faulty."

"So what do we do? Leave it for the janitor to clean up?"

The twins stared down at the floaters in the toilet bowl.

"Wow, those look gross. I think you did more—"

"—than my last one. Let's try to flush it again, but much harder this time."

So they did, this time with each of them placing a thumb on the flush button.

Then they both shrieked as one, and leapt back in fright as the entire toilet fixture folded itself up and sank into the floor. They watched pink ceramic tiles pop out of the floor and cover the space that the toilet had occupied. Simultaneously, a blast of deodorant spray from an unseen aperture quickly eliminated the smell of Berry's excrement.

"Wow!" one of them said.

"Hey, look," the other one said. "Yeah!"

Right where the toilet had previously stood, there was now a large opening in the wall.

"Looks like we found the guns, sis. Yep, this sure—"

"—looks like a gun closet to me."

The girls helped themselves to the weapons, each taking the same things from the racks—a small revolver, a survival knife, and a small axe. And each twin stuck the weapons in exactly the same place as her sister: axe in belt on the left, knife in belt on the right; revolver in right-hand pocket of jacket.

Then they stared at the small pink chainsaw in deep regret.

"Too bad there's only one of those."

"Yes, and that makes me very angry, because—"

"—there should be two chainsaws because there's two of us Poole twins. This is—"

"—the show's producers' doing. They're stacking the odds against us. Oh, screw them. We'll win anyway. Won't we?"

"Yes, screw them. We will win—"

"—no matter what dirty tricks they try to play on us."

Invigorated and motivated by this perceived discrimination against twinship, Cherry and Berry Poole left the one-time toilet and departed the house.

They stood side-by-side on the small front porch, peering through the darkness beneath the trees.

The darkness was troubling. It *sounded* wrong. And this was because although the ROC had imported vegetation down here, they hadn't imported the creatures that went along with that vegetation, particularly the insects. Everywhere here was as silent as a frozen-over graveyard in the dead of winter when the wind is still, which was the intention.

Finally, one of the twins asked the other: "So where do you think our money is hiding from us?"

"Oh, that's a no-brainer. It has to be—"

"—somewhere in the tower." Shielding her eyes with her hand as if from intense sunlight, Berry stared forward at the glittering vertical surface from which the light from the overhead projectors was reflecting across the foreground.

"How much do you remember of the tower's layout?" Cherry asked.

"As little as you do."

"Yeah, you're right. And I've forgotten most—"

"—of what I remember anyway."

"Me too. But—"

They ducked into cover as a hulking malformed shape skulked through the trees ahead of them. It was walking without caution, restlessly shaking leaves and branches, and making a lot of noise as it went by. It was breathing heavily too, snuffling almost like a pig.

They remained silent until it vanished.

"Hey, was that a boogeyman?"

"Dunno, don't wanna find out. But I think it had more than two legs. Hey, or maybe it—"

"—had more than two arms."

Twin yelps of fright. "Boogeyman alert, boogeyman alert!"

"Why the hell didn't we shoot it then?"

"I dunno. Maybe 'cos we've—"

"—never shot anything or anyone before? Yeah, that has to be the reason. And it's a good reason too. We really don't want—"

"—to kill anyone unless we want to. And we won't want to—"

"—unless we have to. Unless they—"

"—really pissed us off. In which case we'll be really hard—"

"—and evil psycho bitches."

They heard some more loud rustling noises, this time coming from behind the house. As if the creature they had earlier spotted was now circling around behind them.

Berry stared at Cherry in fright. "You know what, sis? Let's just get—"

"—the hell away from here before it comes back."

"Hell yeah!"

They set off quickly through the trees, heading to where they remembered the road to the black tower was.

CHAPTER 11

Fatima

"So where do you think the money is hidden?" Fatima asked Emily. "Seeing as you work here, you must have a good idea of how your employers think."

Emily nodded. "Yeah, ideally that would be the case. But in this instance, seeing as they know that I'm competing too, they're likely to have gotten even more devilishly creative than usual. For instance, I'm sure that they didn't set me down anywhere close to the prize."

Fatima nodded. "That seems logical to me too. You'd be too likely to spot it."

On Emily's warning that they not stray too close to the pond for fear of what might lurk beneath its seemingly placid surface, the two young women were currently walking around it, keeping under the trees. They held their guns at the ready, ready to dispense death to anyone seeking it. Their destination was a parked motorbike twenty yards ahead.

"It's a much faster way to navigate the play zone," Emily had told Fatima. "I ride very well. My ex-husband was a biker."

Fatima had just nodded. She found it upsetting, hearing a person of about her own age speak of being divorced, when she was yet to even lose her virginity.

Wow, have I really been missing out on life, she thought.

She'd already asked Emily where they were. "I know that we're underground; but where underground? You can tell me that much, right?"

Emily had laughed. "I honestly don't know the answer myself. The ROC has several subterranean facilities like this around the world—I know there's one in China and another in Saudi Arabia, and one in Brazil also; although we may still be in the USA." She'd shrugged. "I'm as much in the dark concerning our current location as you are. I was asked to wait alone in an office, and then gassed in there; and then I woke up in a luxurious underground suite."

Fatima had been gassed in the lounge of the office where she had an appointment to meet Miriam Heller. The receptionist had walked across to her and sprayed a blue mist in her face and that was that.

"Try not to think about it," Emily had suggested. "It really makes no difference where we are. What counts at the moment is finding the money and winning the game."

They walked on towards the motorbike, going slowly and stepping cautiously, very aware that there might be death lurking in the trees around them.

"Hey wait!" Fatima told Emily as they approached a small clearing in the woods.

"What? Did you notice something?" Emily asked after they had stopped.

Fatima shook her head. "I just have a really weird feeling right now. Like there's lots of eyes watching us."

"You're right," Emily agreed. "I can sense them too. Someone *is* watching us." She tugged on Fatima's sleeve. "I think we need to get out of here right now. Let's hurry across to the motorbike."

"No, no," Fatima said, holding her back. "That's the problem: the danger seems to be ahead of us."

Emily waved her gun at the twilit trees across the clearing, which now seemed impregnated with evil. "So what now? Do we double back and try to reach the bike by coming down the road?"

Fatima nodded. "Yes, I think that's the best—What the . . . !?"

She stopped speaking because all of a sudden the air over the clearing was filled with pale winged shapes which were launching themselves from the tops of the trees opposite them.

"Shoot them!" Emily yelped as the winged things slashed and snapped at them.

Fatima was already doing so. Adrenalin kicked in and she swung her gun left and right, firing at the creatures.

She felt like she was in a deranged video game, one where the monsters were flesh and blood. Because the things attacking them were bat-men. Though if standing upright none of these flying freaks could have been more than two-and-a-half foot tall, airborne they were a dominating force, with their insane human faces, muscular torsos, and huge pale wings which ended in foot-long fingers that clawed at Fatima and Emily. The bat-men's pygmy-short legs ended in equally long-and-clawed toes.

One of the bat-men scratched open Fatima's arm, then spread his jaws wide to bite into her neck. The man-creature's eyes were filled with a completely insane and ravenous hunger that made her want to wet herself from sheer fright. The freak was silent though—all the bat-men were—and now that his mouth was open, she could see why: he had no tongue; just a slobbering black hole of a mouth that contained a few horribly long teeth.

Shuddering but resolute, she stuck the gun in the winged freak's face and pulled the trigger. He was blown backward, his brains exploding out of the rear of his head as he flopped out of the air to lie dead in the clearing, with his wings folding over him like a collapsing tent.

The bat-creatures filled the air. Fatima shot one more of them in the chest, then chanced a glance at Emily. Emily was firing both of her guns at the freaks, several of whom already lay dead or bleeding to death on the ground by her feet. She was shooting calmly and without hesitation, like she'd spent hours training at a shooting range.

Beyond Emily, the black tower was broadcasting their battle in glossy color.

This is crazy, Fatima thought, swinging back to her own battle. *Well, Mrs. Heller did warn me it would be dangerous!* She was glad that she and Emily had agreed to work together. Alone, there was no way they would have survived this assault. She also realized that they were lucky they hadn't yet stepped out into the clearing and so the flying freaks couldn't surround them and attack from all directions at once.

She ducked as one of the bat-men swiped at her with his claws, then as he flew past, she stuck her gun between his buttocks and pulled the trigger. The bullet seemed to paralyze the freak, and then flung him across the clearing to slam against a tree.

Fatima's gun clicked empty. She flung it down and pulled the other one from her waistband. She aimed the gun at a bat-man, but it didn't fire. After the freak had clawed her arm, she realized she hadn't cocked the gun yet.

The bat-man who'd clawed her arm seemed to think she was harmless now and flew at her head-first with his mouth wide open.

"Screw you, dude!" Fatima yelled and fired point-blank into his mouth. In an explosion of brilliant color, his head seemed to bloom like a red flower and then he collapsed dead to the floor.

"I think they've had enough," Emily said.

Fatima looked around and understood what she meant. The bat-men were fleeing. As silently as they'd descended, they once more lifted into the air and seemed to vanish.

The two courageous young women stared at each other and at the corpses on the ground. There were nine dead freaks and two that were still alive, though both were gurgling on blood from clearly fatal wounds.

Emily quickly put the wounded out of their misery with shots to the head. She seemed to have completely escaped injury. Fatima's arms were bleeding a little from the scratches she'd suffered at the hands of the bat-men, but her wounds were all superficial and she found she could ignore them. Behind Emily, the giant tower screens broadcast the end of the battle and then began a replay of the action.

"It's sickening how they make no noise," Fatima remarked through her heavy breathing. "And did you see their eyes? There's utterly no humanity left in them."

Staring at the winged corpses that now littered the forest clearing, and remembering that all of these monstrosities that looked like midget extras from the set of a vampire movie had once been humans like herself made Fatima shudder and filled her with an intense fear. Yes, truly there were some fates worse than death.

"I told you the ROC is an *evil* organization," Emily said, as if reading her face. "You still doubt that?"

Fatima shook her head. "Hell no. You more than convinced me of that the first time out."

"You've got a lot of fight in you," Emily said, approval evident in her voice.

"I didn't know I had it in me," Fatima replied. "Hey, how'd you learn to shoot like that? Bang, bang, bang, like Dirty Harry."

Emily shrugged. "When you're married to a biker, you're around lots of guns. And you gotta learn to use 'em too, 'cos we were always having beef with rival biker gangs who wanted to steal our turf or our drugs." She laughed. "I told you I like excitement."

"So why'd you quit then?"

"I got pregnant and decided I didn't wanna raise a kid anywhere near all the drugs and violence that being a biker's wife brings you in contact with. So I divorced Tommy and settled down in Attleboro in Massachusetts . . . the rest is her-story. Then, a year ago, I applied for a nursing job at the Raynham Outlook Clinic—which is owned by the ROC, though I didn't know that then—and by stages I found myself getting sucked into the organization."

Fatima was about to question her further, but was stopped by a loud thud.

She almost yelped at the sound, and instantly swung her gun that way to shoot any new attacker, but then she saw what had made the noise: a black video drone had just crashed on top of the dead bat-men.

Fatima heaved a sigh of relief. Two of the drone's propellers were busted, and it rotated madly on a freak's body, unable to get aloft again. After spinning around twice, it flipped over and landed upside down on the grass, where its two working propellers jammed for good.

"I wonder which one of us shot the little metal guy," Emily joked.

Fatima was about to reply her, when something hard hit her on the back of the head. Feeling like her mind had just opened up to let the night in, she slumped to the ground.

She lay there on her back with the musky smell of the dead freaks in her nostrils, staring up at Emily. "Help!" she croaked.

But Emily was in trouble now. A huge boogeyman had her. To Fatima's stunned senses, the boogeyman was more of a shape than a certainty. She could tell that he was wearing a hoodie, but that was about all.

Emily got off a single shot and then the boogeyman disarmed her, knocking both of her guns to the floor. Then he lifted her off the ground and carried her away from Fatima, back into the woods.

Fatima watched the freak walk off with her kicking and squealing friend. Through the haze that threatened to put her to sleep, she noted which way the boogeyman went.

Oh great, now I've gotta go rescue Emily, she thought. *I just hope the rest of the bat-men don't come back now. Stunned like this, I'll be easy pickings for them.*

CHAPTER 12

Miriam

In her Control Center, a comfortable room where she sat monitoring all the action on a bank of huge video screens, the games-mistress Miriam Heller nodded in approval.

I was right about this girl Fatima. She's definitely got what it takes to be on this show. She might even win it!

Now, to prevent herself being captured by the bat-men if they returned, Fatima was rolling her body back under the trees, which was very smart of her, because the winged men were almost useless on the ground.

Miriam twisted on her plush couch and checked her monitors for the other contestants. The Poole twins seemed to be on their way to the tower. The police detective Karen Rogers was looking through a house, clearly trying to locate the treasure. The hooker Lexi Austin was hiding from a boogeyman.

Nothing too interesting there. But otherwise Miriam was satisfied for the present. Besides, the show had only been on for thirty minutes; she knew the blood and guts and gore and body count would only increase as the duration extended.

In this respect, it was good for the show's online ratings that the Hillman pair of stepmother and stepdaughter had died quickly. Their deaths would spur up the viewer's interest and make the betting much more intense.

The eight contestants' profiles had all been uploaded online for everyone to check out.

The current favorite to win was the cop Karen Rogers. The ROC nurse Emily Ford was in second place, while, maybe because of her surprising show of violence towards Karen, Lexi Austin was now in third place in the viewers' ratings.

Personally, Miriam put Fatima above both Lexi and Emily—the girl just had 'something' that was certain to shine during this bloody contest.

The Poole twins? Miriam felt there was zero chance of either of those two winning. The pair of them were already showing how incompetent they were, with their total interdependence merely complicating things further. And that weird way they had of speaking—completing one another's sentences as if they were the same person? Ugh! Cherry and Berry Poole were the show's comedy act and also, eye candy for its male and lesbian viewers.

Because, oh God, how lovely those two girls were.

Miriam couldn't have children, but if she'd been able to, she'd have sold her soul for twin daughters as beautiful as the Poole twins.

But everything has a price, she thought grimly. *Maybe their joint mental deficiency is God compensating them for their perfect looks.*

Fatima and Emily's fight against the bat-men had been really exciting though. While watching the young women fight for their lives, Miriam had felt the blood pounding through her arteries; she'd felt an intense desire to be down there competing herself. She suspected that most of the show's female viewers had felt the same.

And now that Emily Ford has been caught—the screen showed the boogeyman carrying her around the side of the tower—*there's surely more excitement to come shortly.*

She stared back at Fatima; an angled overhead shot from a camera mounted in a tree opposite her. The young woman was out of danger now. She was lying beside a tree and trying to sit up; grunting in pain as she did so. Down but definitely not out.

Great, she's a real fighter. But . . .

There was something odd about Fatima Noori. Each time Miriam saw her, she had the feeling that she knew her from somewhere else. And knew her quite well too.

Yes, I know this young woman, but not on this show. But maybe I'm just being silly or overcautious. Because, unlike with the other contestants, I've met Fatima more than once—we met several times earlier in the year. She was supposed to be on The Virgin, but she fell ill and then . . . yes, I'm sure that's it.

On the giant composite screen in front of Miriam, Fatima had succeeded in sitting up and was now rubbing the back of her neck. After a while, she got to her feet, walked back to the clearing to retrieve her guns, reloaded both of them, and then stalked off through the woods in the direction that the boogeyman had carried off Emily.

That's one really serious-minded young woman, Miriam thought approvingly as she watched Fatima Noori. *And yes, I'm certain I've met her somewhere before, and quite recently too. Was it in a mall while shopping? Or in a restaurant somewhere? Where did she say she works again?*

Miriam's husband Aaron appeared then in an inset onscreen window.

"How's it going, honey?" he enquired with that boyish smile of his that she'd always being unable to resist.

Just like on their own *Virgin* show, she and her husband were working in different rooms. Aaron was currently with the ROC's video editors.

"Oh, I'm fine, dear," Miriam replied airily, knowing the room's hidden microphones were picking up her voice. "Things are starting to heat up, don't you think?"

"Yeah, certainly looks like it," Aaron replied. Then he looked away from her for a few seconds and nodded to someone off-camera. When he turned back towards her again, she noticed that he seemed a bit stressed. "What's the matter, darling? Trouble at your end?"

Miriam had been in the ROC's giant surveillance room—the place was enormous, with literally hundreds of huge monitor screens. Being in there had given her the impression that, when not producing shows like this, the ROC might be occupied with spying on the entire planet.

Anyway, Aaron was over there now with their imported staff, handling the video feeds, while she monitored things here in her Control Center and also ran security for the show. (Except for areas in which they'd personally requested assistance, the ROC had hands-offed and let them present the *Final Girl* game show their way.)

The term 'run security' was misleading anyway. The ROC's security was practically airtight. No one could either get in or break out of here, this secret facility up in the snowy wastes of northern Alaska. It was late October now and with the advent of the long Alaskan winter, the hidden entrances to the ROC's underground complex had become even more unnoticeable than usual.

Aaron shook his head in response to Miriam's question. "Oh, nothing serious. Just a few malfunctioning video cameras. They keep blinking on and off in a straight line, which has the tech guys here suggesting a computer virus of some kind. Hopefully it won't affect the video feed when anything interesting is happening, or we'll have to either show it as a replay or start tracking the failing cameras with airborne drones, which is okay, except when tracking action that's occurring beneath the trees or inside the houses."

He grinned. "But it's really just a little thing, honey; nothing to worry your head about. I'm sure we'll soon fix it."

Miriam nodded. A project this complicated—there were sixty-four drones and three thousand film cameras down in the play zone, and at least another thousand microphones—couldn't help but have some bugs.

"Ok, honey, gotta go, just checking on ya," Aaron said. He blew her a kiss and signed off, his inset image being replaced by one of Fatima Noori's grim face, which once more had Miriam wondering where she remembered the girl from.

Then her thoughts shifted to her temporary employers instead.

***

When the Red Octopus Corporation had contacted Miriam and Aaron Heller, asking them to help set up and host their reality show *The Final Girl*, the couple had had little idea of what to expect.

True, husband and wife already had some idea of the ROC's biotechnological wizardry, but this knowledge was completely eclipsed but what they soon discovered.

And there were additional levels to the ROC that Miriam merely suspected; and she suspected, other levels that she didn't even suspect existed.

To be most easily understood, the ROC was a clandestine worldwide religious organization cum secret society, sort of like the Illuminati on steroids.

They worshipped a kind of 'anti-god' deity they called 'Sinis' and like devout worshippers generally do, were trying to evolve themselves to become like it.

Miriam had been shown an illustration of a Sinis. It was a shapeless tentacled and winged monstrosity, something that had had Miriam questioning anyone's desire to worship it, let alone evolve to become like it.

Still, each to their own, she'd thought.

She and her husband Aaron had both balked at their hosts' offer to show them a living Sinis.

"Hey, guys, how 'bout if we leave that alone for the moment and just concentrate on this *Final Girl* show you want us to run for you," Aaron had said with fear on his face.

Thankfully, the offer to show them a living Sinis hadn't since been repeated. Miriam had no desire to view such a monstrosity in the flesh. And she suspected too that the creature wouldn't actually be divine at all, but instead something that the ROC had grown in their laboratories, much like humans regularly made idols of stone, wood, metal and pop stars.

But religion aside, the ROC's worldwide reach was truly stupendous. It was like an exclusive and powerful club, one in which race, gender, age, income level and publicly expressed political creed was meaningless. A place where well-known public opponents were found to be allies working for the same cause of ROC world dominion.

Miriam knew for certain that at least three recent US presidents were high level ROC members, as were a large number of other world leaders.

Miriam and Aaron's own reality show *The Virgin*, had been designed to make money via the Dark Web (or underground internet).

However, even though it had a Dark Web feed for non-ROC viewers, this *Final Girl* show was more of a whim than anything else, just voyeuristic, violent fun for the club members. The prize was twenty-four million dollars simply because that was the number one got by multiplying the numbers eight and three, both numbers holding deep significance to the ROC. The number 'eight' was important because an octopus had eight legs, while 'three' was significant because this was apparently the third year since the ROC had found their Oracle, a living person who could communicate directly with their deity, the Sinis.

This explanation was of course over Miriam's head. Just more crazy religion she could live without.

I'm just here to run their show. And they're paying Aaron and I a lot of money, so hell yeah, we're gonna run it for them.

Staring at the play zone on her monitors, Miriam couldn't help but be impressed. Anyone walking across the iced-over Alaskan surface up at ground level, would find it impossible to believe that there was a manmade tropical forest 200 feet underground. Like a resort in Florida, complete with palm trees and a pond.

The ROC had accomplished a miracle here; about that there was no doubt. And the play zone was merely part of a giant underground complex, the true extent of which had been hinted to Miriam and Aaron Heller, but which they'd not been permitted to tour, making them both wonder what the hell else the ROC were hiding down here. Indeed, Aaron was certain that the Red Octopus Corporation was doing some work for the Pentagon, most likely in the area of biological weapon development.

***

Onscreen, other than for Fatima's dogged pursuit of the boogeyman who had abducted Emily Ford, nothing much was happening. On a left-hand screen, the Poole twins were still looking equally gorgeous and confused; while above them, Karen Rogers was searching yet another house for the prize money.

Karen seems to know what she's here for, Miriam thought. *None of the others are looking for the cash yet.*

There was a tentacled boogeyman two houses away from Karen, but the freak seemed unaware of her presence nearby.

***

Miriam, who was herself interested in body-modification, had enquired where the ROC got their experimental subjects. The answer had been readily given:

Sometimes the ROC abducted people to experiment on. Other subjects were people they were paid to dispose of—much more effective and convenient than hiring a hitman or murdering someone oneself and then wondering how to get rid of the corpse. Some test subjects were ROC betrayers, or media spies . . . and weirdly, some were people who volunteered to be turned into vampires or mermaids or boogeymen. Some of this last category were suicidal, but others merely wanted the thrill of a different sort of life from that to which they were accustomed. Almost like a human being desiring to become a dog or a cat so they could be someone's pet.

Miriam definitely drew the line at the fish-babies, however. Modifying human infants like that was totally unacceptable.

***

Watching Karen onscreen suddenly reminded Miriam of Lexi Austin, who for some reason, she found it as easy to forget as it was easy for her to generate false memories of Fatima. She looked around for Lexi, but the red-haired prostitute seemed to have walked off-camera for the moment, into one of the play zone's few dead spots.

Miriam's central monitor, the one which displayed the most important happenings in the play zone, had been showing Karen opening a suitcase, but now it suddenly went blank. Then it shifted to the interior of another house, where a nauseating boogeyman was descending a staircase. Then that monitor also went blank.

Miriam realized what had just happened: the computer bug or virus that Aaron had mentioned had now swept around to where Karen was.

Miriam was just about to call her husband and ask how far they had gotten with resolving the technical difficulties with the video cameras, when the blanked-out image was replaced by one of Lexi Austin's face. Thankfully this image stayed. So, yes, it was just the system virus acting up.

Miriam was intrigued by the look of surprise on Lexi's face.

Girl looks like she's just gotten herself into some trouble.

She settled back in her couch to view the action.

CHAPTER 13

Lexi

Lexi blamed herself for not killing Karen. *I screwed up big-time when I shot at her and somehow missed. Yeah, yeah, it was a wonderful plan until I didn't kill the bitch, and now she's gonna be after me all through the show, and I need to watch my damn back.*

Since leaving the house where she'd shot at Karen, Lexi had entered two other buildings to search for both the money and fresh weapons. She'd not found the money, but at least she was armed again. A wicked knife with a serrated blade. Being more of a gun person, the weapon didn't fill her with confidence, but it was something.

She looked up nervously at a sound. Since seeing Fatima's and Emily's fight with the bat-men Lexi had been scared of trees and clearings.

She was making her way towards the black central tower. It seemed obvious to her that that was where the money was hidden. Dealing drugs with her boyfriend had taught her that: it was best to conceal things right out in the open. She couldn't count the number of times that the police had tried to bust Johnny Walker, only to leave frustrated, while the drugs they were looking for were right beside them—one of Johnny's favorite places of concealment was to glue the white cocaine packets to the top surface of the two ceiling fans in his bungalow. With the fans working, no one would ever suspect that that's where the drugs were hidden.

If you worked it right you could even take the drugs into the police station with you. One time when the cops had hauled Lexi in for questioning, she had been wearing both a padded bra and butt pads that were full of cocaine. Another thing Johnny Walker did was put cocaine into fake external hard drives, remote controls, and CD cases. He'd quit on the CD cases thing when one rookie detective who was a Slain Jane fan had taken out the band's *Antidote for God* CD from Johnny's CD rack. The only thing that had saved Johnny Walker from a long jail term then was that the older detective had told the rookie to "stop screwing around with that shit," just before he'd have opened it up and seen the circular packet of white powder it actually contained.

So, to Lexi's mind, the prize money had to be in the tower. *That's the most obvious place here. Or maybe the cash is up in one of the trees. Hey, what was that noise?*

She paused, but it was nothing. She'd been walking out in the open, darting from house to house while watching the indoor sky. She found it frustrating how, even though the road she was on led directly to the tower, it curved so much that following it might actually be thrice as long as just walking straight through the trees.

But the trees hold danger. And besides, out here on the road I can see who's coming after me!

Doggedly following the road had brought Lexi to the pond. The pond was about a hundred and fifty feet wide and extended across to a concrete walkway at the base of the tower, whose screens were now idling again. On Lexi's side of the pond, a log cabin stood twenty yards away on her right; and a long wooden pier extended out from this into the lake. Four water bikes were tethered to the end of the pier.

On seeing the water bikes, Lexi thought a bit: *This blasted road curves beside the pond and heads back into the trees again, which is sure to take me back towards that bitch Karen. Shit, I should've killed her. How the heck did I miss like that? It was the cocaine that threw my aim off, I'm sure of it.*

Despite which certainty, Lexi got the cocaine jar out of her purse anyway and sniffed a lot more of the white powder.

The cocaine seemed to inflate her head with courage. Snorting like an enraged bull, she turned and strode off towards the log cabin. Now she made no attempt to walk stealthily. There were no bat people in the air, and she figured that if they did show up, she'd be safe inside the cabin before they reached her.

The cabin was new, with its front half suspended on wooden poles sunk into the water. Lexi climbed up onto the pier and walked to the cabin's front door. She peeked inside the house and saw that it was empty, then proceeded down the pier towards the water bikes at its far end.

Here the water was crystal clear and maybe five feet deep; she could see the sand on the pond bottom, along with several very weird fish that swam away before she could get a proper look at them.

Hey, what if the money is hidden in the cabin?

That thought took her mind off the weirdness of the fish for a moment and made her look towards the wooden house again. *Yeah, the money might be in there; I'd better search it before leaving here. I'd feel real foolish if after heading for the tower I see on a monitor that someone else—maybe the twins—found the money out here.*

But then a larger fish swam into view and stared up at her and she gasped in shock.

The 'fish' was a human infant. Or it would have been a human infant if it still had any arms or legs. At the moment this human 'fish' was just a baby torso with hands attached to its shoulders and feet attached to its hips; with both these hands and feet having webbed, foot-long fingers and toes that functioned perfectly as fins. The 'fish-baby' was completely hairless and had sets of gills along its neck.

Lexi was horrified. Like most women, she adored babies; and to see someone do this to one of them—lines of surgical scars clearly visible on the baby freak's body as it circled in the water showed it hadn't been born this way—was almost unnerving to her.

She stared up at the black tower and then back down at the fish-baby in the water. It too was staring up at her with bright blue eyes. Then it bared its teeth at her—they were few but looked razor-sharp—and swam up to the surface. She stepped back, and not a moment two soon, because the freakish thing next leapt up out of the water at her, snapping its teeth and almost clamping its jaws over her hand before she yanked her hand away.

The fish-baby splashed back into the water. Lexi stood there shivering. Then she heard more loud splashing behind her, on the other side of the pier.

This time she didn't get out of the way in time. She felt a sharp pain in her left forearm. She looked down at it. Another fish-baby was clamped on her arm, its razor-sharp teeth dug deep into her flesh like it was a piranha feeding. This little freak's eyes were black as coal and seemed to burn with hunger. As it dug its teeth even deeper into her flesh, it clawed at her breasts and side with its long webbed fingers, and its gill slits fluttered.

Oh my God!

But Lexi still had her knife. Without thinking she stabbed the fish-baby in the side and dragged the serrated blade across its belly. In a rush of nauseatingly warm blood, the fish-baby's guts spilled out like those of an actual fish. It began shuddering on Lexi's arm, dying in agony but unwilling to let go of its prey.

She jabbed the knife into its mouth and tried to lever its upper jaw out of her flesh. She almost succeeded, but then had to duck as two more fish-babies flew at her, both of them coming from the water beneath the log cabin.

It occurred to Lexi then that she'd be much safer inside the log cabin. Once she was locked in there she could slice this dead fish-baby off of her arm.

Making it to the end of the pier was totally out of the question now. The fish-babies were certain to eat her up before she could untether one of the water bikes. And even if she did somehow evade them and get a bike free, she saw no chance of herself crossing the pond; the fish-babies would have reduced her to shreds by the time she was halfway to the tower.

Being about halfway down the pier now, she prepared to run the gauntlet back to the cabin. She clearly heard the splashing in the water on both sides of the pier as more fish-baby freaks prepared to leap out at her.

For a moment, Lexi's attention was taken up by the realization that her struggles with the fish-babies was being broadcast on the tower walls across the pond. A whirring sound overhead made her look upwards; two drones hovered over her, filming everything.

Lexi turned to run. But then, something hooked her ankle and she tripped up and fell flat on her face.

Her fall stunned her, but not for long. Falling had also slammed her left arm onto the pier and the pain from the creature attached to her forearm was like an adrenalin boost to her brain.

She tried to get to her feet but couldn't. And in addition, something was now dragging her off the pier—from her feet to her knees, the lower parts of both of her legs were out in the air.

And it felt like human hands gripping her ankles.

What the hell?

Lexi rolled onto her side and stared in horror at the two mermaids who had hold of her legs. Both were beautiful, but grotesque in the extreme, with long flaxen hair, bright blue eyes that glowed with intense madness, and sensual lips curved in hungry smiles. Like the fish-babies, the mermaids' hands had foot-long webbed fingers, the nails of which were dug like hooks into Lexi's calves, setting free freshets of blood.

One of the mermaids licked up the blood with a long tongue. The other one hissed at Lexi, revealing teeth even longer and sharper-looking than those of the fish-babies. Both fish-women's torsos were completely out of the water, as though they were standing on their tails, and their breasts were pressed against the side of the pier. Neither fish-woman had any nipples. The gill slits in their necks pulsated with their excited breathing.

They too had clearly once been human, as the surgical scars across their chests and shoulders revealed.

"Let go of me!" Lexi screamed desperately as the mermaids hauled her towards them, towards death. She began feeling around for her knife, but she couldn't find it. However, she did find her handbag and she began beating at the mermaids' hands with it.

"Let go of me, you water bitches! Oh God, I need a gun! I need a gun!"

The mermaids' grip was as relentless as their hunger, but Lexi was desperate to survive. She dug her fingers between the pier slats and held on tight with both hands, refusing to be dragged down to a watery doom.

For a few moments it was a stalemate.

But then a fish-baby flipped up out of the water and sank its teeth deep into Lexi's left breast.

Howling in agony, Lexi let go of the pier.

By the time she realized her error she was already down in the water and the mermaids and fish-babies were ripping into her flesh with their razor-edged teeth and were shredding and eating her. She kicked and tried to get free, but her adversaries were in their native element now and she had no chance in hell of escaping them.

She tried to scream but she'd already been pulled underwater. Water flooded her lungs and suddenly she was drowning. Her death was fast and merciful but nonetheless seemed agonizing slow.

Lexi Austin's last conscious thought as she died was: *You mean those ROC assholes actually put video cameras UNDER the pier to record scenes like this? Oh, how gruesome can you get!?*

Lexi died and the cameras captured it all. And the tower showed it all.

CHAPTER 14

Karen

Watching Lexi's miserable death give Karen no satisfaction whatsoever.

No, she hadn't liked the redhead one bit. After all, Lexi had twice tried to kill her.

But the gruesome nature of Lexi's death left a bitter taste in Karen's mouth.

This is one hell of a dirty game. And yet I feel compelled to play it to the end, as if some basic insecurity drives me on. Oh well . . .

She'd watched Lexi's death in the living room of the current house she was searching. She'd turned off the TV when the six or seven mermaids eating the redhead had began arguing over her bones, pulling Lexi's now almost fleshless skeleton between them as if they were having a tug-of-war. The corpse hadn't been able to survive such stress for long; it had quickly separated into pieces, with most of its torso falling to the pond bottom, where the gruesome fish-babies instantly swarmed over it, picking away what little flesh was left on its ribs.

Well at least I don't have to worry about Lexi Austin shooting me again. I mean, how unrepentant can one get?

Karen had left the house shortly afterwards.

This is the fourth building that I've searched out here, she thought, heading for the tower, which was just thirty yards away now. *I'm starting to think that maybe the money isn't in—*

Then she caught a flash of motion to her left. Spinning towards it, she saw a boogeyman coming at her. Naked from the waist up, this boogeyman was short and squat, with bulbous eyes that made him look something like a toad, an impression that was confirmed seconds later, when he opened his giant mouth and shot out a six-foot-long tongue at her.

Thanking her stars that she'd always had great reflexes, Karen flung herself sideways.

She hit the ground hard and then rolled over, trying to get a shot at the freak. But his tongue had snared her around the ankle and he was already reeling her in as if she was a hooked fish, his muscular tongue dragging her over the grass towards him with scary ease.

As she got closer to him, she saw that his large hands ended in sharp claws that were poised in midair, waiting to dig into her body. But just before they could tear into the soft flesh of her legs, she got her gun properly sighted on his deformed face, and then it was over for her attacker.

Two bullets, each one perfectly placed in a bulging and grotesque yellow eye, and the toad-man collapsed backwards, with his tongue instantly uncoiling from around her ankle.

Shaken, she got to her feet and ran for the black tower.

This side of the building had three doors at ground level, the middle one of which was a set of glass double-doors.

Karen headed towards this middle entrance and pushed it open. It opened noiselessly. She glanced back once to ensure that no one was following her, and for a moment her gaze climbed over the forest and scaled the sheer stone wall that she'd been suspended on just a short while ago; the access platform was once more perched halfway up the wall.

Then she forgot the outside world and stepped inside the tower.

***

Glass and steel. Plastic and wood. Furniture. More doors.

She was inside a deserted lobby. Everything inside here was spic and span, as clean as a hospital or a mortuary, where out of respect to the ill and the dead, dust and disorder were considered unwelcome. Or maybe disorder was related to good health; and hospitals and mortuaries were merely clean because their residents no longer had the strength to dirty them.

Alright, now where have the ROC hidden the money?

The lobby had two elevators, both of them open and waiting for passengers. Karen strode towards the right-hand one and stepped inside it. She was about to press the button for the second floor when a bad smell made her pause and step out of the elevator again.

That's the smell of . . . dammit, why can't I remember anything? But still, I know this frigging smell!

Intrigued, she forgot about the elevator and instead left the lobby by one of its side doors, tracking the strangely familiar odor.

***

The source of the smell proved to be close by, less than five yards down the first corridor that Karen stepped into. A right-hand door stood open, and when Karen peeked inside she saw corpses on tables.

Lots of corpses on tables.

It's a morgue! she realized. For a moment the sight of the corpses threatened to unlock her vault of memories. *I've been in mortuaries before—I'm certain of it. Yes, I'm a police detective, so it's natural that I'd have to identify the dead. And that also explains why the smell in here is so familiar.*

But nothing more came to her.

A brief glance around this mortuary revealed it to be a huge place, one that maybe occupied a third of the tower's ground-level space. It contained a huge number of autopsy tables, about half of which were occupied by the dead, most of whom had already been autopsied, with the Y-shaped incisions in their torsos neatly sewn up again. Several of these bodies were missing their heads, while others were missing limbs; a few of them were nothing more than torsos.

Over at the far end of the giant chamber, although she couldn't be sure because of all the tables and support pillars in the way, there seemed to be an indoor pool beside the wall. Closer to her, a huge TV monitor hung on the wall.

Karen was about leaving the dead to rest in peace, when she noticed something that made her change her mind.

Okay, now that's frigging weird. She stepped properly inside the morgue for a better look.

What she'd noticed was that two of the nearer corpses seemed to have the same face, which wouldn't have been entirely strange, except that one of the bodies was that of a middle-aged man, while the other was a pregnant woman. This pregnant woman had the same bearded face as the man.

Karen shivered as she walked over to examine the bodies. Her physical reaction was as much from her surprise as from the room's temperature. Because this place was freezing, which of course explained its lack of storage lockers for the dead.

Wishing she had a jacket to help her deal with the cold, Karen hurried over to the pregnant woman to get a proper look at her face. It was possible that the dead lady was wearing a mask, a sick joke that Karen now knew the members of the Red Octopus Corporation were very capable of playing on the contestants.

But no, the dead woman wasn't wearing a mask. This duplicate face—because the original had to be the man's, right?—this male face appeared to have been grafted onto her head. It was stitched in place, from her neck to the blonde hairline above her temples; and the woman's ears were also part of the skin graft.

Karen studied the woman's torso for a moment, with her eyes first trailing the repaired Y-incision down between her breasts, and then up over her bulging belly, before once more falling to her crotch. The line of stitches on the woman's fetal bulge was so precisely set in its middle that Karen wondered if perhaps the crazy mortician—because who other than an insane person would graft a man's face on a dead woman's corpse—had Y-incised her unborn child also.

She couldn't dwell on this for too long though, because now another thought occurred to her; this one almost as disturbing as the woman's face was.

Hey, I know this face from somewhere! Yes I do! But who is he? Oh, damn it, I can't remember! Curse this memory loss of mine!

She turned from the woman to the man on the next metal table, to see if a proper look at him might jog her memory, because his name seemed to float around the edges of her mind.

But here she was in for an even greater surprise. Because she now saw that this man's face wasn't his own either. It too had been grafted in place on his scalp. Just as with the woman, a precise line of surgical sutures ran beneath the man's chin and behind his ears and below his dark hair.

And touching both corpses' faces confirmed to Karen that no, this wasn't plastic but real flesh and blood on their heads.

So who had the original face? she asked herself, looking away from the dead man, and staring around the morgue, praying that this wasn't the face of her own unremembered boyfriend Jake.

And it was now that Salt Lake City detective Karen Rogers got the shock of her life. Because now she saw that every single corpse in the morgue had exactly the same face.

"What in the world is going on in here?" she asked aloud in horror. "Is someone trying to drive me crazy?"

"Oh no, not at all," a deep male voice replied her. "You've merely stumbled in on an art project of mine."

Shocked by the intrusion, Karen instantly swung around with her gun raised to fire.

And then, on seeing who had spoken to her, she felt powerless to shoot and let her gun-hand fall to her waist.

"Who-who-who-who are y-y-ou?" she gasped at the strange apparition, feeling as if in a few seconds her mind and body would melt like wax from sheer terror, and she would expire as a puddle on the morgue floor, out of the *Final Girl* reality show and her own life for good.

"My name is Operator and I run this place," the intruder replied.

Karen sort-of nodded at him, feeling powerless to speak.

'Operator' was about seven feet tall. But his towering height was the least odd thing about him.

The most odd thing? The giant had six arms. The topmost set were normal, and were attached to his shoulders, while both of his lower sets of arms projected from the sides of his abdomen and were really just forearms attached to unseen elbow joints; unseen because Operator was wearing a formal white lab coat with three sets of sleeves. His topmost set of hands gripped a scalpel and a forceps; the other sets of arms were crossed across his belly like the legs of a dead insect.

"Yeah right . . . Operator," Karen finally said, with a frightened glance around at the gruesome array of similarly-faced corpses. "Dude, the name really fits you."

He laughed as if she had paid him a huge compliment.

His face was hairless, maybe-late thirties in age, and seemed normal enough, though his eyes were hidden by large dark goggles. His hair, however, was a mass of long red tentacles, thick and coiling like snakes.

Operator was standing two tables away from Karen. Now he stepped towards her.

"Just stay back!" she hissed at him, raising her gun again.

"You needn't fear me," he said while continuing to walk towards her. "I'm not in the contest, nor am I one of your boogeymen. Science is all that interests me, not the naughty uses humankind puts it to. Though I must admit that you girls are putting on quite a show tonight. Try to win, Karen Rogers—I'm betting on you."

Operator reached her and stepped past her, not heeding the gun that she now swept around to cover his broad back. Karen felt dwarfed by him, she hardly reached up to his chest.

And, looking around at all the corpses—those corpses all having the same creepy middle-aged male face, a thought had come to her mind.

"Hey," she called to Operator, just as he reached the pool at the far end of the room. "Hey, man, are you one of the surgeons who helped revive me?"

He laughed and turned to face her, and she saw that he had plucked out a severed head from the pool. He turned its face towards her; it was the head of the Hillman girl, the stepdaughter.

"Yes, I did operate on you," he said. "Bringing you back from the brink of death was quite a challenge, but I'm glad we succeeded."

"Thanks," Karen said, feeling a bust of gratitude towards the six-armed giant, "I'm glad you succeeded too. But why can't I remember anything?"

"Don't worry about that. Your memories will return. Just concentrate on winning the show."

She gestured at Megan Hillman's head. "What are you going to do with that?"

He looked down at the head he was holding, his red hair-tentacles writhing across his shoulders as he did so, as if they contained additional brains and were thinking along with him. "Whatever comes to mind," he said, and dropped Megan's head back into the pool. "Unfortunately, she's already dead. Even *my* knowledge of science has its limitations."

Karen nodded slowly. "O.K., big guy . . . but why do all these corpses have exactly the same face? And I think I know this man too, but my memory won't give me his name."

"Like I earlier told you, it's an art project of mine," Operator said, walking over from the pool to stand beside her. Close to her like this, his two sets of auxiliary arms were at the level of her head. The lower, more delicate set of arms, seemed to have once belonged to a woman. Karen felt a fresh surge of dread.

"Yes, an art project," the giant continued. "Sometimes, when bored, I do things like this to help pass the time." With Karen following, Operator walked over to a table that held a child's corpse. From the size of his body, the boy must have been about seven or eight years old. But he too had the same middle-aged-man's face as all the other dead people in the morgue.

"This is just so damn creepy!" Karen protested. The little boy had been Y-incised open and had had all of his internal organs removed, but he hadn't yet been sewn up again. Operator's lowest set of arms—the delicate female pair—now picked up an S-curve needle from the surgical cart and began suturing shut the gaping hole in the child's torso.

While working, Operator nodded down at Karen. "Yes, I know it's creepy; but I'm working on a very creepy piece of art indeed. The model for their faces was a criminal I saw on a poster somewhere; a very nasty fellow—I think he was a contract killer—a hitman—up in Boston, but I no longer remember exactly."

Karen nodded. *Yes, yes, he has to be a criminal, but which one? Oh, how I hate being unable to remember anything!* "Can you at least recall his name?" she asked Operator. "For some reason his face keeps bugging me. It's like there's something about him that I should remember, but which I just can't."

With a sad smile on his face, Operator shook his head. "I'm sorry, Karen, but I've forgotten his name. Edwin or Edmond or Edward . . . or something like that. His name was never important to me anyway—names never are—it was his nasty face that intensely interested me. Seeing that seemingly soulless visage made me wonder about the nature of the human soul itself. Would his face still seem equally creepy transposed onto the bodies of a wide range of persons, of different ages, genders, and races?" He pointed over at a black male body with long dreadlocked hair but the same (though in this case dark-brown) face. "Anyway, that's the whole point of the thing."

Then Operator indicated a large glass tank on a table by the near wall, in which several more identical middle-aged faces floated on hangers in a bubbling yellow liquid. "Once I've done a few more of them, I'll bring some cameras in here and film them in a variety of poses."

Karen stared at him open-mouthed. "That's all? And what are you gonna do with the bodies afterwards?"

Operator shrugged his uppermost set of shoulders; now his middle set of hands had joined the lower pair in closing up the young corpse. "Well, the mermaids always need feeding," he replied. "I took these bodies from their meat-storage lockers."

He grinned. "Of course, this is merely one of several art projects that I'm presently working on. But interesting, don't you agree? Imagine a world where everyone has the same face. Male and female, good and bad, old and young, black and white. A society where everyone looked exactly the same."

Karen shook her head to clear it of the crazy concept. "Dude, you're insane."

"No, I am Operator. I operate." He sighed. "And yes, just so you don't ask, in another life, I did operate a switchboard and make lots of phone calls."

Karen figured she'd seen enough. There was something about the blasé way this six-armed giant beside her was going about his gruesome business that assured her that if she didn't win this show tonight, she too might wind up as part of his next crazy art project.

"Hey, man, I gotta go," she told Operator. "The clock isn't waiting for me. And besides, this place is so frigging cold that I'll get frostbite if I hang out with you any longer than I already have."

Operator smiled warmly down at her. "Yes, of course, Karen. It's been an absolute pleasure meeting you."

He'd gotten the child all sewn up now and was sitting him up on the autopsy table, twisting his arms and legs into a variety of poses.

Karen stared at the face atop the kid's neck and shuddered. Its eyes, visible once Operator propped them open, were a chilling soulless gray.

Wow, you talk about evil. This guy was that for sure. But who exactly is the more evil one here: the guy whose face Operator used, or Operator himself? Because anyone who'd think up a deranged 'art project' like this one here has to be really messed-up ethically.

More than a little frightened, Karen hurried across the morgue to the door.

"Win the game, Karen Rogers!" Operator called after her. "Make me proud of you!"

She paused at the door and turned back to wave at him. "Thanks, big guy! I'll do my absolute best. I'll—!"

But there was no one in the morgue anymore. Operator was gone.

Wondering how that was possible—how a seven-foot giant could seemingly vanish into thin air, and silently at that—Karen got out of there fast.

With her body still shivering from the intense cold it had just been subjected to, she hurried out to the lobby again and caught the nearer elevator to the third floor.

CHAPTER 15

Cherry/Berry

The twin's attempt to reach the tower was cut short when a flock of bat-men attacked them just as they were stepping out of the woods.

"Get back under the trees!" Cherry yelled at her sister, and the pair instantly retreated again and began firing.

Soon there were a number of winged corpses on the concrete expanse outside the woods, one of them even killed by a ricochet off the tower, which seemed to be bulletproof.

However, both girls felt very frustrated. The tower was less than twenty yards away, but attempting to reach it through the aerial swarm would be pure suicide.

A reckless and hunger-crazed bat-man threw caution to the winds and soared beneath the trees with his jaws yawning open to bite Cherry, whose revolver had just clicked empty.

Berry leapt to her sister's rescue however, jumping in front of her and blowing the flying freak's brains out. The bat-man fell to the grassy floor and flapped himself to death, with blood squirting from his shattered skull.

"Ugh, that's just so gross," Cherry said.

Berry was already aiming out at the bat freaks again. But she too had just used up her last bullet and her revolver also clicked empty.

She looked at her sister. "We need to—"

"—reload. Yeah we do, but I seem to have lost my box of bullets."

"I've still got mine. Hey, how do you—"

"—open up these silly guns?"

"Good question, sis. I'm not—"

"—sure either. Here lemme see."

***

102

So, keeping a cautious eyes on the bat freaks swooping back and forth a few yards away from them, the Poole twins tried to work out how to crack their revolvers open, so they could reload them.

Neither girl, however, was aware of the boogeyman standing just three yards behind them.

The boogeyman had been trying to catch Fatima, who, to escape him, had climbed up into the tree behind the twins and had been keeping the boogeyman at bay by jabbing at his face with her knife, having lost both of her guns when he'd initially startled her.

Fearing that the Poole twins would shoot her if they saw her, Fatima had also kept very quiet, so that now the first hint that Cherry and Berry had that they weren't alone there beneath the trees was when the boogeyman grabbed them both around the neck and shook them hard.

***

"Shit!" one of the twins yelped in fright as the huge hand closed around her neck. The shock made her drop her gun, and a moment later, her sister also dropped her own revolver, though whether she too did this from shock or from trying to emulate her sister was debatable.

"Hey, he's got me, Cherry!"

"Me too! Hey, let go of us, you freak!"

The twins managed to twist around to face the boogeyman, and then they began kicking and pummeling him, trying to reach the forest floor and pick up their guns. The boogeyman was hooded, so they couldn't see his face in the shadows, but he stank a lot. Oh, dear Jesus, how he stank.

Then, remembering their other weapons, the girls pulled their axes and knives from their belts and stabbed and hacked at their captor, but somehow, neither of these edge weapons seemed to cut him deeply. Either his skin was too thick to penetrate, or maybe he was wearing some kind of body armor. Still they hacked away, until finally, grunting, the boogeyman swatted the weapons out of their hands.

Outside of the woods, the swirling and swooping bat-men seem to be losing interest in the twins, as if angrily realizing that the boogeyman had stolen their meals from them.

With a huge hand clamped around each of the twin's necks, the boogeyman began dragging them off through the woods.

"Hey, freaking let go of us, you—"

"—God-damned freak, goddammit!" Cherry and Berry yelled at their captor.

Then they saw Fatima jumping down from the tree they were just being dragged past.

"Hey, Fatima, give us a hand!"

"Yeah, stab this brute for us—"

"—or shoot him with our guns! Just freaking—"

"—help us before this thing kills us or—"

"—rapes us. Or worse yet, eats us!"

While making this loud plea for help, the twins had prevented themselves from being dragged away by grabbing two adjacent tree branches.

Fatima stopped and stared at them. For a moment she seemed to be seriously considering their request, and they felt some hope that they'd be saved from the boogeyman.

But then to their horror, Fatima burst out laughing.

"Help you?" she asked, still laughing. "Are you two frigging nuts? Duh, this is a *competition*, you twin morons. I'm not *supposed* to help you, and I'm not going to. Wow, the pair of you act so dumb, you should be blondes."

The 'blonde' reference really stung the twins, because, beneath all their red and blue hair, they *were* blondes. Incensed by the stereotyping insult, they both let go of the branches they were clinging to and raged at Fatima:

"We'll get you for this, you bitch!"

"If we get raped it's—"

"—your fault, Fatima! Oh, we're gonna—"

"—pay you back for doing this!"

"Yeah, just wait and see if—"

Cherry (and Berry) stopped talking because their boogeyman captor, tired of their ranting and their refusal to move, had smacked both of their heads together, knocking them both unconscious.

CHAPTER 16

Miriam

Miriam Heller shook her head at the sight of the Poole twins being carried off.

"Looks like they'll shortly be off the show," she groaned aloud.

She felt pleased however. This was shaping up to be a great reality show. According to Aaron, the ratings were through the roof already; their ROC and Dark Web audience were delighted with the spectacle.

Miriam wondered if tonight's *Final Girl* show would 'break' the Dark Web like the last edition of *The Virgin* had.

Lexi's death had gone over extremely well with the bloodthirsty internet spectators. Miriam had been unable to watch it however. She'd looked away and almost thrown up while the mermaids were feeding.

And now that that boogeyman has the twins, there's the promise of more blood and gore to come soon; and maybe even some sex. And no one has found the money yet. I just hope it's not in the pond, 'cos if it is, it's going to be quite a challenge reaching it without becoming mermaid food in the process. Those fish-girls are badass to the core!

Miriam had no idea where the money was hidden. All she had to do to find out was ask her husband Aaron, but she wanted the thrill of discovering it at the same time as her contestants did.

Oh God, not again! she silently growled as a screen that had been showing Fatima Noori suddenly went blank. *Aaron, darling, you've got to sort this out before it ruins our show for us!*

CHAPTER 17

Fatima

It was with intense relief at her own escape that Fatima watched the boogeyman sling the Poole twins over his shoulders and tramp off through the woods with them.

If they get raped it's my fault? Who the hell gave birth to you idiots? You two are an absolute disgrace to twin-kind. I'm a twin too and me and my sister don't behave anything like you two guys. We act normal, like other folks.

Still disbelieving that the twins could be so dumb as to actually expect her to jeopardize herself to save them, Fatima hurried over to their dropped guns.

One of the revolvers was half-loaded, the other was empty. She searched the forest floor for the spilled bullets and properly loaded both guns. Then, holding one revolver and sticking the other in her waistband along with her knife, she turned and hurried through the woods, in the opposite direction to that in which the boogeyman had carried Cherry and Berry Poole.

She realized she was giving up a great chance to enter the tower now that the bat-men seemed to have dispersed, but she was a very loyal person and not one to desert a friend in need.

At the moment Emily needs me and I'm going to do my best to rescue her.

Fatima paused beside a road she'd reached to check for winged freaks flying overhead before crossing. She was near the road's merging with the tower courtyard and she looked over at the immense black building that seemed to hold up this entire underground chamber.

And besides, that tower is so huge that it's silly for just one person to expect to search through it and find the money. But then, twenty-four million dollars is a lot of cash; it should be rather easy to spot.

She ran across the road and into the woods opposite. The greenery swallowed her up like a mouth, its leaves licking her like thirsty tongues.

The money will either be hidden in a large safe, or in a number of briefcases . . . or maybe hidden in some suitcases. In any case it should be quite easy to recognize. Keeping hold of it will be a different matter altogether though—that's gonna be really hard for one person to manage.

Fatima stopped running. After first peering up and making sure nothing lurked in the branches overhead, she leaned against a tree trunk, tapping her foot on the dark grass. *Hey, I need to be more careful. There's certainly other nasty things hiding in these woods; more human centi—*

Then a loud scream cut through her thoughts: "NO, NO! STOP NO!"

Hey, that's Emily!

Fatima dashed towards the noise.

***

Emily's screams were coming from a nearby bungalow. From the loudness of the yelling, Fatima imagined that she was already too late—that Emily was already being butchered. Or raped—the possibility of rape was one that the virgin Fatima Noori considered worse than death.

But when she got to the house and peered in through the window, she was surprised. Emily was neither being butchered nor raped. Well, Fatima decided the second case had to be properly defined.

What was going on was that the boogeyman was ejaculating on Emily's face. He had tied her down to a large wicker chair and was masturbating by her head, while she yelled obscenities at him. "Get away from me, you sick fuck!" and such like.

The boogeyman paid Emily no mind. He worked his penis with a calloused hand and grinned like an idiot as he splattered her with his semen.

Fatima now got her first good look at Emily's abductor. He was squat and had three eyes instead of two. He also had no neck, his head being merged with his chest, with his beard running all the way down his torso till it became his pubic hair. Now he was completely nude and his body rippled with muscle.

Fatima just stared. She'd never seen a naked man up close before, and was surprised by how large the boogeyman's sexual organ was: thrice as thick as her forearm, for sure. His testicles were also huge—like a donkey's.

In fact, once she paid closer attention to them, Fatima realized that the boogeyman's genitalia seemed to be several men's genitals assembled into one. And he was definitely ejaculating like more than one man, squirting a flood of semen into Emily's eyes and hair and mouth, while she sputtered and coughed like some of it had gotten into her lungs, and screamed and railed at him; although, considering the monster size of the freak's organ, Fatima honestly thought her friend should be grateful that the boogeyman was only ejaculating on her and not trying to have sex with her; because, even to Fatima's inexperienced mind, there was no way the boogeyman was going to get that immense sexual organ into Emily's little body without some serious ripping and tearing happening.

Wow, if that penis was any bigger it would be a fire hydrant!

"Stop! Stop it, you bastard!" Emily howled as the freak drenched her in white goopy come. "Just stop it already!"

But the boogeyman seemed to be done ejaculating anyway. After a few more shakes of his monster penis, he grinned down at Emily and then stepped out of view.

Fatima almost burst out laughing. Emily looked horrible. She was a complete mess; as drenched in semen as if she had swum through a sperm bank.

Fatima relaxed. Neither Emily nor the boogeyman were aware of her presence at the window and her friend clearly wasn't yet in any real danger.

All I have to do is untie Emily and we can both take out the boogeyman and then head for the tower. But maybe it'd be better if I sneak around to the front door and shoot the freak first . . . surprise him . . .

But then Fatima heard footsteps behind her.

"Yeah, the slut's doing exactly what you expect a slut to do. Watching porn!"

Fatima knew that whispering voice. But here, of all places? No, it couldn't be!

She tried to turn around, but the unseen speaker already had a firm grip on her from behind, pulling her back and out of sight of the window.

And the next moment, before she could either shoot or scream for help, to her immense surprise Fatima felt the sharp blade of a knife stab into her neck. The pain was brief but intense—razor-sharp steel slicing her throat open from ear to ear and then cutting further back to the bone, fatally separating her arteries and veins with absolutely no way back; death dealt by a resolute hand.

"Die like the dirty slut that you are!" the familiar voice hissed in Fatima's ear.

And then Fatima Noori was lying on the ground, bleeding a river and dying, and staring up at the mocking face of her twin sister Khadija.

Fatima was certain she was hallucinating. Surely there was some mistake here! She reached up a hand as if to ask Khadija for help. And Khadija bent down as if to assist her.

But then Khadija slammed the blade of her knife into Fatima's chest, deep into her heart, and Fatima knew that it was true, that her own twin sister had just murdered her.

But why? That, unfortunately, she would never know.

CHAPTER 18

Khadija

Once Fatima was dead, Khadija dragged her corpse behind the house, and rolled it into a deep pit.

Then she quickly stripped off her own now blood-splattered clothes and exchanged them with those in her knapsack. Her new clothes were an exact duplicate of what her sister had been wearing. Her own clothes went into the knapsack, which then followed Fatima into the pit.

She smeared some of Fatima's blood on herself . . . and dirtied herself up too. Painting the blood on her face felt almost like applying war paint, which she thought fitting, as she wasn't here for fun and games.

Next Khadija quickly covered up the pit with brush and branches. She straightened up, surveyed the result with satisfaction, and nodded. There, her twin sister was now out of sight and out of mind.

Khadija had been following Fatima for quite a while. There were only three places in the play zone where it would be convenient to kill her sister. Not because of the cameras—Khadija was carrying a special signal jammer, which was why Aaron Heller's surveillance cameras kept blanking out when she walked past them—but because those were the three places where she could hide Fatima's body and not expect it to be found. Well, not found until the show was over.

Once she'd successfully hidden Fatima's corpse from view and had also made certain she was now dressed (and bloodied up) exactly the way the *Final Girl's* viewers would remember last seeing her, Khadija Noori walked back around the side of the house to replace her in the show.

"Okay, everyone, let's get this show back on the road!" she said.

***

For Khadija Maryam Noori, killing her identical twin had felt immensely satisfying, as if she'd just freed herself from herself. It had felt like she'd just disposed of a useless part of herself; something that had been weighing her down since birth.

It was entirely by accident that the ultra-conservative Khadija Noori had discovered what her more liberal twin sister was up to.

Two months ago, Khadija had dropped her cellphone and broken it, and had then borrowed Fatima's phone to make some calls and also check her work emails. Fatima had been drowsy at the time and had just handed her phone over, forgetting that she'd not closed the Yahoo Mail app.

And this was how Khadija had discovered that Fatima had been scheduled to compete on *The Virgin* reality show and now planned to appear on the follow-up *Final Girl* show instead.

The stupid slut! she'd raged. *She's just like our mother! She's going to peddle her flesh for money.*

Khadija's first thought had been to tell her father what Fatima was up to. But then she'd smiled coldly to herself and replaced the cellphone on the nightstand beside her slumbering sister.

After that, by borrowing her unsuspecting sister's phone a few more times and also conducting some online investigations of her own, she'd kept track of Fatima's plans.

It was inconceivable to Khadija that a well-brought-up Muslim girl would even consider appearing on *The Virgin*. Reading those emails had revealed to her that her twin sister had been totally led astray by Shaitan, and was about following in the footsteps of their slut mother. And as Khadija had told both Fatima and their father Saeed more than once: "If I ever have a daughter that goes astray like our mother did, I'll murder the bitch myself to keep her from sullying our family name."

The vehemence with which she made this statement always took even their conservative father aback. Because, now that his beautiful daughters were of marriageable age, Saeed Noori had begun wondering if he'd not raised them too strictly for New York City, as neither girl showed any interest in men.

And Khadija had meant every word she'd said about killing any future wayward daughter of hers. Unlike her sister, who had recently begun speaking sympathetically of their mother Jamila, Khadija had no time for that 'prostitute bitch spawn of Iblis.' All these years later, her deepest regret in life was that she'd been asleep the morning her father had chased Jamila down their street with a meat cleaver. She would have loved to have joined in the pursuit and helped him catch her and butcher her.

But what to do about her own wayward sister?

If Fatima was milk, Khadija was acid; if Fatima was honey, Khadija was drain cleaner. If Fatima shat in the public's eye, Khadija was the outraged watcher who would make her lick that defiled public eye clean and also force her to eat her own turds. The former wanted peace and quiet; the latter clamored for the noise of battle. One sister merely wanted a chance to be herself in the world; the other wished to alter the world to suit her personal vision of it.

Khadija Maryam Noori was the sort of personality for whom an ideal must be taken to its most extreme conclusion. Had she been a Christian, she would have ended up as a nun; either the cloistered kind who lived out their lives making extreme penance for the world, or the Mother Teresa type who served in war zones and fed cities of starving children. But seeing as she was a Muslim, here too Khadija looked for the ultimate sacrifice one could make on the altar of faith. Because Khadija could never be one of the many Muslim women around the world who made a difference through participation in politics or success in a career, for instance; or even just by being good wives and mothers.

No, her own extreme personality goaded her towards taking equally extreme measures.

And so, just like Fatima had long searched for a means to escape their ultra-strict family, Khadija too had long been searching for a way to properly express and affirm herself.

And this was how, six months ago, she'd stumbled on the organization known as MPJ. And MPJ—whose tentacles extended worldwide—had recently gotten her employment with Miriam Heller and Miriam's *Final Girl* reality show.

***

Khadija walked back around the house to the window where she'd killed her sister.

After a brief glimpse into the window, which showed her that Emily Ford was still trussed up in the wicker chair and dripping with the boogeyman's disgusting sperm, she bent and retrieved her sister's gun from the grass.

This done, she dipped her left hand into her jeans pocket and switched off the signal jammer hidden in there, automatically turning back on all the video cameras around her. Khadija was unsure how long the cameras had been off for, but she hoped not long enough to have aroused suspicion.

Well now I'm in the decadent reality show!

Looking back in at Emily, Khadija considered leaving her where she was; the woman deserved to die too. But she realized that doing so would be completely out of character for 'Fatima': *If I came all this distance to rescue her, why would I change my mind at the very last minute? And besides, at the moment we're quite far from the tower. I need to make it across to the tower, to where MPJ left that package for me.*

She had just gotten done making up her mind on this when she heard a loud buzzing noise from within the house.

It took Khadija just a split-second to work out what the sound was.

That's a chainsaw!

The source of the chainsaw noise soon appeared. Still naked and with his penis hard again, the three-eyed boogeyman flung the door open and walked in, whirling chainsaw in hand.

"Cut cut cut cut cut cut cut cut cut cut cut!" he giggled moronically while advancing on his bound captive.

"Stay away from me, you creepy son-of-a-bitch!" Emily screamed as he advanced on her. She unsuccessfully began trying to overturn her chair, so as to escape the chainsaw blade.

Khadija just managed to prevent herself from first shooting the boogeyman in the penis—a virgin like her sister, the organ's unnaturally large size and rigidity terrified her.

But just in time, seconds before the boogeyman began slicing the terrified and loudly screaming Emily Ford into two, Khadija came to her senses and put three bullets into the freak's head.

Bang bang bang! Like a brownstone tenement hit by a wrecking ball, the boogeyman's head disintegrated into red and white mush on his shoulders.

But even then it was still touch-and-go for Emily for a few seconds, as there was a chance that the dead freak might drop his chainsaw on top of her. But thankfully this didn't happen. The boogeyman fell backwards away from Emily and his chainsaw fell on top of him and began chewing him up.

After an interval during which, judging from the new fecal smell in the room, Emily must have shit herself from fear, she stopped screaming and turned around and finally saw Khadija standing by the window.

"Dammit, Fatima," Emily growled at her as the chainsaw turned itself off, "couldn't you have managed to get here earlier?"

"Just fucking say thanks, bitch, and go have a bath," Khadija growled back at her, hoping she gotten the pitch of her sister's voice right. "You stink like a whorehouse that's collided with a truckload of drunken sailors. And that's not mentioning the poop!" Like her slain twin, Khadija was also unused to using profanity. Calling men 'dogs' and women 'bitches' or 'sluts' was generally as far as she went. But, due to her job at a homeless shelter, she was very familiar with less savory vocal expressions.

The bound Emily stared at her in shock. "Fatima, when the hell did you start swearing like that?"

Khadija shrugged. *Oops, maybe I overdid the cussing bit*, she realized.

"Since I upgraded myself," she replied Emily. "This is now version two-point-oh of me, a.k.a 'the badass version.' Not my fault—this freaking reality show is grating on my nerves."

Emily quickly nodded. "Whatever, girl. And yeah, thanks from the bottom of my heart for coming to my rescue." She threw a horrified glance down at the dead sliced-in-half boogeyman, whose blood now covered the floor, then looked back up at Khadija. "Hey, please come in and untie me so that I can go clean up and we can resume searching for the money."

"Yeah, sure thing. I'm coming right away."

Certain now that her identity switch with her sister had gone undetected, Khadija Noori hurried around to the front of the house to go free Emily.

CHAPTER 19

Miriam

Miriam was relieved when the video feed came back on just in time to catch the climax of whatever had been going on with Emily and the boogeyman. Fatima blowing away the boogeyman like that was pure reality show gold; and once more reinforced Miriam's faith in her to win the show.

However, the interim period hadn't been boring in the least. Most of that time had been spent watching Karen Rogers battle an eight-armed freak she'd encountered while searching the tower's third floor. Karen had forced open a bedroom walk-in closet and the spider-man freak had leapt out at her.

Miriam had almost vomited on seeing the creature; it was truly one of the ROC's most grotesque creations. It had no legs at all, just eight arms sticking out of its body at random. Its mouth was a vertical slit through the center of its head, with two long fangs growing in its purple gums on each side. Its body was covered with short bristles, and like an obscene joke by its makers, as if they were driving home to the viewer the fact that the spider-freak had been made from four different people, the creature had four penises growing next to each other.

Somewhere beneath it—maybe near its anus (although Miriam was too scandalized by the sight of the thing to really want to know), was the spinneret from which it shot webs.

This was the monster that Karen had battled for eight long heart-pounding minutes, with the freak swinging at her from the ceiling and walls, and twice gluing her to a wall, while she barely escaped from it.

But the creature's mode of feeding was also its weakness, as it kept going for Karen's neck, wanting to sink its fangs into her and drain her dry. And, although clearly terrified, Karen Rogers had shown herself to be very brave and also to have incredible reflexes, literally snatching victory from the jaws of defeat.

Karen's second escape from the creature had been particularly thrilling, because even though she had lost her gun during the skirmish, she'd also succeeded in hacking off two of the monster's arms with the fire axe that had been hanging on the hallway wall.

After this damage, which Miriam suspected might be fatal to the creature, the spider freak had retreated under the bed and had not re-emerged.

Holding the fire axe at the ready like a battle-scarred Amazon, Karen had finished searching the suite and left it. She'd tried to free her gun from where the freak had glued it to the wall, but that had proved impossible, so she'd left it behind and gone to search the next room.

Miriam was herself beginning to wonder where the money was concealed.

Twenty-four million bucks shouldn't be very hard to find; that much money has to take up some obvious, visible space. I suspect that the girls simply aren't looking in any of the right places yet. The cash has to be in a giant crate somewhere, or stashed inside a fridge or . . . please don't tell me it's in the trunk of that car parked over by the far side of the lake.

But at least Karen *was* searching for it, which was more than could be said of the show's other four surviving contestants, though not through any fault of their own.

The Poole twins were still unconscious captives. Those two weren't searching for anything until they woke up; and first they'd need to escape from their boogeyman captor.

Miriam looked at a right-hand monitor. Karen was standing in the middle of a corridor and seemed to be trying to make up her mind on something.

"That's odd," a female voice said behind Miriam. Miriam looked back at her personal assistant Teresa Coombs, who'd just entered the Control Center.

"I thought you might want some coffee," Teresa said, setting down a tray on the table beside her boss and then filling a cup for her. Teresa was a beautiful brunette who'd been runner-up on the last edition of *The Virgin*.

Miriam accepted the steaming cup of coffee from her. "Teresa, you just said something was strange. What were you referring to?"

Teresa pointed at the center screen, which now showed Fatima Noori sitting in a living room. Fatima was reloading her revolver from a box of bullets, while Emily was putting on some clothes she'd found in one of the bedrooms. They were men's clothes and several sizes too large for her petite frame (the tee shirt looked like it was a dress, and the guy's shorts looked like trousers on her), but Emily clearly wasn't about putting her own messy clothes back on.

"This is what's strange," Teresa said, stepping up close to the monitors and tapping on the small MPJ tattoo on Fatima's right shoulder, which appeared from beneath the hem of her tee shirt sleeve time each time she turned to say something to Emily. "I don't recall that tattoo being there before. In fact, I'm certain she didn't have it this morning."

"Oh, you must've missed it," Miriam replied. The tattoo bothered Miriam too, but not because she thought it had suddenly magically appeared on Fatima's body. The tattoo bothered Miriam because she didn't think Muslim girls with a strict upbringing got tattoos in places where their parents might see them. Actually, she didn't think Muslims got tattoos at all. She didn't recall too much about Fatima's background, but she knew she'd wanted to compete on *The Virgin* because she wanted to leave her unpleasant family situation.

Why get herself tattooed where her fanatical parents might see it? she mused to herself, and that, coupled with her previous worries that she remembered Fatima Noori from somewhere, made her call her husband Aaron on the Control Center's automatic microphone hookup. "Darling, I need you to do two things for me."

Aaron Heller's face instantly appeared onscreen. "Which are, honey? Sorry if I sound rushed; we're still trying to discover the source of those video feed blank-outs. They've stopped for the moment, but we need to work out what's causing them before we lose some more of the action."

Miriam nodded. He indeed looked hassled; handsome and hassled. "First thing, please set up a video call with Sheik Ibrahim Khomeini for me. It's very urgent and very important. He's not ROC, but we sent him a private invite so he's certain to be watching the show."

"Sure, no problem. And the second thing?"

"I need you to run a background check on Fatima Noori. I need you to find out everything you can about her. Every single thing."

Aaron's expression turned a little concerned. "Any trouble, honey? I think she's doing a great job so far. Wow, did you see how she killed that last boogeyman?"

Miriam nodded. "Oh yes, she's wonderful; better than I ever expected. But please, run that background check on her. Find out everything you possibly can about her; down to when she has her monthly periods. And as fast as you can."

He frowned. "That serious, huh?"

She nodded again. "I don't know why, but I've a hunch that the information might be vital tonight."

Aaron nodded. "Okay, hon, I'll patch the call to Sheik Khomeini through myself and set two of the boys to research Fatima's life story. Sorry, gotta go now."

Aaron's image faded from the screen.

"You know, there's something really odd about that girl," Teresa said as the central monitor image shifted back to Fatima for a moment. She sat beside Miriam on the couch and added, "Yeah, I can't shake the feeling that I know her from somewhere."

Miriam looked at Teresa in horror. *You too? What the hell is going on tonight?*

Miriam's left leg was artificial, the original one having been amputated after a teenage accident. Now, as sometimes happened when she was nervous, she felt twinges of pain in the leg stump and gently rubbed what remained of her left thigh between the straps that held her artificial leg in place.

But then, taking her mind off the stump-itch, the center monitor shifted from showing Fatima and Emily to showing the Poole twins, who were just waking up in captivity.

"Alright, now this looks damn interesting," Teresa said.

Miriam gave the screen her full attention. Yes, this situation the twins were in did look very interesting.

CHAPTER 20

Cherry/Berry

Cherry and Berry Poole awoke to find themselves both shackled to a wall in a large and very untidy room. In addition, the boogeyman had partially undressed them while they were unconscious, removing both their jackets.

After groaning a bit from the twin headaches they'd both gotten from the boogeyman knocking their heads together, the girls sat up with their backs against the wall. Once they were upright, one of them touched her belly and winced.

"Hey, Cherry, when's our period supposed to start?" The twins synchronized their monthly periods with contraceptive pills. The only problem with that was that they couldn't fix the time of day when they'd start bleeding down to the exact minute.

"Day after tomorrow, I think. Why?"

"My belly hurts, sis. Almost like I'm gonna start—"

"—bleeding right now? Yeah, that must be because the nasty—"

"—boogey-monster punched me there. It's not time yet—"

"—and that's good, 'cos we don't have any tampons here with us."

That settled, the twins looked around at their prison.

"This has to be the basement," one of them said; it really didn't matter which one of them it was.

"Yeah," her sister agreed. "There's no windows and just that door over there."

"And it also smells of stale food. Hey, why does—"

"—this place smell of stale food?"

The other twin shrugged. "Beats me, sis. But hey, maybe it's 'cos those cartons by the wall—"

119

"—contain spoilt animal food. Yeah, I think you're right." She looked around, taking in the dirty room at a glance. "Maybe the stuff in here is what—"

"—the freaks and mermaids feed on when there's no contestants available for them to eat."

"You know, Berry, I think we're in deep shite now."

"Sis, let's get this straight: *I* am Cherry, *you* are Berry. We've enough trouble on our plate—"

"—without adding an identity crisis to it. I know, I know."

"So try to remember . . . ?"

"Ok, I got it now. I am Cherry; you are Berry."

"No, no! You have blue hair and I have red hair, so—"

"—what does it matter anyway, right? I think we scheduled an appointment at the hairdresser's tomorrow. Yeah, if we—"

"—survive this show. What colors are we dyeing our hair again?"

"Purple for me and platinum for you, or maybe it was the other way around. It doesn't—"

"—really matter anyway, seeing as we both look—"

"—exactly the same and think exactly alike."

"Yeah, exactly. But if we want to make it to the salon tomorrow we need to—"

"—survive today. Yeah, you're right. We need to come up with a plan of escape before the damn boogeyman comes in—"

"—and starts fucking us to death."

"Or killing and eating us. Oh, that would be so terrible and disgusting."

"And very painful indeed."

"Which part?"

"The sex or the killing and eating?"

"Say, did you even see the boogeyman's face? I'm wondering if—"

"—maybe he had very long and sharp teeth."

"No, I didn't notice. Long and sharp teeth will really hurt if he bites us."

"I remember he smelt very bad!"

"But we didn't see his face because he was wearing that damn hoodie and then he knocked us out."

"Sis, all of this is Fatima's fault. If she'd helped us we wouldn't be here now, chained up like dangerous convicts. I'm not gonna—"

"—ever forget that. Or forgive her either. Hell no, we Poole twins can be cruel twins too. Just wait till we catch you, Fatima—"

"—you bitch. We're going to kick all of the stinking poop out of your ass."

"Hell yeah, we will."

"All right, sis, let's think about how to get out of here. Now we've got additional—"

"—motivation. We're going to survive this so we can—"

"—kick Fatima's skanky ass as well as get our hair done at the luxury salon tomorrow."

The girls hugged one another, then fell silent and began thinking.

Aside from the boxes reeking of stale food, this basement room contained a tall metal cabinet in one corner, a table and a metal chair. The wall paint was a peeling off-white and the single gray door was situated directly opposite the twins.

Disturbingly, the yellow-tiled floor they were sitting on had several dry brown stains on it, which both twins independently realized were bloodstains, but which neither mentioned to the other for fear of scaring her.

And as with all the other places they'd so far visited in the play zone, neither young woman saw any sign of the video cameras which they knew were recording their dire straits.

The twins were restrained similarly, by a single metal hoop around their wrists which was connected to the wall by about three foot of chain. The hoop was hinged at the end that connected to the chain and was locked at the other end by a sturdy padlock. So, there would be no escaping from it except they had the key. Cherry was chained by her right wrist and Berry by her left wrist, which they'd noticed but weren't too upset about because it still looked symmetrical; like staring at themselves in a mirror.

"I don't see how we're getting—"

"—out of this without some help. Damn Fatima! If—"

"—the greedy bitch had just—"

"—helped us. But no, she wants all of the money for her—"

Their recriminations against Fatima Noori might have continued had not the door swung open then and their captor strode in.

"Shit!" Cherry and Berry both yelped at their first proper sight of him.

The boogeyman had now removed his hoodie, and was naked from the waist upward.

"Oh, shite, this just had to be our bad hair day!" one twin lamented.

"Yeah, how come we get the really ugly and icky one!" her twin agreed.

This boogeyman had a single yellow eye in the middle of his forehead and a protruding snout like a pig's. Even worse, his skin was all leathery and cracked up like a gator's. This leathery texture was clearly why their axes and knives had earlier done little harm to him, though now they could see the shallow bleeding slashes and gashes their weapons had caused to his muscular chest and belly.

His body was also tattooed with surgical scars, as if he'd already fallen apart several times and had had to be reassembled. The scars were all over his scalp too.

"I think he might actually be covered—"

"—in real gator skin," Cherry whispered. "But that's impossible, isn't it? How—"

"—can a real human have an alligator's skin?"

"Or maybe it's fake like Momma Poole's handbag? But I—"

"—don't think so; it really looks like his actual skin. Oh, how gross!"

"Oh, how we hate the ROC!"

The boogeyman was also shoeless now and both his hands and feet ended in horrible, cracked yellow nails. The thought of him touching them made both twins cringe in horror. And yes he did smell; of seemingly bucketloads of stale sweat.

But their grotesque captor's looks and stench quickly proved to be the least of their problems. Because they'd gone from lying down to sitting on the floor and hadn't gotten to their feet yet, neither Cherry nor Berry had yet seen what lay on top of the table opposite them. And besides, a large box blocked off a complete view of the tabletop anyway.

On noticing they were both awake, the boogeyman scowled at them.

"One-Eye hate two-eyes," he spat, revealing that he had almost no teeth in his mouth. "Must correct eyes!"

"What's he talking about?" Cherry asked, as the boogeyman grabbed a spoon off the table and advanced on them.

"I think he hates the fact that we've both got—"

"—two eyes, while he's got just one!"

"Yeah, I can understand that, but what has that—"

"—got to do with us? Oh no, I think he wants our eyes!"

The boogeyman had now reached them. He yanked Cherry to her feet by her blue hair and once she was properly upright, took hold of her head in his scaly hands.

"Hey, let go of me!"

"Yeah, let go of her!"

But the boogeyman didn't let go. Instead, he dug his spoon into Cherry's left eye socket and expertly scooped her eye out.

Almost before either twin realized what was going on or the pain had even set in, Cherry's left eye was dangling on her cheek. And then the boogeyman leaned forward, sucked the eye into his mouth, bit through its optic nerve and swallowed.

Yes, he ate Cherry's eye.

Now pain hit the mutilated young woman, blood squirted from her face, and she began howling in pain.

"You nasty bastard, what have you done?" her sister screamed at the boogeyman, and then realized that he was already turning his attentions to her.

"No no, don't!" she squealed as he hauled her too to her feet by a handful of hair, then grabbed her head and thrust the bloody spoon at her face also.

"Yes yes, do it!" her twin squealed to the contrary, with a hand clamped over her ruined eye. "Make her look exactly like me!"

"Yes yes, make me look exactly like her!" Cherry or Berry squealed as the spoon dug into her own eye socket also, she being consumed by a tornado-like delirium of pain and confusion; but most of all by the terror of being different from her beloved sister in any significant and visible fashion.

Then the stinky lizard-skinned boogeyman had eaten her own left eye also, and she felt both traumatized and grateful.

But both girls also felt enraged, and the closer of them to their assaulter (equally mutilated as they were, it mattered not which of them it was) dug her left thumb into the boogeyman's single eye.

"You one-eyed bastard, we're gonna blind you for—"

"—this and then you'll have no eyes at all!" they screamed in joint agony.

Now it was the boogeyman's turn to howl in pain. Dropping the blinding spoon, and clutching at his poked eye, he staggered away from the twins.

But no, they hadn't successfully blinded him. A moment later he grabbed something else off of the table and lunged at them again.

"I punish bitches!" he growled as he grabbed Cherry's left arm.

"No no no, we're very sorry, sir. We won't—"

"—ever do it again!" the twins screamed as one on realizing that the maniac was now gripping a meat cleaver.

"Bitches must respect I and eyes!" the one-eyed boogeyman said, placing Cherry's left hand against the wall and smashing the cleaver hard against it. Cherry screamed again and slumped to the floor in a faint, with both her left thumb and left index finger severed from her body.

"ME TOO, ME TOO!" Berry screamed at the boogeyman, swinging her own left hand at his face and seemingly doing her best also to blind him, but intentionally not succeeding.

Her action however produced the desired result, because, screaming "TEACH YOU BITCH LESSON RESPECT I AND EYES TOO!" the maniac grabbed her own left arm and hacked both her thumb and forefinger off also, although in her own case it took two swipes of the cleaver to get it done, by which time the red-haired young woman had fainted beside her sister.

But neither of them were out cold for long, because suddenly one of them felt a burning on her mutilated hand and jerked awake screaming, to find the boogeyman cauterizing her hand wound with a handheld propane blowtorch. (Had she been calm enough to pay closer attention to their captor, she'd have seen that he was also busy chewing on one of their severed thumbs.)

Cherry/Berry instantly fainted again from the pain, while their brutal captor swallowed the thumb he was eating, and turned his attention to her twin, who similarly woke up, screamed at the agony and the sight of what he was doing to her, and promptly fainted again also while he completed his fiery task.

"Bitches not bleed to death now. I fuck very hard when bitches wake up. Many many times fucking bitches. Teach them good respect for I and eyes."

Satisfied, the boogeyman turned off the blowtorch, replaced it on the table, and then left the basement for a while.

CHAPTER 21

Karen

After almost becoming dinner for another human centipede, Karen decided that she'd had enough of searching the third floor for the time being.

I need to regroup, she thought. *I need to find some guns somewhere.*

She didn't feel tired, which was good. In fact, since her recovery her body had felt great. Nowadays, she hardly felt fatigued at all.

She frowned. *If only my memory worked as well as my body.*

She descended the stairs to the second floor and began searching again, although this time her focus was on finding some weapons, stuff she could use to defend herself in case of an attack, or to launch an attack of her own.

She was however unsuccessful. She found food in a kitchen and helped herself to both an energy bar and a Coke. Miriam had informed them that all of the food was safe.

While sitting in the dining room next to the kitchen, she stared out of the tower at the world below, this enclosed space called the play zone. She could see outside because there were windows in the giant external monitor screen to let air into the building.

I wonder where the others are and how they're getting on in the game. Has anyone found the money yet?

This kitchen had no TV, and without a weapon of some kind (she didn't consider kitchen knives really useful against the sort of monsters the ROC had created) Karen wasn't about going into any apartment just to watch television and keep abreast of the show's happenings.

She finished her Coke and, after slipping a few energy bars into her back pockets, hurried out to the elevator.

It had just occurred to Karen that maybe all of the weapons on the show were hidden outside of the tower. And she was on her way back outside to get herself some.

***

While crossing the concrete yard that separated the tower from the encircling woods, Karen found herself wondering for the first time about the incredible amount of technology built into this so-called 'play zone.'

Realizing that she was only-God-knew-how-many-hundred-feet underground, with (how many?) million tons of rock overhead, was a scary thought. The play zone was too big for her to truly feel claustrophobic in, but she felt a very similar dread.

She stepped beneath the trees, and almost immediately felt a heavy and calloused hand on her shoulder.

She reacted on instinct, policewoman training, ducking back, grabbing the arm attached to the hand and flinging the person forward over her shoulder in a judo throw.

She paused for a moment to see who it was, saw that it was Miriam's original pincer-armed boogeyman Pluto, and then while the giant struggled back to his feet, she took off running through the trees towards the nearest house.

After she'd covered a short distance, loud noises behind her made her look back.

The boogeyman was hot on her heels. And he wasn't alone. Running ahead of him were two creatures, once-men altered by the ROC's infernal mastery of surgery, once-men who had six legs attached to their bodies—not arms like the spider-man had had, but six actual human legs, two at their shoulders, two where their ribs ended, and the last two in the normal place, at their hips, although this 'normal-positioned' set of legs was angled forward like a beast's, so that the freak could run on all six limbs like a wild animal.

Their heads were abnormally large, and their open mouths yawned from ear-to-ear and, in contrast to those of the other freaks that Karen had so far seen on the show, were packed with long and pointy teeth.

Hunting-dog-men, she realized, turning to flee again as her pursuers narrowed the distance between them.

She heard them getting closer and closer, but made it up the steps of the closest bungalow and got the front door open.

She slammed the door shut and locked it, then stood with her back to it, surveying the apartment. This wasn't one of those she had earlier searched.

Karen didn't delude herself that she was safe now. The boogeyman after her was over two meters tall and ripped with muscle, not to mention that those pincers he had in place of hands would surely make firewood of this front door in no time at all.

So, I need a weapon. And I don't have time to search this entire house! Where can I . . . ?

She could hear them behind her now, climbing the front porch. The six-legged dog-men were snuffling like pigs out there; and the boogeyman's steps sounded as if he was trying to cave the porch in with his feet. It was a terrifying combination of sounds.

Karen ran across to the kitchen. *Lexi found guns in the fridge!*

She reached the fridge and opened it up. There was no gun case in there, just six-packs of beer. Then she pulled open the freezer section. Still no guns, but amongst the frozen sausage packets lay a large survival knife.

It'll have to do for now! she thought, grabbing the knife. Out in the living room, the front door was already splintering to thunderous noises.

Karen ran back into the living room just as the front door exploded off its hinges and flew halfway across the room.

She paused a short distance from the door. Action stance; knife held straight out; ready to stab the boogeyman.

But he didn't come inside. He sent in the man-hounds instead. The pair of six-legged freaks leapt into the living room and advanced on Karen. Seeing the knife she was holding, they slowed down and a look of instinctive cunning entered their hungry eyes. Now, instead of walking directly towards her, they moved off to her right and left sides, trying to outflank her. But she understood their aim and quickly stepped back until she was right next to the wall. She was close enough to the kitchen entrance to duck inside there and lock the door, but she realized that doing so would mean boxing herself into a small space, and that would be suicidal.

The boogeyman stepped inside the living room now and watched the man-hounds.

Staring at the freaks' glowing yellow eyes, a scary thought came to Karen—that those weren't actually human brains functioning inside their huge heads, but that the ROC had transplanted animal brains into their skulls.

Stop thinking like that, she warned herself. *That's just crazy talk.*

The two dog-men paused two yards from her and grinned at her with ear-to-ear smiles full of jagged teeth. Karen waved her knife at them, urging them back. But instead of retreating they advanced on her.

Finally one of them leapt at her with his jaws open, seemingly ready to rip her head off.

She ducked out of his way and stabbed him in the belly—between his middle and rear legs—as he went past. She tried to hold onto the knife, but it had apparently gotten wedged between two of the dog-man's bones, because as the creature slid past her, the knife both ripped a fatal gash in the freak's side and wrenched itself out of her hand.

Trailing intestines and blood, the dying dog-man slid past Karen and into the kitchen. She had just enough time to slam the kitchen door behind him, and then the second dog-man was on her.

And now she had no knife.

The creature rode Karen to the floor, slobbering spittle all over her. His jaws were wide open and he was trying to fit them over her head to maybe bite her face off, but she locked her hands around his throat and got her arms straight, so that all he could do was claw at her. But his damn claws were damn sharp. Karen almost screamed when one of his middle feet—and these were actual human feet, though the toenails looked like they came from a lion or an eagle—sliced her left forearm open down to the bone.

Galvanized by her fear and agony, Karen began strangling the dog-man. She squeezed her fingers as deeply into his throat as she could.

When the dog-man realized what she was doing, he began struggling to get away from her. She took advantage of his fright to slam his head against the wall and then, while he wheezed in a daze, to grab a flower vase and hit him with that instead. She kept hitting him with the flower vase until his head was pulp.

Then she leapt to her feet.

Okay, where's big brother?

The boogeyman 'Pluto' was already heading across to her. He was leering at her, his excitement clear in his three eyes; sweating, and with the surgical scars holding his gruesome face together gleaming like worms crawling over his head. His pincers were already open, ready to snip her up like they were scissors and she a bit of fabric.

He was however advancing cautiously, clearly shocked by the death of his two 'pets.'

Karen wondered what course of action would be best here.

There's no way in hell that I'm gonna beat this monster without a gun! All I can hope to do is evade him and try to make it out of the front door alive and in one piece. So do I duck back into the kitchen and retrieve my knife, or do I duck to his right or left and . . . ?

And then, in a rain of shredded flesh, the boogeyman's head exploded off of his shoulders.

Karen first thought that she was dreaming. For a moment, the giant freak stood there headless, with his arms still raised and his pincers ready to descend, and then another shotgun blast in the back knocked him to the ground.

Karen looked over the corpse at Emily Ford, who was making a point of blowing the smoke from the muzzle of her shotgun. Emily was now dressed differently from earlier on in the show, in a tee shirt that was much too big for her petite frame and a pair of similarly oversized man's shorts. She looked like a little girl playing dress-up in her father's clothes.

Behind Emily, Fatima Noori waved at Karen. "Yeah, I know it's supposed to be every woman for herself on this show, but the nurse in Emily couldn't just leave you to die," she explained.

"Thanks!" Karen wheezed at both young women. She leapt over the dead boogeyman and headed for the door.

"You're bleeding," Fatima told her.

Karen looked down at herself and saw that it was true. In addition to the blood that had splashed across her clothes during her fight with the freaks, her left forearm now streamed with blood where the dog-man had sliced it open. This new wound continued where her earlier bullet wound left off, resulting in a single large tear in her arm that looked distressingly dangerous.

Emily put her shotgun down and examined Karen's arm. "We've gotta get that seen to or you're soon gonna bleed to death," she announced. "Problem is, where to find surgical supplies around here."

"We can find them in the morgue," Karen instantly said.

"The what?" Fatima asked. "I mean, the where?"

Karen explained. "There's a morgue in the tower. I found it while searching. I met this giant guy in there named Operator. He was stitching up a corpse and—"

"Operator?" Fatima asked dubiously. "That's the guy's actual name?"

"Yeah it is," Emily said, tying a curtain cord tightly around Karen's upper arm to serve as a tourniquet until she could patch her up. "I've worked with him in the past."

Karen wanted to ask how the hell Emily, who was a contestant on the show, could previously have worked with Operator, but she'd begun feeling weird. She wondered if maybe it was the blood loss from her wound making her feel this way. Or maybe it was simply her dread of returning to the mortuary and encountering all those corpses; those corpses that all had the same face, a face that she felt she should remember, but yet couldn't place no matter how hard she tried.

Fighting to remember the past just wore her out.

And there was something else too, that made Karen wonder if she was losing her mind. This 'Fatima Noori' seemed somehow different from the one she'd met earlier. This 'Fatima' seemed more hyper, more aggressive, more determined, more . . .

"I'm version two-point-oh of myself," Fatima informed Karen on noticing her questioning glances. "View it as me having Dissociative Identity Disorder if you like, I don't mind." Then she nodded to Emily. "Hey, let's get her into the tower and to that morgue she mentioned before she bleeds to death on us."

Emily nodded to Karen. "Yeah, she's right. I've stopped the bleeding for now, but I do need to stitch up your arm before we get involved in any more action."

Karen let them shepherd her out of the house and back towards the tower. She walked in front, with Emily supporting her, while Fatima brought up the rear, walking backward with her guns pointed at the trees.

They made it to the border of the woods without incident.

"The thing now is to make sure there's no bat-men about," Fatima said. "I don't wanna tangle with those flying freaks again tonight."

The others nodded. Together, they carefully studied the crossing to the tower to make certain they wouldn't be dashing into danger.

The tower was showing a one-eyed boogeyman bending over the Poole twins, both of whom seemed to be both unconscious and bleeding from their faces and hands, though because they were both slumped over and the video camera was overhead, the exact nature of their wounds wasn't clear.

"Ugh, I just hope he won't pull his dick out and start . . . you know . . ." Emily said with disgust written all over her face.

Fatima giggled. "You would know, wouldn't you?"

Emily glared at her. "Don't you dare remind me of that!"

Karen wondered what they were talking about. *Did something happen to Emily that I missed? And why is she dressed in a man's clothes now?*

The boogeyman walked away from the twins and the screen faded to black again.

"Thank God they took that away," Emily said.

"Well, at least we know the twin goon squad haven't found the cash either," Fatima said. Then she abruptly yelped, "Oh, heck!"

The other two women turned worriedly to her. "What's the matter?"

"I forgot our boxes of ammo back at the house. I'll have to go back for them."

"Leave 'em there. We're sure to find some more in the tower," Emily said.

Karen shook her head. "Don't count on it. I've been through that building with a toothcomb. Didn't find a damn thing in there—not a single bullet, speak less of a gun."

"Sorry," Fatima apologized, with a willingness that made Karen suspect she was lying. *Or does she think the money is hidden back there?*

"Listen, Emily," Fatima said, "you take Karen across to the tower and I'll be back in a short while and join you guys inside the morgue."

"Try not to get captured," Emily whispered as Fatima ran off between the trees. "We're never gonna find the cash if we have to keep saving ourselves all night."

Emily handed Karen a gun, and then, after once more scanning the area for bat-men, they crossed the courtyard to the tower entrance.

"There's definitely something creepy about that girl," Karen told Emily as they crossed the concrete.

"Well, she already told us she's got multiple personalities," Emily agreed, pushing open the door and letting them in. "Though I must admit I felt safer with mental-version-one of her around. There's something spiritually unsettling about this version two-point-oh of her. Something almost fanatical."

CHAPTER 22

Miriam

Sheik Ibrahim Khomeini was a withered 80-year-old man, despite which he maintained both an unhealthy habit of hedonism and a habit of acquiring exotic wives—twenty-seven at last count, if Miriam remembered correctly.

At the moment, the sheik was dressed in a powder-blue bathrobe and had on a pair of thick glasses, so he could see Miriam clearly while addressing her.

Sheik Ibrahim was very well connected internationally. He was Qatari by birth, and as a young man had initially begun a career in politics, from which he had been banned for life, on threat of death, when the Qatari government had discovered how unscrupulous and dissolute he was.

The old Sheik was fabulously rich, a fact clearly revealed by the opulent surroundings from which he was replying Miriam's video call. He was sitting on a white leather couch in a living room, one which had a swimming pool in one corner in which a number of nude young women were swimming and splashing water on each other. One of the ladies was Asian, two were Caucasian and one was a Negress. Miriam couldn't tell if the frolicking young women were some of the old man's wives, his concubines, or just some high-class prostitutes he'd employed for the night's enjoyment, either before or after watching *The Final Girl* show.

At the moment, however, Sheik Ibrahim wasn't enjoying himself. Miriam had told him about Fatima Noori's strange tattoo, and asked if he knew what it might mean. She'd known something was wrong when all the color instantly drained from the sheik's face:

"Empijay? Oh, my dear glorious Allah, not them, not them!"

"Who are MPJ?"

"The initials stand for My Personal Jihad," the old man miserably replied. "They're supposedly a decentralized branch of the Taliban, whose members carry out suicide bombings on targets of their own choosing." Sheik Ibrahim now looked even older than he was. "We Muslims however suspect that MPJ is really sponsored by westerners who want to give Islam a bad name. They recruit the young, impressionable, and disgruntled—who of course abound in every culture—and both give them a cause and the weapons to carry it out."

Miriam was very shocked by this revelation. *Personal jihad? Suicide bombers? But . . . but that easygoing girl just wants to escape her repressed family life. Why in the world would she join a terrorist organization?*

Sheik Ibrahim sighed. "Oh, I wish I could make it illegal for such beautiful maidens to become suicide bombers. Let the ugly ones go— I won't miss them at all. Yes, the ugly ones, fine, but not beauties like this. Allahu Akbar."

"How extensive are MPJ? I mean, how internationally networked are they?" Miriam was still trying to decide if the sheik's revelation meant anything other than that she had a fanatical contestant on her show, when the sheik sadly added:

"Oh no, you mean she plans to kill herself onscreen? What a waste of tight Persian pussy. And beautiful too—like Miss Universe or a divine houri. Please beg her for me not to kill herself. I'll marry her even if she loses."

Despite her confusion, Miriam had to laugh. "Old man, you never quit!"

Sheik Ibrahim nodded. "But it's true. It's so true. Suicide is such a waste of beauty and life." Looking very pained, he went on:

"Oh, these goddamn young people and their endless intifadas. They all seem hell-bent on preventing us from spending our God-given oil money in peace. Damn fools. Had I blown myself up as a young man—and my uncle Farouk did encourage me to do so, so his sons could inherit my father's oil fields—how would I be alive today to be enjoying Allah's sweet blessings. And oh, this Fatima girl is so lovely too—gorgeous like the houri promised to the faithful in paradise. And she plans on dying. Oh, I am made so, so sad at the thought of it."

Sheik Ibrahim clearly had nothing more to tell Miriam. Waving a weary and saddened goodbye at her, he cut the connection.

***

Once the old man had signed off, Aaron's face immediately filled the screen. He looked worried. Miriam instantly felt her own worries increase.

"What's the problem, darling?" she asked her husband. "More failing cameras?"

He nodded. "But that's only part of the problem. Honey, the boys just got through running that background check on Fatima Noori that you requested." He waved a printout at her. "I'll quickly summarize what they found out. Nice girl, college graduate with a degree in Education. She lives with her dad and works as an elementary school teacher."

Miriam nodded. "That's as much as I remember too. So why do you look so worried?"

Aaron sighed. "Well, there's one more thing, honey. Our Fatima has a twin sister Khadija . . . an identical twin."

A girl's face was now inset beside Aaron. "Here's her twin sister. Recognize her?"

"Hey, I know *her*," Miriam said, staring at the face. "This is Nancy Carter from the logistics department for this show. She's been working for us for six weeks."

Things were starting to make sense to Miriam now. Nancy Carter was Khadija Noori in disguise. Blonde wig, green contact lenses. Braces. Thick Goth makeup—red eyeliner, black lipstick and nail polish, striped white-and-red tee shirt and tights, and black jacket, skirt and boots. Beside this 'Goth' picture Aaron now put up another one where 'Nancy' wasn't wearing makeup and was revealed as the spitting image of her sister.

Utterly impossible to know it's the same girl, Miriam agreed as she studied the side-by-side images. *So, that's why I kept thinking I knew her. But made up like that, even if she was in the same room as Fatima, I'd never have thought they were sisters, talk less of identical twins.*

'Nancy Carter' hadn't been supposed to travel to Alaska with them, but last week, Jeff Greely, Nancy's boss in logistics had suffered a hit-and-run accident that had left him with two broken legs. So gothic Nancy, who'd already shown herself very capable of handling Jeff's job, had immediately been deputized to take over; and she'd performed better than expected.

*And she's also a member of MPJ—My Personal Jihad—which sponsors
disgruntled Muslim youth worldwide to blow themselves up. Shit, and she's on my
damn show!*

Miriam's worries had her unconsciously scratching her left thigh.

She quickly filled her husband in on her discoveries. If MPJ could
infiltrate them this easily, they were clearly very well connected
internationally, up to the point of having moles in the ROC. An
infiltration from 'inside' was something neither she and Aaron nor the
ROC had foreseen happening. It even seemed eerily poetic and ironic:
one mad worldwide organization trying to destroy another one.

Aaron was horrified by Miriam's revelations. "Oh, shit! Nancy was
responsible for shipping everything up here. I don't want to imagine
what else she transported here along with those movie editing
consoles I ordered."

"I figure the inventory included at least one heavy-duty bomb,"
Miriam said. "Darling, where is Nancy now?"

Aaron frowned. "That's the thing. No one's seen her since the start
of the show. Not too unusual of course, since most of her work was
done beforehand. She might be relaxing somewhere . . but . . . but . .
."

"Aaron, I think the crazy girl has a bomb on her. And she wants
to blow this place up."

Aaron shook his head in dismay. "What about her sister Fatima?"

"Darling, we both already know the answer to that one. The real
Fatima Noori is either knocked unconscious or dead. I suspect she's
dead—why keep her alive if you're going to kill everyone else
anyway?"

Aaron Heller nodded. "So we've a suicide bomber on the set and
we need to find her ASAP. The problem is—and that was what was
bothering me when I called you back—she's gone again?"

"Darling, what do you mean by 'gone again?' "

"She was together with the policewoman and the nurse, but then
she left them—"

"Yeah, I saw that."

"Well, since then, she's vanished." He looked off-camera for a
moment, asked, "Hey, Carlos, any luck yet?" and then turned back to
his wife. "Sorry, honey, just checking on something. Okay, now where
was I? Okay, yeah . . . Nancy or rather Khadija Noori has vanished.
None of our cameras or drones are picking her up anymore. Which

means she's using a signal jammer." Then something seemed to occur to him, because he smiled coldly. "But hey, our gothic terrorist girl isn't as smart as she thinks she is."

"What do you mean? Darling, explain it to me. Can we find her, and if yes, how?"

Still smiling, her husband nodded. "Oh, we can find her alright. Now that we know it's not a virus affecting the dysfunctional video cameras, we'll just track the failing ones. They'll show us where she's heading. The signal jammer she's using apparently scrambles the feed of each camera as she comes near it, so we'll know when she's approaching one and also when she's walked past it. And also, since she doesn't want anyone to know what she's up to, she'll likely be going slowly, because she needs to watch out for cameras that are out of range of her signal jammer; far-off drones, for instance. The way I think our girl is thinking? . . . When you plan to commit suicide, what difference does ten more minutes make if you're going to die at the end anyway? And despite being a suicide bomber, she'll also be wary of both boogeyman and monsters. I don't think Khadija Noori wants to be murdered or eaten before fulfilling her explosive destiny. The little bitch really wants to make a showing tonight."

He looked off-camera again. "Hey, have you guys been paying attention to what I'm saying? Good, start tracing the dead cameras. . . . You're already doing so? Great . . . Okay, they're gonna line up towards a specific location in the play zone. Let me know when you've gotten a fix on where Nancy is heading."

Miriam was already on her feet and waiting impatiently when Aaron turned back to her. "Okay, I'm off to my jeep," she told him while clipping a walkie-talkie to her hip. "Honey, alert security that I'm on my way and ask Teresa to meet me at the car port, and call me with Khadija's location as soon as you have it."

"Will do," Aaron said. "Let's pray she's not yet armed herself."

"I don't think she has," Miriam replied. "Last time we saw Khadija, she didn't look like she had a bomb on her. So she must have secured it somewhere in the play zone where we wouldn't think of looking for it. We either have to reach the bomb before Khadija does, or reach her before she can detonate it."

And then Miriam Heller was out of the control room and running down the corridor.

Some terrorist girl wants to blow up my reality show? Oh no, darling, you're not going to!

CHAPTER 23

Cherry/Berry

The same agony that had put the Poole twins to sleep now woke them up again.

Tee shirts and skirts smeared with blood, they sat up and stared at each other, each young woman with tears in her single remaining eye and a mess of blood in the other eye socket.

"Damn it, sis, have I got a headache! And you look—"

"—exactly like me, so I look like total shit now. I look like one-eyed—"

"—shit. Yes, I know. I look exactly the same as you do, Cherry."

"*You're* Cherry. Red hair alert, bitch. Red hair."

"Sorry, the blood in your hair made me think it was red. Oh, God dammit—"

"—how my hand hurts! Like someone—"

"—lit a fire inside it."

"Shit, Berry, that boogeyman son-of-a-bitch mutilated us! He plucked out our eyes and cut off our thumbs and fingers. I think he ate the fingers too."

"Yeah, the asshole did!"

"And now he's gonna want to fuck our assholes too!"

"Yes, he is. He definitely is. And that's gonna be so shitty. Because—"

"—even if he does fuck both of us at once, we don't have a stopwatch to time how long it's gonna take him to come in our asses, or to make us come either."

"Cherry, we're not gonna come. The one-eyed son-of-a-stinky-bitch is gonna be raping us—"

"—and we can't ever come while being raped. Rape hurts. Afterwards we should make leather handbags and boots out of the croc-skinned son-of-a-bitch's hide. Oh, sis—"

"—what are we gonna do? I need some painkillers. Aspirin or something stronger! My left hand feels like it's on fire!"

"Mine too, sis. Oh, it looks really really ugly now, like roast beef and I hate it. And I also hate it how now we can't see anything—"

"—on our left without turning to look that way."

"Shit, we feel like we're in hell."

"Yeah, we do."

After hugging one another for comfort, the girls fell silent for a while, staring at themselves and continuing to silently weep from their single remaining eyes. Both were very aware that time wasn't on their side, that at any minute now the dread boogeyman was certain to return and subject them to the evil and dreaded sodomy. Because, although both twins had in the past joked and fantasized about being raped by an anonymous stranger, neither of them actually desired to experience such a horrible thing in real life.

And then Cherry(?) made a startling discovery:

"Hey, sis," she said, "if I try, I think I can get my hand free now."

"You can?"

Cherry nodded and demonstrated. Now that she no longer had a thumb and forefinger on her left hand, the rest of the hand easily slipped through the metal hoop around her wrist, although she grit her teeth in agony when the hoop scraped against the cauterized edges of the ghastly wound.

Berry nodded with delight, even though she couldn't free herself, because in her case the shackle was around her right wrist.

"Hurry, look for the keys before he comes back!" she whispered to her sister, who now leapt to her feet and hurried over to the table from which their captor had gotten the tools he'd hurt them with.

Cherry was back with the keys to the padlocks a few seconds later, and soon freed her sister too.

And then both one-eyed girls stared grimly at the array of nasty implements on the table. Their tee shirts were now plastered to their skin by both sweat and blood and they both felt uncomfortably itchy.

"You know I really like this drill," Berry said, picking up the portable power tool and running her bloody fingers along its long and spiral-grooved metal bit.

"Yeah, I really like it too," her sister readily agreed, also running her fingers along the drill bit. "I think the boogeyman was going to use it to drill us. To drill us—"

"—in our butts, I'm sure. The impotent jerk. To drill and kill us!"

"Yeah, if his dick worked and he had a girlfriend and had sex often he—"

"—wouldn't feel the need to torture and kill pretty young woman like we used to be."

"Asshole!"

"Too bad there's just one drill, yeah."

"Are we gonna kill the boogeyman, Cherry?

"I think I'm actually Berry, Cherry. And yeah, we're gonna kill the boogeyman—"

"—because we need some killing practice. So far on this show, we haven't demonstrated how badass we can be."

"Badass Pooles are one-eyed jewels!"

"Oh, sis, my hand hurts, can't we—"

"—find some analgesics around here?"

And then, shifting her gaze from the tool table to the rest of the basement room for a moment, Cherry (or Berry) was struck by a sudden thought:

"Hey, sis, what if the prize money is in one of these boxes in here? It would be—"

"—really sad for us to miss the money after suffering so much down here. Yeah, they smell of moldy pet food but let's search anyway—"

"—'cos I don't trust Miriam Heller not to trick us again—"

"—like she keeps doing by leaving just one of things everywhere."

"Let's search quickly, before the boogeyman comes back."

"We may even find some painkillers in the boxes. Or some—"

"—clean clothes we can change into."

"And afterwards we'll either escape or wait and give the boogeyman some payback. 'Cos payback's—"

"—a bitch—"

"—and we Poole twins are twin bitches when we wanna be!"

"And so this time it's gonna be twin paybacks!"

"We're gonna do unto that boogeyman like he did unto us!"

"Damn straight, bitch!"

They got down to searching the stacked boxes. Seeing as both twins only had one good hand now, it was a very untidy search, with Cherry and Berry simply toppling the basement's many cardboard boxes onto the floor and kicking them open.

Every now and then one of the girls would accidentally scrape her mutilated hand against something and howl in agony.

There was no money in the boxes, which mostly contained moldy pet food in plastic bags. But in one carton they did find a first-aid kit with a bottle of Tylenol 'Extra-Strength' in it.

And then, to their grinning delight, in the last carton they opened, the twins came upon two identical pump-action shotguns and several boxes of shells.

"Sis, we were very wrong about Mrs. Heller. She loves us after all," the girls told themselves while picking up the shotguns. Of course, handling the weapons with no left-hand thumbs took a bit of practice, but they finally worked it out, and even managed to cock the shotguns too.

Cherry grinned. "I really hope the boogeyman comes back soon," she said, after gobbling down about seven or eight Tylenol caplets.

"Oh, what a lovely warm reception we'll have for him now," Berry agreed, grabbing the bottle of painkillers from her sister and following suit.

***

The unsuspecting boogeyman returned two minutes later and was met by a hail of shotgun fire the second he stepped through the door.

The one-eyed freak stood no chance at all against the angry twins. Cherry and Berry literally splattered him against the wall. And then, when he lay on the basement floor, with blood gushing from the huge holes in his torso, clutching tenuously to life and gasping his last breaths, both girls set their shotguns down on the table and picked up the portable drill instead, both gripping its handle.

"An eye for an eye, asswipe!" they yelled as they switched the drill on. Then they leapt on the dying freak and sank the drill bit into his single eye. "This is for mutilating us!"

Not caring that the boogeyman died immediately they splattered his eye open, Cherry and Berry drilled through his head until the metal bit broke on the floor beneath him.

Sweating and exhilarated, as their overdoses of Tylenol had now begun cutting through the pain they were in, they got up and high-fived with their good hands.

"Let's go look for the money!"

They replaced the drill on the table and retrieved their shotguns, then stepped towards the door.

They peeked out and nodded to one another. "Coast is clear. Sis, let's—"

"—get the hell out of here."

After a brief hug for reassurance, they set off.

CHAPTER 24

Karen

A human centipede kept Karen and Emily trapped in one of the tower elevators for almost ten minutes.

The creature, apparently the same one that Karen had successfully avoided on her previous trip into the tower, had been descending the lobby's left-hand staircase when the two young women had entered the building. It saw them at the same time as they saw it. The freakish creature was blocking the way to the morgue, and there was no way around it.

Even by the weird standards of its own bioengineered species, this particular human centipede was *odd*. In addition to the fact that a good number of its torso segments had breasts, meaning it had been made from a combination of both men and women, its segments were also of different skin colors, with about half of the unwilling donors that had formed the creature clearly having been Caucasian, and the rest a mix of Negro, Asian and Latino.

"What the hell now?" Emily asked, firing two shotgun blasts at the creature. But it was already in motion, and both shots she got off missed its terrifying head and instead blew off two of its limbs.

Wounded and angered, the human centipede charged at them.

"Don't waste your ammo!" Karen screamed at Emily as she was about to fire again, pulling her back as the creature surged toward them like a sea wave. And so they ducked into the nearer of the two lobby elevators. Even then it was a close call, with the human centipede's front head almost squeezing inside the cage with them before the elevator doors shut. But Karen kept the monster out by placing a boot between its grape-like bunches of eyes and kicking hard.

"Now what?" Emily asked once they were safe, throwing a concerned glance at Karen's arm. The tourniquet had stopped the bleeding, but the wound still gaped open, and it clearly would take very little to make the bleeding resume. "I really need to see to that arm of yours as soon as possible."

Just as had been the case back when Lexi had shot her, Karen wasn't in much pain from her wound this time either. Which she was certain she could thank the ROC doctors for.

She considered Emily's earlier question for a while. "Tricky," she said. "We're in here and it's out there. We can't get out and it can't get in. And of course we want to get out and it desperately wants to get in so it can eat us."

"Girl, maybe the blood loss has begun affecting your brain, because you're merely stating the obvious."

Karen shook her head. "No, no, my point is that its hunger for our flesh is our escape from it."

Before Emily could question her further, she leaned forward and punched the button for the third floor.

"What did you just do that for?" Emily asked as the cage began rising. "We've got guns. We could simply have opened the elevator doors and blasted the damn thing to smithereens."

"Yes, we could," Karen agreed, "but you're forgetting that until Fatima returns we don't have enough ammo, and we might meet other creatures we need to fight. And what if something happens to Fatima and she can't come back? I already told you how sparse the weapon stores seem to be in this building."

Her comment made Emily laugh and tap the side of the elevator cage. "Yeah, I guess the good old ROC don't want their pretty space-age building shot to pieces. The tower's external monitor screens are bulletproof, but its interior isn't." She grinned at Karen. "Alright, I'm with you. What exactly do you have in mind?"

The elevator had reached the third floor now and was opening.

"Simple," Karen said. "We wait for the centipede to climb the stairs and reach us again. Then, once it gets here, we return the elevator cage downstairs. Assuming there's no other freaks waiting down there, we'll be safe inside the morgue before it figures out that we've tricked it."

Emily laughed. "You're a frigging genius, girl."

They waited for the human centipede to arrive on the third floor.

CHAPTER 25

Khadija

As she stepped into the log cabin beside the pond, Khadija Noori felt filled with a desperate tension. It was one thing to desire to prove your dedication to your faith by making the ultimate sacrifice; and another thing entirely to carry it out.

Now that the glorious moment was so close, Khadija wondered if she was doing the right thing.

While walking through the wooden house to the place of concealment, she realized that her biggest regret would be leaving her father behind. He was certain to be utterly devastated by both of his daughters dying on the same day.

Sorry, father, some things were fated to be since we were kids. If our whore of a mother had stayed home, none of this would have happened.

Khadija didn't even think of her dead sister. At the moment she felt as if she'd been an only child; that there had never been anyone named Fatima Noori.

She stepped behind the television in the living room of the log cabin and pulled off its rear. There was nothing inside the TV except her bomb. Enough cutting-edge high explosive to turn an apartment building into rubble, packed inside a bulky leather jacket. She hadn't built it herself; her sponsors My Personal Jihad had provided it, just like they'd gotten her her logistics job with Miriam Heller. Just like they'd also engineered Jeff Greely's hit-and-run accident. She continued to be impressed by MPJ; by the sheer extent of their deadly reach.

In addition to easily sneaking Khadija into this infidel fortress, MPJ had provided her with detailed blueprints, showing her exactly where to detonate her bomb for maximum effect.

And so here I am now. Ready to take on the world. The infidel dogs and their sluts will all die!

Khadija felt no more fear as she pulled on the bomb-jacket. The jacket's deadly weight was reassurance that she was on the right track, reassurance that she was about to do the right thing. She was ready. She only hoped Allah and His holy prophet would accept her sacrifice.

Have I done enough? She knelt, bowed her head to the floor, and muttered a silent prayer.

Then, rising again, she put her hands into the jacket's pockets and slipped her fingers through the twin detonation loops. The loops were a protective measure to ensure she didn't accidentally blow herself up before she wanted to. All she had to do to set off the bomb was pull them both at the same time. Because of all the wireless signals in the play zone (including those from her own signal jammer) the bomb had no countdown timer.

For a few moments Khadija wondered how different blowing herself up would feel from shooting herself in the head. Then she took her hands out of her pockets, picked up her gun, and stepped to the door of the log cabin. Time to go.

She'd now begun feeling impatient, looking forward to her death as if it was her next birthday. But it wasn't yet time to die. She had to get into the tower and climb to the top floor—she had passkeys.

In addition to holding up the roof of the play zone, the black tower also lay directly beneath the fuel tanks for the giant subterranean generators that powered the entire complex. My Personal Jihad had calculated that an explosion on the tower's fifth floor would collapse the entire play zone in on itself and also take out all the upper floors of the underground complex. Everyone on those floors—several hundred people, including herself—would die. And the US government would have no choice but to investigate the giant sinkhole that had suddenly appeared in the middle of the northern Alaskan wastelands.

Before making this trip, Khadija had asked a friend at the homeless shelter where she worked to deliver a 'birthday present' to her father tomorrow, a package that contained a letter explaining what she'd done and why she'd done it, and asking him to watch the news for confirmation of her success.

The last thing I want is for dad to spend years hoping Fatima and I might come home some day.

Keeping an eye out for hungry mermaids and fish-babies lurking in the pond, she stepped down off the pier and ducked between the trees again. Yes, with the signal jammer working she could run directly to the tower, but any drone flying towards her from its opposite end, or hovering across the lake, would be out of the signal jammer's range and might transmit images of her to the show's organizers; who could then simply cut all power to the tower and lock it down before she scaled it.

So now, a quick dash through the trees and I'll be inside. I gotta make certain Karen and Emily don't see—

Khadija was suddenly grabbed from behind. Next, someone punched her in the belly, making her drop her gun. Before she could stick her hands into the pockets of her bomb jacket to detonate it, the bomb jacket was slipped off her shoulders, and her hands were forced behind her and cuffed together.

She stood there confused, unable to run because three burly men in black jumpsuits and ski-masks were holding her firmly in place; unable to think because this wasn't something she'd expected to happen tonight.

"Well, well, well, if it isn't the maiden from hell," Miriam Heller said, stepping in front of Khadija.

Oh no, the infidels have caught me! Khadija finally realized. *It's over.*

CHAPTER 26

Miriam

Miriam Heller stared at the captive girl. "Khadija *Maryam* Noori," she said gently, smiling coldly at the frustration in the girl's eyes. "You're lucky that you and I share the same name, else I'd have already fed you to the mermaids."

The girl stared back at her defiantly. "Shaitan! Iblis! Anti-Arab witch!"

Miriam shook her head. "Khadija, I'm neither anti-Arab or anti-Islam; I'm just anti- being blown up by anyone."

While Khadija angrily mused on that, Miriam looked over at the tower. None of this was being recorded. Aaron had already switched off all the video cameras on this side of the tower and those across the lake that might be tracking the action. In addition, all the drones had been herded off elsewhere in the play zone to track the freaks and boogeymen.

The tower screens currently showed Karen and Emily exiting an elevator on the ground floor.

While defusing this terrorist threat, Miriam and her husband were being extremely cautious. The Red Octopus Corporation had no idea that any of this was happening. Just as with the composition of Aaron's video crew, these security staff who had apprehended Khadija were the Heller's own employees, men and women they could trust with their lives.

But of course, that's just half of the problem, Miriam thought angrily. *This terrorist bitch here still has to be dealt with.*

The Heller's security operatives had already found and removed Fatima Noori's corpse. Miriam had seen a picture of Fatima's almost decapitated body. She stared at Khadija in frightened disgust: the girl must have ice water running in her veins. Miriam found it horrifying that Khadija could do that to her own twin sister; butcher her like she was a sheep. The murder seemed even more horrifying because both girls were so identical; hadn't it felt to Khadija like she was killing herself?

But her father's a butcher, right? So maybe she's been practicing? Or what else explains such brutality?

"Okay, Khadija, now listen," Miriam finally said. "So long as you're not trying to kill me, your sibling rivalry and religious fanaticism are your own business, but . . . but you just screwed up my reality show. Now I'm one contestant short. But, thankfully, no one else has realized what's happened and so that can still be fixed." She stared deep into the girl's eyes. "Alright, now here's the choice I'm giving you: Either you compete in the game in your sister's place or I'll ship you off to Qatar to marry Sheik Ibrahim Khomeini. He's already in love with your sorry ass."

Khadija mused on that a bit and then smirked at Miriam. "A sheik, you say? That doesn't scare me. I'll happily marry him if he's young and handsome and rich. At least he shares the faith I was about dying to protect."

Miriam rolled her eyes at the girl. "Bitch, he's eighty years old and has twenty-seven other wives. I'm sure he'll think he's in Paradise while making it with you, but you'll think you'd died and gone to Hell."

"Ugh!" Khadija snorted in disgust, her eyes widening. Then she studied Miriam's face to see if maybe she was joking. "For real? Eighty years old?"

Miriam laughed, amused by how quickly the girl seemed to have acclimatized to her defeat; and how, now that her previous intention to kill herself had been foiled, she'd instantly switched back to the normal worries of a twenty-something woman. She reached out a hand and tweaked Khadija's right nipple. "Damn right, he's that old . . . and he'll love to play with these funbags of yours every night."

Khadija visibly shrunk back at the very thought, though with three beefy men holding her in place she couldn't actually move far. "Hell no," she spat. "I'd rather die first! Yeah, yeah, okay, I'll play the damn game. So, tell me, what do I do?"

Miriam smiled coldly. "Nothing that you aren't already doing, except that we're taking the bomb away, and your signal jammer too." She snapped her fingers. "Teresa, get the signal jammer off of her. I believe that's it in her left pants pocket."

She waited until her ski-masked PA had found Khadija's signal jammer and switched it off, then resumed addressing the girl: "Okay, now you're officially joining the search for the hidden money. From this point on you're officially your twin sister. And you keep on being her even if you win. Understood?"

"Yeah, whatever. Anything not to be sent as a mail-order bride to Qatar. That's white slavery, you know."

Miriam smirked at Khadija Noori. "Do you honestly think I give a fuck about that at the moment?"

Khadija looked around at the heavily armed ski-masked men and woman surrounding her and didn't reply.

Miriam went on: "Okay, now, also remember that this show's sponsors don't know you've infiltrated them. Let's keep it that way, okay?"

Khadija's eyes widened in some surprise. "You're scared of them— I mean, the ROC—aren't you? Scared they'll find out that I broke through their security."

Miriam laughed. "Not as scared as *you* should be, girl. Where do you think the ROC got the segments for their human centipedes from?" She pointed at the nearby pond. "Or the women they turned into mermaids?"

Khadija gulped in fright then. Miriam laughed again. "Young woman, right now you've actually a choice between four evils— become a mermaid yourself, become mermaid food, get shipped as a bride to the Middle East, or compete on the show. As for me and my husband, our concern isn't fear of what may happen to us if the ROC discover you're here. No, we merely don't wish to ruin what is sure to be a lucrative business relationship."

"Goddamn infidels. Shaitan! Money is all you ever care about."

Miriam rolled her eyes. "Don't even go there. Just fight and win, Khadija. You're feisty enough to do it." To the three men restraining the sullen young woman, she said: "Uncuff her and give her back her gun."

Once she was free and armed again, Khadija looked suspiciously at Miriam. "How do I know that you won't still carry out some reprisal against me after the show ends?"

"You don't need to worry about that," Miriam said. "You have my word that we won't. If you win the show, you'll be your sister anyway for the rest of your life, which I suspect should be enough punishment for you. And if you don't win . . . well, next time you'll just have to look for a less well-guarded target to kill yourself in."

Khadija glared at her angrily, and then, without another word, she turned and walked away.

However, rather than head for the tower, Khadija seemed to be heading deeper into the woods.

"Where exactly are you going?" Miriam asked her.

Khadija stopped, turned around and explained, waving her gun at them for emphasis: "I'm almost out of ammo, see? And because Karen says there don't seem to be any weapons inside the tower, I need to go back to the house where Emily and I rescued her to get the boxes of ammo I intentionally forgot there. I told the girls I was gonna go fetch 'em." She shrugged. "Or else when I rejoin them, they're gonna wonder what happened."

Miriam nodded. Personally, she was quite bemused by all this 'rescuing' of themselves that the girls kept doing each time one of them was in danger, as if this was some sorority sisters bonding exercise they were participating in. She wondered at what point these young women would realize that this *Final Girl* show was actually 'every woman for herself.'

They'll stop being friends once they find the money, she decided. *Wealth is well-known to destroy partnerships and even families. Finding that twenty-four million dollars is certain to set them against each other in a big way.*

Khadija set off again. Once she'd vanished between the trees, Miriam called her husband on her walkie-talkie.

"The explosive situation has been neutralized, darling," she told him, heaving a sigh of relief at their narrow escape from catastrophe. "The disaster has been averted and everything is under control again. You can turn all the video cameras back on now."

Then she headed back to her jeep and the Control Center.

CHAPTER 27

Karen

The patchwork human centipede arrived on schedule, lumbering hungrily towards them like a locomotive made of meat.

Karen waited until the freak was about to lunge into the elevator before hitting the button to close the doors. Sensing that it was once again about to be deprived of its meal, it lunged anyway; the two women heard its claws scrape the exterior doors as the lift descended.

Once back down on the ground floor of the tower (and with the human centipede for the moment stuck up on its third floor), Karen and Emily quickly made their way to the morgue.

Walking through the mortuary door, Karen felt a moment's rush of fear at the prospect of meeting the giant Operator again. But the room was empty.

It was still as cold as ever however. And as if the giant six-armed surgeon/mortician had returned here in her absence to prepare more of his gruesome art props, there now seemed to be even more of the same-faced corpses lying on the autopsy tables.

Karen once more found herself trying to remember whose ugly and evil face this was stitched on all the unfortunate dead in here.

Emily however, was very unimpressed: "Operator keeps doing stuff like this," she informed her companion. "He calls it art, but I think it merely reveals how diseased his mind really is."

Karen figured that anyone who grafted extra limbs onto his own body couldn't exactly be right-minded to start with. And, maybe because of the blood she'd lost, the freezing temperature in here was starting to bother her.

Emily seemed not to notice how cold it was. While steering Karen through the sea of Y-incised corpses towards a table with a loaded surgical cart beside it, she said, "Once, Operator got it into his head to swap around all the body parts on almost thirty corpses."

"What?" Karen was staring at the 'little-boy' corpse that Operator had sutured shut when she was previously in here. *That face. Why can't I remember that face?*

Emily walked over to one of the shelves by the wall and took down a bottle of denatured alcohol. "Yeah, he did. And if I recall correctly, he called it 'A Study of Human Reconstruction in the 21st Century.' Total B.S. if you ask me. You can just imagine how horrible the results were, what with a mix of different genders, ages and races—you'd have kid feet attached to old-people legs, black female legs attached to white male bodies; genitals and eyes switched around, and any other combinations he could come up with. It was a gruesome mess, but Operator completed it, photographed it, and, craziest of all in my opinion . . . he afterwards painstakingly separated and properly rearranged them all again, supposedly because, according to Operator, even the 'evil dead deserve some respect.' After which the bodies all went to feed the mermaids anyway."

Karen was once more about to ask Emily Ford how she knew so much about the workings of the ROC's grotesque mortician, when Emily, who'd just begun cleaning the wound in Karen's left arm with a cotton wool swab, paused.

"Hey, I think there's something stuck in your arm. Looks like part of a twig. It must have gotten lodged in there while we were making our way through the bushes."

"The arm's a bit numb," Karen agreed. "That's maybe why I didn't notice. I can hardly feel my wounds."

Karen waited while Emily fiddled in the long cut with a pair of tweezers. Then Emily began looking more and more puzzled.

"What's the matter?" Karen asked, when she saw Emily staring up at her in surprise.

"Karen, this isn't a twig in your arm. It's a wire. And it's running alongside your radius bone. What I mean is—it starts and ends inside your wound, like it's a part of your body."

The news shocked Karen herself. *A wire inside me? How can that be?* She looked inside her forearm and saw that Emily was right: a white wire about two millimeters thick could be seen emerging from the torn muscle near her elbow and vanishing into the muscle near her wrist.

"It looks exactly like a small nerve," Emily said. "The only reason I discovered it wasn't is because the freak that hurt you peeled its covering off. See?"

Karen nodded as the nurse indicated the bared portion of the wire, which revealed a copper-colored core.

"I wonder what'd happen if I tapped it with the tweezers," Emily said.

"Don't," Karen yelped in sudden fright," pulling her arm away. She was very scared of discovering what the results of such probing might be. "Listen, Emily, according to Operator, I practically died and it was a huge battle to revive me. With that taken into consideration, a wire in my arm doesn't mean too much."

Emily was insistent. "No, you misunderstand me. I'm not suggesting that you're a freak too. But I know Operator and those ROC surgeons. They may have augmented you in some way."

Karen frowned. "Like sci-fi? You're suggesting they've given me superpowers now?"

Emily nodded. "Exactly. Like super-strength or X-Ray eyes . . . or you might even be able to fly now."

Karen laughed. "C'mon, girl, be serious."

"I am serious."

Karen shook her head. "Well, I don't feel any different. I can't lift things any easier than you can, I definitely can't see through walls, and I'm very sure I can't fly now." She placed a hand against her forehead and sighed. "It's just that I can't remember anything." Which brought her previous question back to her mind: "Emily, when I met Operator earlier and asked him whose face he was stitching onto all these bodies, he told me he'd forgotten. All he could remember was the guy's first name. Edward . . . or Edwin . . . something like that." She focused her gaze on her companion. "Emily, you seem to know a lot about this place. Do you know who this middle-aged face belongs to?"

Emily turned and looked at the arrayed corpses. "Yeah, someone told me. It's Edward . . ."

"Edward . . . what?"

"Ed . . . now what was his surname again? Yeah, I remember! Edward Sanders." She looked searchingly at Karen. "Edward Sanders. Does the name mean anything to you now?"

But Karen was already smiling. "Yes, it does. Edward Sanders, the million dollar loser." Her memory was still cotton wool filling her brain; a white cloud that adamantly refused to rain on her mental desert; but this man's name and exploits forced their way through the hazy past.

"Let me sew the arm up now," Emily suggested. "We'll worry about that little wire later. It's likely just there to compensate for some nerve damage."

"No, no, no, not yet," Karen said. "Listen to me, Emily. I think we just found the money."

Emily laughed. "Here in the morgue? Wow, hon, all that blood loss *really* is getting to you."

Karen laughed too. "Emily, I'm not joking. The money is hidden in the corpses. Operator sewed Edward Sanders's face on these bodies as a clue to the contestants. He was lying when he told me he didn't remember the man's name."

Emily had stopped laughing. Now she turned and looked around at the array of corpses in the morgue. "You're serious?"

Karen nodded. "Yeah, I'm dead sure. Edward Sanders was a Boston mob bookie who worked for kingpin Marko Velli. He stole a million dollars in cash from Marko and needed to flee the country, but the problem was how to get the money across the north border into Canada. So a surgeon friend of his suggested to Edward that he open him up, pack the cash in his belly and sew him back up again. The plan was that once he made it across the Canadian border, another doctor would remove the cash from him."

"Hey, that won't ever work," Emily quickly objected. "As a nurse, I can tell you there isn't enough space in a person to hide that much cash." Then she scowled. "Except if they . . ."

Karen smiled. "Yeah, the surgeon took out most of Edward's guts so he could fit the money in there. He froze the guts and they were supposed to be replaced once Ed made it to Montreal. They were gonna simply fly Ed across to Canada as an elderly invalid."

"Aw, this is simply too complicated," Emily objected. "Why not just . . . oh, I don't know—it just sounds too stupid and dangerous."

"That's why he's called a loser—because he went along with such a dumb plan," Karen said, trying to dredge up the rest of the sordid story from her memory. "But see, what Edward didn't know was that the doctor friend who'd operated on him actually worked for Marko Velli, who'd already discovered Ed's theft and just wanted to have some fun with him. So imagine Edward's horror, when on making it up to Montreal, he's rolled into the operating theater to find none other but Marko Velli himself waiting for him."

"Ugh," Emily said. "After all that trouble?"

Karen nodded. "You can imagine the rest." She laughed. "I guess Marko was in a somewhat forgiving mood that day. Long story short, Marko incinerated Ed's intestines while Ed watched helplessly, and then Ed was operated on without anesthetic and the money taken out of him . . . but he survived. Edward left the hospital with just two feet of small intestine and almost no colon at all."

Emily winced. "But still, he's dead, right? So the shock of everything must've killed him after all."

Karen nodded, then shook her head. "Yeah, Ed's dead, but no, that's not how it went down. It was the Vegas mobsters who killed him. He was owing the Las Vegas casinos about half-a-million bucks in gambling debts, which was apparently why he stole Marko's money in the first place, and when Edward couldn't pay the Las Vegas crew what he owed them, they gutted him again, and this time cut out every organ left inside his body, including his heart and lungs." She shrugged at Emily. "Of course, all this is hearsay, it's how the underworld grapevine said it happened. But the Vegas police did find Ed's corpse in a casino dumpster, with all of his innards in a plastic bag nearby."

"What a loser," Emily said, shaking her head. "But, hey, let's confirm your theory about the money." She set down the needle she'd intended using on Karen's arm and picked up a scalpel instead.

Karen smiled. "Trust me; Ed's got the money. Just count the number of corpses. Excluding this kid here, who I already know is empty, there should be twenty-four others."

After saying this, Karen looked towards the morgue door, which was obstructed from view by a large freezing unit. She hoped they'd remembered to lock the door. It would be insane if the human centipede cornered them inside here.

"I just wanna make sure," Emily said, stepping up to one of the nearer male corpses. "Once that's done we can plan our defense."

"Whatever you say," Karen replied, then she patiently watched as Emily expertly slit the dead man's belly open again.

"Wow, you're right," Emily gasped in delight as the corpse's skin parted to reveal wads of hundred dollar bills wrapped in clear plastic. "The cash really is inside—"

Then she yelped in fright and leapt back from the dead man.

"What's wrong?" Karen asked.

Emily gaped at the body, then gaped at Karen while pointing at the body. "He moved! He isn't dead. He's . . . he's . . . !"

"He's a frigging *zombie*," Karen said drily as the clearly 'dead' man began trying to sit up. "Trust the damn ROC to pull a swerve like this. Now that we've found the money, we've got to fight to keep it."

"Oh, my dear God, please tell me this isn't happening now," Emily groaned as all the other corpses in the morgue also began sitting up on their autopsy tables. "Yes, yes, I work here, but I never suspected we could do this too."

Several of the dead people had now gotten down off their tables and were shambling zombie-like across the floor towards Karen and Emily with their arms outstretched to grab them. It was one level of dread watching the dead return to life; but that dread was completely upgraded because these walking dead all had the same ugly face, with the same fishlike gray eyes.

The dead man that Emily had slit open grabbed her arm. As he pulled her towards him, packets of dollars fell out of his belly.

"Let go of me!" Emily shrieked in fright, reaching for her shotgun, but with her fingers falling short of it.

In addition to each one of them having Edward Sanders's ugly face, all of the zombies had big-cat dentition, like a lion's or tiger's teeth. The zombie who'd caught Emily was already bringing his spread jaws towards her neck when Karen stuck her pistol into his mouth and pulled the trigger. The dead man was blown backwards against the table he'd been lying on. Emily disentangled herself from him, ran forward and picked up her shotgun.

The 'dead' zombie collapsed to the floor, and more money spilled out of him.

Karen quickly analyzed the developing situation. The morgue exit was behind the zombies; no way out there. And the zombies were advancing, closing in on them. And even if Karen couldn't read the expressions in their dead eyes, there was no mistaking the language of their sharp gnashing teeth and grasping fingers.

These undead guys and girls are hungry. For real.

"We're gonna have to hold them off somehow," she told Emily, pulling the other girl backward before another zombie grabbed her.

"Yeah, yeah," Emily agreed, "but what the hell is animating them? That guy you shot—he has brains dripping from his head; it isn't like he's some kinda machine. If he was dead, how could he also be alive?"

Karen pulled a table between them and the approaching dead horde. "I don't see that it matters. What's important is that from the look of their teeth, they're gonna be trying to eat us. And we don't have enough ammo to stop them all."

"Where the hell is Fatima when you need her?"

"She's most likely dead now. Running off all alone like that was dumb of her."

Emily helped Karen pull another table between them and the zombies. The zombies now had them pegged into the far corner by the corridor wall, a short distance from the start of the pool in which unused body parts were soaked.

For Karen, the most scary thing about their attackers wasn't the fact that they were the living dead. No, it was that male face that they all shared. And even here, the problem wasn't Ed Sanders's uncontestable ugliness. No, it was the perverse grotesqueness of his face's superimposition on a variety of human shapes. Seeing that middle-aged face atop a little girl's neck was obscene to say the least. The three or four pregnant 'Eds' looked even worse—the lines of sutures down their bulging bellies looked like the result of a botched caesarian operation.

To Karen's relief, the zombies clearly couldn't think very well. They kept walking into the tables and bouncing back, looking both frustrated and confused that they weren't able to reach those they wished to consume.

"Okay, that's holding them for now," Emily said as she and Karen braced themselves against the middle of the two tables that separated them from being eaten alive. "But . . ." and then, right out of the blue, she began laughing.

"What's funny about our situation?" Karen asked, discharging her pistol point-blank into the head of an 'Ed' that had managed to grab her arm across the table. The zombie's head splattered open and he fell back like a felled tree, parting the ranks of his morbid fellows like a knife as he vanished from view.

Still laughing, Emily pointed at another member of the front line of zombies, whose belly had been ripped open by one of the steel tables' corners so that it now yawned wide open, revealing the wads of cash packed inside it. "Well, this is the first time in my life that my money has ever tried to eat me."

Karen didn't find the joke funny at all. She stared through the ravenous undead mob, trying to figure a way out of this crazy mess.

CHAPTER 28

Khadija

Khadija Noori fumed with rage as she ran towards the house where she had left the spare ammunition.

Now I am in the damn game for real. I have really let My Personal Jihad down, and I'm sure both Allah and His holy prophet are disappointed in me for not making the ultimate sacrifice. I can't believe I was so weak, so careless that they caught me. So I came here just for nothing? Well, winning the twenty-four million in prize money will be quite some compensation. And yes, I am going to find and keep the money. But oh, glorious Allah, please be merciful to me. Having to live as stupid Fatima from now on? Oh, that really is a horrible punishment.

But she was terrified of the alternatives—particularly of being shipped off to Qatar to marry a lecherous old man her grandfather's age.

For Khadija Noori, who was young and ripe and almost bursting at the seams with repressed sexual desire, imagining her toned virgin body crushed beneath the withered and flabby body of an octogenarian was one of the most nauseating images that her mind could conjure up. The thought of a toothless aged mouth sucking on her firm young breasts and of such an ancient erection entering her inexperienced genitals made her want to throw up.

Oh hell no. I really meant what I told Miriam. I would rather die than have a disgusting man like that as my first lover ever. If only he was younger but just as rich . . .

Still considering how lucky she was to have escaped that horrible fate, Khadija almost missed the sudden motion on the porch of the house she was heading for.

But once she saw it she immediately fired three shots in that direction.

She was so confident that she had hit the target that she did not even stop walking, and her confidence in her stellar marksmanship was rewarded when a few seconds later, the tentacled body of a boogeyman fell forward onto the front porch.

Khadija's expertise with firearms was no fluke. Once she'd joined My Personal Jihad, they had trained her for every eventuality, including in the use of knives and in unarmed combat. Under the pretext of having extra work to do at the homeless shelter, many of her weekends over the past six months had actually been spent meeting her instructors, a grim middle-aged Yemeni couple who ran a shooting range and who'd taught her to kill.

But they didn't really prepare me for every eventuality, she thought grimly. *They certainly didn't prepare me for damn technological malfunctions. Because the only way Miriam could have realized that I'd substituted myself for Fatima was if my signal jammer failed at some point.*

Because Miriam Heller had forgotten to mention it, Khadija still had no idea that she had been given away entirely by her uncovered MPJ tattoo, which still peeked out occasionally from beneath the right sleeve of her tee shirt when she moved her gun arm. My Personal Jihad had given her a choice of places to have the tattoo, and even the option of not having one at all, as many Muslims considered tattoos to be haram (i.e. forbidden). But Khadija had desired the tattoo as something that would help keep strong her determination to use her body as the ultimate weapon. If being tattooed was a sin, she had believed her impending sacrifice was sufficient to cleanse away that sin.

Thinking back now, she was surprised that she'd managed to successfully conceal her double life from her sister and father for so long. Of course it had helped that Miriam and Aaron Heller's operational headquarters was in New York where she lived, but the endless identity switches between herself and 'Nancy Carter' over the past month and a half hadn't been easy. Neither had been juggling two jobs. The fact that her employment with the Hellers hadn't been full-time until her boss Jeff Greely had had his 'accident' had also helped a lot.

Khadija reached the porch steps. She paused with a foot on the first step and stared down at this latest abomination that the ROC had unleashed against her.

The boogeyman was dead, no doubt about that: one of Khadija's bullets had hit him in the head and ripped away most of the rear of his skull. Blood and brains were spread out behind him.

But what remained of the boogeyman's head was horrible enough to behold.

His face was just a disfigured mess, something that seemed to have been assembled by surgeons from leftover flesh. And his body wasn't much better, it was also a mess of horribly scarred skin. And his arms? No they weren't tentacles like she had originally thought, just seemingly boneless; both were twisted and coiled in strange directions like dead snakes. And both flexible appendages bore long surgical scars that seemed to mark where their bones had been removed. And of course, as expected, the dead man's arms and feet ended in too-long fingers and toes which themselves ended in long black claws.

Khadija shivered as she stared at the revolting transhuman corpse.

Oh, my dear God, and that infidel bitch Miriam actually threatened to do something similar to me? To have me surgically turned into a mermaid? She truly is an agent of Shaitan.

Resolving to be a very good girl henceforth, Khadija leapt over the boogeyman's corpse and hurried into the house to get the boxes of ammunition.

CHAPTER 29

Cherry/Berry

The short corridor leading from Cherry and Berry's erstwhile prison opened into another, longer corridor, at the right end of which stood an elevator.

As they had no idea where they were, the girls at first ignored the elevator and walked in the opposite direction, where, through a doorway they could see windows.

Then they stepped into an empty conference hall and realized that they hadn't been held captive down in a basement at all, but were actually up on the tower's third floor.

"How'd we get up here?" Berry asked, leaning out of a window. "Damn that—"

"—evil boogeyman," Cherry finished for her, stepping up beside her and also peering down at the tower courtyard. "Now we have to get back downstairs again!"

Covered in blood from head to toe and both looking like a pair of escaped prisoners-of-war, the twins turned away from the window and re-crossed the conference room to its door. The overdose of painkillers they'd taken had shaved the pain off the injuries they'd suffered, so that now the headaches they'd both gotten from having their left eyes plucked out had shrunken to a mere niggling throb in the backs of their heads, and their left hands no longer felt like someone was roasting them in an oven.

But, just in case, they'd brought the bottle of Tylenol 'Extra Strength' along with them.

Their two main problems now were getting used to seeing with just one eye (they were having difficulties telling how far-off or nearby objects were) and holding their shotguns steady (the twins' lack of left-hand thumbs meant that, once raised, their shotguns kept slipping sideways onto their forearms).

And the girls were now both very angry. They'd enjoyed dispersing payback to the boogeyman who'd eaten their eyes and fingers and now shared an unspoken desire to hurt someone else, anyone who dared piss them off.

And it was while they were in this dangerous state of mind that the hungry and equally angry human centipede which Karen and Emily had lured up to the third floor came upon the Poole twins.

And the freak made the mistake of attacking the girls.

**

The human centipede swept towards the two girls like a derailed locomotive intent on demolishing everything in its path. Its similarity to a train was reinforced by the racial-patchwork nature of its construction, all those different races blended into one in a way that the United Nations would love to accomplish on the third planet from the Sun. The centipede's tiny brain was aflame with hunger and the pain of the limbs that Emily had shot off. In addition, it could smell the blood on the twins and realized that they too were hurt; and it felt they would make easier prey than the two women who'd wounded it.

And so it rushed at them, with its head raised well off the floor like that of a lion poised to strike and its many claws tearing the corridor carpeting to fluff, and its smell of sweaty masculinity and femininity filling the air.

**

Cherry and Berry had been walking along the corridor towards the elevator, when they saw the human centipede charging at them. They took one look at the onrushing engine of destruction and began laughing their heads off like madwomen.

"Hey, centipede, we're the Cruel Twins, and we're so pissed off right now—"

"—that we're gonna shit on your damn bad karma and flush you down your own toilet! So—"

"—come and die, freak!"

And then, with that 'twintuition' the girls so often displayed, they began moving like parts of a perfectly synchronized machine. One girl stepped to the left of the corridor while the other went right, and then they both knelt down, swept their shotguns into firing positions and then:

Bang! Bang! Bang! Bang!

The human centipede never knew what hit it. One moment it was hovering over the two girls, trying to decide whether to first attack the one with red hair or the one with blue hair, and the next thing, it was being blasted into pieces, with pieces of its horrible face and brains and its first two leg-arms flying off its body like red rockets and splattering the walls and ceiling, then raining down onto its rear body segments. One shotgun blast turned the 'bunch of grapes' mass of its left eyes into jelly, while another blast tore out the entire right side of its neck, so that what now remained of its head immediately toppled sideways, where the twins destroyed it even more. This was one time when they felt no need to do exactly the same thing, their 'twintuition' in accomplishing their shared objective was deemed sufficient.

Then, once the human centipede's front head was complete mush, Cherry and Berry nodded at each other and simultaneously leapt to their feet. Then after slapping their palms together, they ran along the centipede's fast collapsing body.

"Hurry! We gotta kill its other head before it dies on us!"

"Yeah, yeah. Dammit, Cherry, this sonofabitch monster actually thought it—"

"—was gonna eat us. And, hey, I'm Berry . . . or am I? This gets confusing in a fight. Can we just have the same name and be—"

"—the same person sometimes? Hey, that's—"

"—not a bad idea. Yeah, right!"

They were breathing hard by the time they reached the other end of the creature. The corridor wasn't wide enough for it to turn around, but its rear head howled in anger and anguish as it heard them approach it from behind. It was still deadly though, raking the corridor walls with its claws in its attempts to reach them and claw them into edible pieces.

The twins stopped behind the creature and pointed their shotguns at the back of its head. They began dancing and singing:

"This how we flush the poo! Flush the poo-poo when we're through! One, two, one two . . . go, sis, go!"

Click! Click! The sound of firing pins striking empty chambers.

"Hey, our damn shotguns are empty!"

"Hey, monster, don't go anywhere. Give us a few moments to—"

"—reload and then we're gonna kill you anyway!"

Cherry pulled a handful of shotgun shells out of her pocket and the girls got down to reloading. They took their time doing so, occasionally looking at each other and giggling, while the human centipede's rear head, realizing its crisis and still unable to turn around and attack them, now tried the opposite tactic of dragging itself to safety instead.

Cherry and Berry finished reloading the shotguns and cocked them. Then they walked up behind the dying centipede-monster and grinned down at it.

"Okay, freak, say your last prayers."

"We're about to dispatch you to monster heaven!"

But then, right before they placed their shotguns at the back of the human centipede's head, it slumped forward and lay motionless. Its mouth flew open and its fat black tongue uncoiled onto the floor.

"Hey, hey, man! Don't you dare—"

"—die on us. We ain't killed you yet! Sis, I think it's dead."

"Wow, how damn unfair can life be to us sometimes."

"Aw well, that's done. Let's just—"

"—get out of here and head downstairs. But its—"

"—smelly corpse is blocking the elevator, sis, and you don't feel like climbing over it and getting its sweat on you. And neither do I. So let's just—"

"—take the stairs. At least now that it's dead—"

"—it can't come after us."

CHAPTER 30

Karen

The impasse with the zombies wasn't ever fated to last long. Still, the two young women, Emily on the left and Karen on the right, valiantly endured, bracing their bodies against the two autopsy tables they'd set between themselves and the zombies, and doing their best to avoid falling into the clutches of the many dead hands clutching at them, hands which sought to grab them and haul them across the tabletops and feed them into the twenty-something sets of gnashing jaws that awaited their soft feminine flesh with a monstrous and inhuman appetite. And of course, overlying and amplifying their terror of being eaten, was that ugly middle-aged male face all the zombies shared, be they black or white, young or old, or male or female.

The two tables were themselves now covered with gore: piles of flesh, pieces of shattered bone, dislodged eyes and teeth, and pulped chunks of brain. The gore made each tabletop slippery and difficult to keep a firm hold on its edges.

Several times while keeping the undead at bay, Karen and Emily had barely managed to escape the sharp teeth of front line zombies who'd been forced onto the tables by the relentless crush of those behind them. When this happened their only recourse had been Emily's shotgun.

And then there had also been the 'pregnant' zombie (although in actuality the seemingly pregnant zombies' wombs were just filled with twice as much money as the others) whom Karen had originally shot in the head, but whom, after falling to the floor, had apparently still had enough of its splattered brain intact to enable it crawl under the table and grab Karen's leg and try to bite her. Emily had quickly remedied that situation by sticking her shotgun into the woman's mouth and firing.

But after blowing three zombies' heads to bits, Emily's shotgun had clicked empty and she had been forced to discard it and instead pull out a small revolver from her back pocket.

Karen wasn't sure how many shots were still left in Emily's revolver. *If I counted correctly, she's already fired it three times to keep the tables clear. Which should leave three bullets in the gun . . . if she'd not used it before we got in here.*

As far as Karen's own gun was concerned, she had no idea how many shots were left in it either. *That all depends on whether or not Emily fired it before giving it to me.*

She glanced across the morgue, at the giant monitor on its far wall, which she knew was turned on—though its screen was darkly idling on standby—and felt grateful that it wasn't broadcasting their current life-and-death struggle; watching themselves in their current crisis would have been too distracting.

Aware from the offset of the siege in the morgue that she and Emily were at an immense disadvantage in terms of the number of foes ranked against them, Karen had been wondering how they could reach the safety of the exit door.

"We can't waste our ammo shooting them," she'd already advised Emily. "Let's just keep them at bay for as long as we can and try to figure a way out of this."

But this 'stalemate' approach hadn't taken into account their need to keep clearing the tables of those zombies who'd been shoved onto it. And strangely, even though she and Emily had now 're-killed' at least ten of the zombies, there seemed to be at least twenty-four 'living' ones left in the morgue. Considering that the prize money for the *Final Girl* show was just twenty-four million dollars, this disparity bothered Karen until she realized the reason for it. Apparently, the child zombies didn't have as much space in their little bellies as the adult ones did, so that freak-maker Operator had placed smaller packages in each of them; cash packages of maybe half a million dollars each; but of course this also meant one needed more of the kids and teens. A reversal of this argument would also explain why the 'pregnant' zombie women had extra cash stuffed inside them.

"My arms are killing me," Emily protested now, with splatters of zombie gore and a strained expression on her face. "I don't think I can hold these damn tables in place for much longer."

"Me neither," Karen agreed. "I suggest we make a break for it now while we still have some ammo in our guns. We'll shove the tables sideways into the zombies. Once those on the sides are out of the way, we'll shoot those in the middle, then we run through the space created when those we shot fall down." She frowned at her companion. "You up for that?"

Emily nodded. "Only real choice we've got anyway. Ready when you—"

But maybe it was a lapse in their concentration because they were talking, or maybe both young women's arms were simply too weak now (Karen's in particular, because of her wounds) to hold the sturdy metal tables in place, but it was right then that the zombies managed to shove the left-hand table out of the way and so break through the barricade that had been holding them at bay.

Because Emily was on the left, she bore the brunt of the zombie attack. They surged forward and grabbed at her, but she reacted quickly, shooting one of them in the face and then leaping up onto the table that had just been shoved out of the way. From up there she dealt out 'death' to one more zombie, but by then the others had her, and this time there was no escape.

"Get off me! Get off of me!" Emily screamed as the undead covered her, while Karen discharged her gun into the backs of two zombies in an attempt to reach and save Emily.

But then Karen quit firing and just watched in horror. It was clearly too late already for a rescue attempt. The zombies had Emily down on the autopsy table and were devouring her, while Emily howled and howled and howled in agony.

Karen felt like vomiting. The zombies pulled Emily apart as if she was a roast chicken or Thanksgiving turkey, yanking her guts out of her belly and chewing on them.

CHAPTER 31

Cherry/Berry

The twins stepped down from the stairs into the tower lobby, heard both the sound of gunfire and loud hungry growling from the nearby corridor, and quickly changed their minds about exploring the ground floor for the prize money.

"Nope, not doing it," one of them said, to which the other one immediately agreed: "Yep, let's just head back upstairs and wait till the shooting stops. If nothing else—"

"—after the gun battle there's certain to be either less contestants—"

"—or less boogeymen for us to deal with. Yeah, you're right."

"Upstairs it is. Also, I wonder—"

"—who is shooting who. But it doesn't really matter—'

"—so long as they don't kill the money as well. Haha—"

"—hahaha!"

They turned back to the staircase, miscalculated their steps and bumped into each other. This had been happening a lot since losing their eyes, and each sister was getting very tired of it. Actions that they usually synchronized perfectly when they each had two eyes and could see one another clearly were now becoming clumsy: it was a totally intolerable situation.

"Dammit, sis," Cherry said after bumping into Berry for the third time, "how I hate being one-eyed. It makes—"

"—seeing things really difficult."

"Oh, we'll get Fatima for this, don't—"

"—you worry. And when we do we'll kick her ass so hard she'll be pooping left eyes for a week."

"Hey, let's just take the elevator. But oh no—"

"—we can't do that because the human centipede's smelly corpse is blocking the way—"

"—and no way are we gonna climb over it and smear all that nasty sweat on ourselves. But, Berry, I'm curious."

"Yeah, me too. The question is, should a human centipede—"

"—seeing as it's made up of close to thirty torso segments from thirty different people—"

"—be called a corpse or corpses? And, sis, I'm—"

"—Berry and you're Cherry, and we're both—"

"—very very very angry one-eyed bitches."

"And we're going to be even angrier if we don't win the prize money!"

While speaking they'd been climbing the stairs back to the second floor.

Almost immediately the twins stepped up onto the landing, they were attacked by one of the flying freaks, the bat-man apparently having flown in through one of the windows in the tower screen.

But the Poole twins were on top of their game now and the hungry airborne man-thing didn't stand a chance.

"Get it before it gets us!"

In a move they'd now perfected, Cherry and Berry stepped aside to the corridor walls, raised their shotguns, and each girl fired once.

The bat-man splattered into meat-pie filling, and the girls strode confidently past its minced remains.

"You know, I just love shotguns," Cherry said as they pushed open the first door on the left. "You don't really have to aim the thing—"

"—just point it in the right direction and pull the trigger."

"Oh yeah. . . . Wow! Will you just—"

"—get a load of this!"

They'd stepped into a chamber containing an indoor swimming pool. The pool was large, bean-shaped, and in its center had a small island complete with sand and two real coconut trees.

"You gotta agree that the ROC know how to enjoy themselves—"

"—when they aren't enjoying themselves watching us kill ourselves."

"It's gonna be great to have money again."

"Maybe we'll even start—"

"—our own reality show. Yeah, I can see it now—"

" 'Keepin' Up With Da Cool Pooles.' Yeah—"

"—folks, we're ba-ack on to-op! You think Momma and Daddy Poole will go for it?"

"Mom? Yeah, for sure. Moms always love reality TV. But Daddy Poole? I sure—"

"—hope we can persuade him."

"No problem, we'll just hire Daddy Poole to work for us then. He's broke now anyway—"

"—which is why we're here in the first place. . . . Yeow, Cherry, something's got a hold of my leg!"

While talking, the twins had advanced to the edge of the swimming pool, sat down there and had begun washing the blood off of themselves.

And so they'd not seen the mermaid until it was almost too late. And anyway, the mermaid had swum towards them on their blinded left side.

This mermaid was black with braided hair, had a very long tail and had even longer teeth than both the human centipede and bat-men had had. The mermaid was grinning, the gill slits in her neck squirting out jets of water, as she pulled Cherry (or was it actually Berry now?) into the swimming pool.

Unwilling to lose her twin sister, Berry matched the mermaid for strength, gripping Cherry under her armpits and pulling hard.

Not wanting to get their shotguns wet, before sitting down by the pool, the twins had placed the weapons on two deck chairs near the wall of the chamber; which meant the shotguns were now well out of reach. Before Berry (or Cherry?) would be able to dash over and retrieve one of them, the mermaid was certain to have pulled her sister underwater.

So it was now a tug-of-war. The black mermaid had a clear physical advantage, but Berry's desperation substituted for strength and she finally managed to haul Cherry completely out of the water.

The twins dashed to the deck chairs for their shotguns. Nodding to each other, they raised them and pointed them at the mermaid.

"We fire on three! One, two . . . WOW! Hold on, sis!"

Cherry and Berry lowered their guns and stared.

Cheated of her prey, the black mermaid had reared up out of the water

"Are you certain she's really a mermaid?" Berry asked in horror as more and more of the lady-freak's body came out of the water. "Her tail is—"

"—so long that she looks like a modified sea snake."

"Yeah, that tail looks close to fifteen feet long. What do you call a sea-serpent woman?"

"Exactly that, I guess. Wow, check out all the surgical scars along her tail, like she's made up of—"

"—lotsa people. Wow, that's just so frigging creepy. Are you—"

"—okay, sis?"

"Yeah, I'm fine. But she gave us a shock for sure."

They aimed at the dusky sea-serpent woman again, but didn't fire. She was staring hungrily at them, daring them to come near to the pool's edge again. She looked ravenous enough to lunge at them (her serpent tail was easily long enough to cover the intervening distance), but their lack of fear clearly made her cautious.

And then, as if she suddenly realized she was endangering herself by being so provocative, she flung up her hands to cover her face and began sinking back down into the troubled pool water.

Cherry and Berry watched the sea-serpent woman vanish underwater, her long black braids floating on the swimming pool surface for a moment before disappearing also. The girls took a couple of cautious steps closer to the water and looked for her, but the edge of the pool now hid her from view.

"Let's go find somewhere else to get clean. We can't wash here with her in there."

"You know," one of them said as they stepped out of the chamber with the swimming pool. "It's really great—"

"—that we didn't kill the sea-serpent woman. Yeah, I know. Because since we didn't kill her, we can—"

"—feed that nasty Fatima Noori to her."

"Yeah, dropping Fatima in there will—"

"—really teach her not to leave us hanging like she did."

"Hope we find her soon; real soon."

"Yeah, I'm hurting so much because of her and I feel so damn bitchy now—"

"—and you know it sucks sea snake eggs to be a one-eye bitch."

CHAPTER 32

Karen

Once Emily was dead and eaten, the zombies turned their full attention to Karen.

Two of their number already had hold of Karen's arms and one of these had begun sucking on her wounded arm and licking up its restarted flow of blood.

Karen fought doggedly against the zombies. She kicked and punched at them with all her might, but she only shot them when she had no other choice. She was very aware that once her ammunition was finished, she would be too.

She discharged her gun into the left eye of the man slurping blood from her arm. His head exploded, and he fell away from her, showering his brain matter behind him.

But how are these zombies being animated? Karen wondered. *It isn't as if there's invisible wires dangling from the ceilings around here, controlling them like puppets. The ROC surely must've used some kind of experimental serum to bring all these dead people back to life. And in that case, while I doubt such a serum's effects can be permanent, I also doubt that I'm gonna survive long enough to witness it wear off.*

But really, this was no time for thinking. Another zombie was already taking the place of the one she'd just shot, and Karen knew she needed to break through them before she got totally swamped by the weight of numbers holding onto her and pulled down and out of sight beneath them.

She started fighting to reach the far-off morgue door. A zombie yanked her backwards and bit deeply into her shoulder. Howling in pain, she fired over her shoulder without looking back at the attacker. The noise of the gunshot so close to her ear almost deafened her, but she was rewarded by the zombie's letting go of her.

She elbowed a female zombie out of the way—but could one actually call her 'female' when she had that horrible male face?—slammed the butt of her pistol into the mouth of a male that was trying to reach her neck, and stomped hard on the belly of a third, 'pregnant' one who'd slipped on some blood and fallen to the floor, but was nonetheless trying to bite her legs. The 'pregnancy' exploded, giving birth to wads of greenbacks bearing Benjamin Franklin's face.

This cash is all mine if I survive this!

But it didn't look like she was going to survive this. There were too many zombies. Simply too many. Karen dreaded the awful moment when her gun would click empty and that would be it for her.

She'd now successfully cleared a space in the middle of the zombies. In the moments before they rushed at her again, Karen seriously considered shooting herself in the head.

I don't want to die like Emily just did; eaten like I'm a hamburger. Another bullet to the brain can't be any worse than the first time. She raised the gun to her forehead and placed it against her right temple.

But then she bravely changed her mind: *Oh no, I'm not killing myself. I can't commit suicide with this much money so close by; money I can have if I can just figure a way out of this mess.*

The zombies closed in on her again; but now too she saw Fatima striding in through the morgue entrance. Karen heaved a sigh of relief, glad she'd refrained from ending her life. Fatima was loaded with weapons; she looked like a walking armory.

"Hiya, I'm ba-ack!" Fatima called out, smiling at Karen.

The zombies turned to face the new arrival and some of them began to shamble towards her.

Karen scowled at the other girl. "What the hell took you so long? All you had to do was fetch two boxes of shells."

Fatima grinned. "Let's just say I had a religious crisis to deal with—terrorists in my brain. But, *wow* in a bad way! I honestly didn't believe my eyes when I saw this happening on the tower screen. Are they all really dead or were they faking?"

"How alive can you possibly be if you've already been autopsied?" Karen responded tiredly. "Throw me a gun, please."

"Here, catch!"

Fatima tossed a pump-action shotgun to Karen, who snatched it out of the air, shoved the barrel into a zombie's mouth and blew its entire head off.

With herself firing at one end of the morgue and Fatima doing the business at the other, they slowly began to 're-kill' the zombies.

CHAPTER 33

Khadija

Khadija Noori's problem now was that she wasn't naturally bloodthirsty. She'd had an ideological justification for her planned suicide bombing/mass murder; but now that that was no longer her motive, she felt somewhat lost at sea.

Take her current rescue of Karen Rogers for instance. It would be much easier (and smarter too) to just let the zombies eat her. But Khadija was too well brought up and schooled in religious virtues like loyalty to stand aloof and watch someone die without trying to help them.

No, she wasn't a coward, and was very prepared to fight for what she believed in, but what she believed in wasn't money. Her faith wasn't in the Almighty Dollar, but rather in Allah, the beneficent and merciful and in His holy messenger Muhammad. Where she was concerned, God and money were polar opposites.

But yeah, money has lots of benefits, she thought while sighting a pistol on a teenaged zombie's head and pulling the trigger. *At the most basic, with twenty-four million dollars in my bank account, I can do a whole lot for the folks at the homeless shelter.*

The zombie in question collapsed . . . *'Re-dead?' Is that the right term for it?*

Guns in both hands, Khadija was fighting her way over to Karen's side. The zombies had Karen surrounded near the center of the morgue, and even with the shotgun Khadija had thrown to her, it seemed just a matter of time before the undead swarmed all over her and took her down.

A runty zombie—a nine- or ten-year-old kid with that same horrible face they all had—was heading for Khadija. She shoved her left-hand pistol into its mouth and pulled the trigger.

The problem in here was that she couldn't fire indiscriminately. The light machine gun slung over her shoulder would make short work of the zombies, but it was also certain to knock Karen out of the picture too. Which, although very desirable in the long term, was something Khadija couldn't do.

Damn me and my damned conscience!

Now, if it had been the Poole twins in such a crisis, Khadija didn't see herself having the same scruples. Cherry and Berry creeped her out big-time.

And well, the other benefit of not blowing myself up is that I get to see father again; but will he ever forgive me for killing Fatima? Yeah, I'm sure he will, once I tell him what she was up to! One thing's for sure though, dad won't dare hand me over to the cops, since then he'll have no daughters left at all. Or, maybe I'll just lie that Fatima died on the show before I reached her . . .

As she pushed her way between the morgue tables, Khadija wondered if maybe the eight contestants on the *Final Girl* reality show had been selected primarily because they basically weren't violent and self-seeking people, or at least didn't appear to be. And if that was so, was the prize money supposed to reveal the depths that basically 'good' people would sink to to enrich themselves? *Emily was a nurse, they're trained to save lives. Karen's a cop, same thing. My sister* (now she felt a twinge of regret), *was a goody-two-shoes to the extreme . . . then the mother and stepdaughter. The stepdaughter was harmless enough, and the stepmom was preggered, so she'd pass as nurturing sort of character.*

Her theory sort of broke down there . . . but she tried to take it to a conclusion:

The twins completely love one another, can't do a thing without each other. And the hooker? Well, a prostitute is sort of a public wife, isn't she? The key word here being 'public,' which implies a sort of misplaced generosity with her body.

She stopped searching for a meaning to the madness, and instead blew away another zombie's head, waited till it collapsed to the floor, and stepped over it.

And then she'd successfully shot a path through the zombies and was standing next to Karen, who'd just rolled a morgue table between herself and the approaching horde. Karen looked a real mess by this point, with zombie gore all over her; lots of zombie brains and blood and pieces of shattered skulls. But except for the wound in her arm which had originally made Emily bring her in here, she seemed okay.

"We need to get out of here already," she told Karen, tugging on her arm. "Let's go, go, go!"

Karen shook her head. "We can't! The money is hidden in the zombies!"

Khadija did a double-take. "Huh, hidden where? What are you talking about, money in the zombies?"

Karen blew a clutching zombie arm away, in the process detaching it from its owner, swiped a mess of exploded undead flesh off her face, and then pointed to the corpses strewn across the morgue floor. "I meant what I said, Fatima. The money is hidden inside the zombies."

Fatima? Just in time, Khadija remembered that she was supposed to be her sister now. She looked down at the corpses Karen was gesturing at and now noticed the blood-splattered packets of money around them. She grimaced when she realized that most of the dead zombies were spilling money from their reopened Y-incisions.

With a horrified look on her face, Khadija turned back to stare at Karen, who was busy reloading her shotgun from a box of shells that she'd placed on the table. "Okay, so we re-kill them all, and then argue over the money ourselves. Is that the plan?" At the moment there were maybe ten zombies left alive in the morgue, but they were having trouble climbing over the bodies of their fallen comrades.

Karen nodded. "Yeah. Except you've a better one."

"This one's fine. We can team up to take on the twin goon squad too."

Karen looked surprised. "The twins are still alive?"

"Yeah, they both look like shit now though. Kinda poetic, seeing as they already act shitty."

Karen shoved her reloaded shotgun into the gut of a fat zombie and blew it across the room. She was about to fire again, but paused when Khadija grabbed her by the elbow and shook her.

"What the hell do you think you're doing?" Khadija angrily enquired.

"What the hell do you mean, what the hell am I doing? I'm doing what we just agreed on: shooting the damn zombies."

"Yeah yeah, I'm cool with that," Khadija retorted. "But don't shoot them in their bellies—that's where our money is hidden and we don't want to perforate it with holes. Shoot them in the head; that's how you kill zombies."

Karen nodded. "That's what I was doing originally, but it's easy to forget they're our paycheck when they're trying to eat us." She turned to shoot a zombie edging around the side of the table. "Don't worry, I'll try to remem—"

Karen had just slipped on some zombie brains. Her legs shot forward, the shotgun flew out of her hands, and as she fell back, her head struck a sharp metal projection on the wall—part of the frame of a shelf that had been removed.

The rod punched completely through Karen's head and exited through her left eye.

If Khadija was surprised by this unexpected turn of events, she was even more surprised when the zombies dragged Karen's corpse down off the metal rod. They tugged her free with such force that her head cracked completely open, the rod acting like a crowbar and levering off the top of Karen's skull.

Khadija gasped open-mouthed. *Why are there wires inside her head? What the . . . ? Hey, there's no brains in her head at all, just a mass of wires! . . . And . . . and is that a hard drive in there too? What is she, a robot? But no, she's flesh and blood too . . . sort of . . . What's the movie name for things like this? Ah . . . ah . . . Android! That's right, she's an android? What the . . . ?"*

Four zombies were already pulling Karen's corpse to pieces, and their dismantling her merely confirmed Khadija's suspicion. A mass of multicolored wires spilled from Karen's chest the moment the zombies got it open, and her heart—which was still beating furiously—seemed half-plastic and had a pulsing green thing sticking out of it.

Oh yes, she is an androi— "Yeow!"

Still horrified, Khadija spun around to find a zombie biting her right arm. She placed the barrel of the pistol in her left hand against the zombie's nose and fired. The gun clicked empty, so instead she shoved its barrel deep into both of the zombie's eyes, bursting them and blinding it. And then, while it tried to understand why it couldn't see her anymore, she shifted her other gun from her right hand to her left and blew the zombie away. Once its brains were gone, she prized its teeth out of her arm.

After one more scared glance at Karen's corpse, Khadija dropped her pistol on the table, unslung the light machine gun from her shoulder and began firing at the zombies.

With no need now to worry about hitting Karen, the battle with the zombies was over almost before it had begun. Mindful of the money in their bellies, Khadija kept the machine gun at head-height and swung it left and right until all of the undead (including the ones behind her who were feeding on Karen's corpse) were properly dead again.

Then, sighing hard, she dropped the machine gun on the morgue table and knelt over Karen's remains for a proper look.

The detective's body had largely been stripped bare of flesh. Multicolored wires were clearly visible trailing her bones.

Khadija searched for Karen's head, which had gotten separated from her body. She found the mostly-intact head underneath a zombie, and picked it up to examine it.

Yeah, no doubt about it—the girl was an android alright. And not the cellphone operating system either.

Though its exterior was clearly flesh and blood, the interior of Karen's head was a combination of plastic and metal, a mass of intricate circuitry with no brain matter at all; and yes, there was a hard drive in there—the small laptop kind but lacking a case—bolted firmly in place. Two fat cables ran from the hard drive into a fleshy white bulb which Khadija assumed to be what scientists called the medulla.

The shock of seeing this was almost too much for Khadija to bear.

I'd never have suspected she wasn't real, not in a million years. She looked, talked and acted like a real woman, with all the right motions: swaying hips, face and hand gestures, and everything. Wow! To be able to do this, the ROC are definitely light years ahead of everyone else in—

"Hey, Fatima, bitch!"

"Yeah, bitch, where are you?"

Khadija winced. *Oh no, not those damn Poole twins.* Then she smiled coldly. Well, here at least were two idiots that she wouldn't mind shooting, if only to rid the world of them.

I'm no longer a twin myself, but those two give Gemini sets a bad name.

She dropped Karen's head and stood up, letting her fingers rest on top of her machine gun.

"Hey, there she is! Hey, Fatima—"

"—you damn evil bitch—"

"What the hell do you two want?" Khadija quickly interrupted before they got into full throttle with their gobbledygook speech. She hated their disturbing and disorienting habit of finishing one another's sentences, with the one who had been interrupted nodding in agreement, as if her twin was now saying exactly what she was herself thinking and had meant to say.

Both girls simultaneously indicated their bloody left eye sockets. "This is all your fault, Fatima. You should—"

"—have helped us back there. But you—"

"—didn't and that damn boogeyman—"

"—mutilated us."

Khadija was already growing tired of being her sister. These two idiots opposite her were obviously angry with Fatima for some silly reason, and now they were blaming her for her sister's mistakes.

Exactly how many other people has Fatima offended in her silly life that I'm going to have to deal with? Maybe I can strike a deal with Miriam and simply revert back to my own name after the show is over. It isn't as if the viewers are gonna be keeping tabs on me. Yes . . . if I go home as Fatima, dad may never know the difference . . .

The Poole twins had been staring angrily at Khadija while she weighed the merits and demerits of her current situation. Both of them had let their shotguns fall to their sides so they could show her their similarly-mutilated left hands.

Khadija laughed at the girls. She found it impossible not to.

"Cherry, she's making fun of us!"

"I'm Berry, not that it makes much—"

"—difference now. The real question is—"

"—how are we going to pay her back for what she did to us?"

Now sensing a determination in the twins, Khadija moved her hand fully onto the machine gun's grip. All she needed to do now was snatch it up and she could easily perforate both young women with lots of holes. There would be no contest whatsoever, because before they could fire at her, the twins had to first swing their shotguns up onto their wounded hands and aim them.

"Oh yeah? So what are you two one-eyed freaks gonna do about it?" Khadija asked in a voice dripping with scorn.

"She's taunting us!"

"Yes she is! She's really pissing us off and—"

"—asking for it. And she's—"

"—really going to get it."

Oh, how Khadija hated this weird way that the Poole twins spoke. But she let them ramble on. There was something incredibly pathetic about them. It was like watching two chickens who had no idea they were about to be roasted.

"Are we gonna kill her?" the blue haired twin asked.

"No, we'll just pay her back in her—"

"—own coin. Yeah, do to her like she did to us!"

"The black sea-serpent woman upstairs won't like it. You promised her dinner."

"Well, that's just too bad, isn't it? We're too angry now. An eye for an eye—"

"—a thumb for a thumb, and a—"

"—forefinger for a forefinger!"

"We're gonna disfigure you too, Fatima, you selfish bitch."

Intense anger on their faces, the two of them began walking towards Khadija, shoving the intervening autopsy tables out of the way.

Khadija decided she'd had enough. It was time to put these two fools out of their misery.

She grabbed the machine gun off the table and fired, sweeping the weapon left to mow down the twins.

But she got off just one shot to the right of them and then the gun jammed.

She stared down at it in horror, while across from her Cherry and Berry gaped back in equal horror.

"Sis, she tried to kill us. Fatima just tried—"

"—to kill us. Oh, she's evil, Berry! She's so damn evil!"

"Am I Cherry or Berry? And which one of us are you?"

"IT DOESN'T MATTER! We'll sort ourselves out later. For now, just shoot the damn bitch!"

"Yeah, let's kill the silly girl! Like she ain't already hurt us enough. Let's get—"

"—the nasty bitch. Don't you dare blame us now, Fatima, 'cos—"

"—this is all your own damn fault!"

While ranting at hyper-speed, the girls were simultaneously swinging their shotguns up and aiming them.

Oh shit, Khadija thought.

She flung the machine gun down and grabbed for the pistol on the table . . .

CHAPTER 34

Cherry/Berry

. . . But the twins were much faster.

The first twin shotgun blasts completely destroyed Khadija's face. The gun she'd been about aiming at Cherry and Berry dropped from her fingers and she stood there wobbling, until a second pair of shotgun blasts blew what remained of her head and neck off of her shoulders.

Khadija's corpse collapsed onto the pile of dead zombies behind her.

"Bye bye, Fatima!" the twins waved.

Then after high-fiving themselves, Cherry and Berry crossed to where Khadija's headless body lay.

"She really should have just let us pluck her left eye out. She should—"

"—have taken her punishment like a woman."

"Hey, Fatima biatch slut, we're the Poole Twins."

"Sometimes also known as the Cruel Twins."

"Screw you, corpse!"

"Yeah, you're in great company here in the morgue!"

"Hey, Berry, something's—"

"—wrong. Yeah, I know. What's this weird MPJ tattoo—"

"—on her arm? I don't recall seeing that earlier. No, I don't—"

"—either. But she must've had it, right? We just didn't—"

"—notice. We must've just imagined that we didn't. Unless you think she's twins too like us?"

"Nah, you're right, we didn't notice it. Fatima, a twin? Berry, that's ridiculous. Twins never act as mean as she did to us."

"I'm Cherry! I'm Cherry!"

"Yeah, and sometimes we're both Berry too. Hey, sis, why is there money scattered all over the floor and—"

"—spilling out of the corpses too? Sis, I think we've found—"

"—the twenty-four million dollars prize money."

"Quick, quick! Count, count! Who else—"

"—is left alive on the show? Let's number all—"

"—the dead. Okay, here I go: Fatima?"

"Dead, stupid bitch." A kick to the fresh corpse, which was dribbling blood from its truncated neck.

"Stepmom and stepdaughter?"

"Both dead too. Mom killed daughter and was then eaten by centiperson."

"Karen the cop?"

"Dead. Zombies ate her for dinner. Here's her head over here. Something odd-looking about it—"

"—though. Yeah, but let's ignore that for now, sis. Keep counting. That's four—"

"—so far. Okay, the hooker?"

"Mermaids and those fish-baby freaks got her. Ugh, who'd do that—"

"—to little kids?"

"That's five now. Still one more person alive besides us. Hey, where's—"

"—the nurse? I think that's her over there. Lemme go see. . . . Yeah, it's her alright, though half of her face is missing."

"That's all six accounted for then. Berry, I think we've won the game!"

"I'm Cherry. Oh, fuck it—Yeah, yeah, yeah, yeah!"

Shrieking in delight the twins began dancing around the morgue.

"YEAH! YEAH! YEAH! YEAH! WE DID IT, BITCHES! WE WON THE REALITY SHOW!"

"Hey, twins!"

Jubilant and triumphant in their celebration, Cherry and Berry at first didn't hear the new voice.

"HEY, MIRIAM HELLER TO POOLE TWINS! I'M TALKING TO YOU TWO!"

This time the voice was much louder than the noise the girls were making and they noticed it. They turned toward its source—a giant monitor over near the morgue door, which despite having been perforated by one of Fatima's bullets, was still working. Miriam Heller's face was displayed on the screen.

"Why doesn't she look pleased with us?" one of the girls asked the other. Then she addressed the screen: "Hey, Miriam, we've won, haven't we?"

"Yes and no. Okay, girls, you've gotten rid of the last competitor, and technically you're the winners, but there's a problem. This reality show is called *Final Girl*, not *Final Girls*. Only one of you can win, not both of you."

Cherry leaned over and whispered to Berry. "I told you the witch hates us! She's—"

"—about stacking the odd against us again."

"HEY, LISTEN TO ME!" Miriam snapped.

They turned to her again. "Yeah? So what now?"

"Well, you've found the money, and there's no boogeymen nearby to stop you. Besides, in your current location you'll easily be able to defend against any attacker coming in through the door anyway, so we'll agree that you've successfully held onto it also. But now, you two must face off against each other. Winner takes all."

"WHAT!?" Cherry and Berry shrieked at Miriam. "NEVER, NEVER, NEVER, NEVER, NEVER!"

The onscreen Miriam Heller rolled her eyes at them. "Sorry, girls, that's the rules."

"Hey, but, Miriam . . ." Berry slowly explained, "both of us, I mean Cherry and I—"

"—in actuality we're just one person. We're really—"

"—one human soul stuck in two bodies. So you see—"

"—there's simply no way that we're ever gonna fight one another."

Miriam shook her head. "Sorry, girls, but that excuse won't work. You've still gotta fight yourselves."

The one-eyed twins looked sadly at each other for a few moments, then leaned their heads towards one another and did some whispering. Then they nodded and turned towards Miriam again. Now they were both grinning broadly.

"Hmmm, alright, if that won't work—"

"—how 'bout this solution then? Hey, we're just wondering . . ."

CHAPTER 35

Miriam

" . . . How about if you use half of one of us and half of the other to make one complete person. Then we can—"

"—both win, right? I mean, that way we won't be breaking the rules and—"

"—we know the ROC has the surgical means to combine us like they did with—"

"—the freaks and human centipedes. Yeah, and so that we're really combined, you can even use half of each of our faces. No, we might like—"

"—to have two heads so we can still talk to each other afterwards and—"

"ALRIGHT, ALRIGHT, YOU BOTH WIN!" Standing in her Control Center, Miriam yelled the words at the Poole twins.

Hearing this, the two bloodied girls down in the tower morgue again began leaping about in delight; while the games-mistress sank down onto her couch and stared at them in horror.

What they'd just suggested was too horrendous to even consider and yet the earnest way the girls had said it—and oh, God, that scary way they had of switching between themselves midsentence—actually had Miriam believing that maybe the Poole twins really did share a single soul.

The really worrying thing was that the now one-eyed girls hadn't been joking; they'd been dead serious, with whichever sister wasn't speaking at the time nodding her total agreement. And Miriam didn't doubt that the Red Octopus Corporation would be very willing to at least attempt to combine the two girls into one person, either with one head or two; something that Miriam certainly didn't want to happen to them, as it seemed a disgusting fate.

That'll just result in a prettier version of a human centipede. Oh, no, I'm not letting that freak Operator anywhere near these two girls.

"They *both* win?" her husband's surprised voice came over the intercom.

"Oh, yes, yes, darling, let them both win," she replied Aaron,. "They're clearly not going to fight one another, no matter what we do, and they look so alike anyway, that it'll still be like just one person won, so . . ."

"Yeah, sure," Aaron readily agreed. "I'll set up a dual banner with them both as winners. I suspect it'll be a popular decision with the ROC viewers too."

Miriam relaxed in her chair and watched the celebrating girls.

Thankfully, on hearing that they could both win, the Poole twins didn't press their request to be cut up and joined together.

However, they did have another request:

"Hey, Miriam, how much will new eyes cost us? We need—"

"—one each. And thumbs too—"

"—and index fingers. Cherry, don't you dare forget our forefingers. We can't—"

"—have just three fingers on our left hands. Yeah, you're very right, sis."

"Yeah, Miriam, Berry and I need two new left eyes and two new left thumbs and forefingers. So how much?"

"Yeah, we know for sure that—"

"—the ROC can clone some for us—"

"—and attach them to us and we don't mind paying for 'em."

"Yeah, 'cos we're rich now!"

Miriam was so relieved that the Poole twins had forgotten their horrid idea of being combined into one person that she felt especially generous.

She laughed. "Oh, considering the fantastic show you girls just put on, your new eyes and thumbs are on the house."

Then she poured herself a glass of sparkling champagne, and, while a golden banner announcing the Poole twins as the winners came over the screen, cast her mind back over the two hours and forty-five minutes that the show had run.

Yes, this *Final Girl* show had 'broken' the Dark Web; its ratings were sky-high. And the ROC sponsors were already asking if they could hold its second edition this year instead of next year.

Miriam didn't mind the rescheduling. *It merely means more money for Aaron and I,* she thought with a smile. But then she stared at the screen and her smile immediately vanished.

But no more twins as contestants, she thought grimly, remembering the whole Fatima Noori/Khadija Noori terrorist mess, and watching the two gored-up winners hug and dance in celebration of their victory. *I've had enough of twins for a lifetime tonight. Who would ever have imagined that looking like another person could turn out to be such a pain in the ass?*

Then, after a sip of champagne, she asked her husband: "Darling, any word yet about that other thing?"

'That other thing' was Karen Rogers. Yes, Miriam had been surprised to discover that the prize money was hidden in the corpses in the morgue. And she'd been even more surprised when those corpses had begun getting up and attacking the contestants.

But she had been completely shocked to discover that Karen Rogers was an android—a robot made of meat. No one had told she or her husband about that.

"Yeah," Aaron replied over the intercom. "The ROC have filled me in on that. Apparently Karen was some kinda defense project that they're handling for the US government. Classified 'top-level security' and all that. Karen was their first finished prototype. They put her in the show as a field test—to find out how she'd cope in a constantly stressed environment, with danger at every turn. Rumor has it that the USA's Joint Chiefs of Staff watched the show tonight."

"But I thought she was a Salt Lake City policewoman. That's what her file said."

"Yeah, she was . . . until that hooker Lexi blew her brains out. So the ROC rebuilt Karen's personality, stored it on a hard drive, and stuck the hard drive in her head . . . then they reanimated her body. To keep the contest fair, they didn't enhance her in any way. She had exactly the same human vulnerabilities as the others." He laughed. "And well, hon, you just watched the rest of it . . ."

The End.

ABOUT THE AUTHOR

Wol-vriey is Nigerian, and quite tall.

He believes there actually are things that go bump in the night.

He writes horror fiction—for adults only, please. And also some surrealist stuff.

Wol-vriey blogs at: *http://oddityfarm.wordpress.com*

WOL-VRIEY
BIZARRO AND TRANSGRESSIVE FICTION

BOSTON POSH (BUD MALONE #1)

In 2028 AD, the USA is a nation ravaged by hungry dragons and dinosaurs. In Boston, Massachusetts, private eye Bud Malone is hired to rescue a kidnapped heiress. But nothing is as it seems.

Malone works to unravel a tangled web involving Boston Chinatown, a 200-year-old woman with a 9-year-old body, white robots, a human-liver-eating psychopath, a golem, a porcelain dragon, and a snake goddess with a crush on him. There's also a woman obsessed with chicken sex. Then Malone meets Posh Lane, a gorgeous call girl who's desperate to quit her pimp.

Romantic sparks ignite between Posh and Malone, but Posh's past suddenly catches up with her in a BIG way. To save Posh, Malone agrees to run a quest for Earth's new rulers, the Forks. But, Malone has no idea that agreeing to the Fork's odd request will send him on the weirdest trip he's ever been on in his life.

BOSTON CORPSE (BUD MALONE #2)

MAGIC CAN BE MURDER! - Drag queen Lucy Tang is back in Boston, and is hell-bent on settling her vindetta against casino owner Sookie Ling. And suddenly, Bud Malone, PI, has the case of his life to resolve.

When Boston's robot police force are baffled by a mind transfer case, they come to Malone for help. The one person who can likely help Malone out here is the witch Soledad Bathory. But Soledad seems to know a lot more than she's telling him. It's a case not made easier when Malone meets Soledad's beautiful cousin, Josephine 'Slave' Bailey. Slave has her own plans for Malone, most of which involve teaching him BDSM and making him her new Master.

Oh, and Rick Rogers owes Sookie Ling a whole lot of money, a gambling debt that's going to be literally Hell to pay!

BOSTON CORPSE - Not your average detective novel!

Burning Bulb
PUBLISHING

WOL-VRIEY
BIZARRO AND TRANSGRESSIVE FICTION

BOSTON LUST (BUD MALONE #3)

"Bless it, Father, for she has sinned."

Seven murdered gay women, all their bodies completely drained of blood. All also with large parts of their bodies dissolved away like acid has been pumped into their veins.

Bud Malone has to find the female vampire preying on Boston's lesbian population.

Then Malone meets the beautiful Trudi Carmen and the case gets even more tangled. Trudi needs Malone's help in recovering a ring that's gone missing. But how in the world is one little black ring related to either the dead women or their killer?

Resolving this case will lead Malone deep into Lucy Tang's legacy—The Abstracta. And then to the city of Genesis.

Boston Lust—Just when you thought Bean Town was safe to visit again.

HELL DANCER

Six people find themselves trapped in Detention, a nightmare realm where the demonic Schoolmaster is hell-bent on reforming them . . . until they die.

Porn superstar Venus Deluxe came to Springfield, MA to party, and next found her life hanging by a thread. One wrong answer will mean her death.

Suspended BPD detective Tanya Rockford was trying to stop one kind of violence, but found a terrifying another. With her and her companion's lives hanging in the balance, it's going to take all of her courage and resourcefulness to escape this hell she's stumbled into.

Porn stud Chad Cannon has made a career from his ten-inch penis. Here in Detention, however, it's his brains that matter. He'll soon be hoping all the pot he's smoked over the years hasn't completely messed up his memory.

The three students, Sherri, Jordan, and Mike? They were all just in the wrong place at the right time. Will anyone survive Detention? The evil Schoolmaster doesn't plan on letting that happen . . .

Burning Bulb
PUBLISHING

WOL-VRIEY
BIZARRO AND TRANSGRESSIVE FICTION

VAGINA MUNDI

Rachel Risk is a professional thief with super-strong hair that can stretch like tentacles to manipulate objects. Ashley Status has both a digitally augmented brain, and 'muscle-purses' in her arms and legs in which she stores inflatable objects—cars, guns, rocket launchers, etc.

When Raye is framed as the fall girl in a jewel robbery, the pair flee Chicago's vengeful robot gangsters and take refuge in the Hotel Bizarre, where the gorgeous 'vagina singer,' Femina, is performing for a week.

But the Hotel Bizarre is even stranger than its name suggests, and very soon Raye and Ash are involved in an deadly adventure, a struggle for survival the likes of which they'd never imagined possible—with loads of deviant sex, drugs, music, and violence at every turn. And just what is the old woman in the skin desert really doing with all those cats glued to her walls?

VAGINA MUNDI—a Bizarro Hymn in praise of WOMAN!

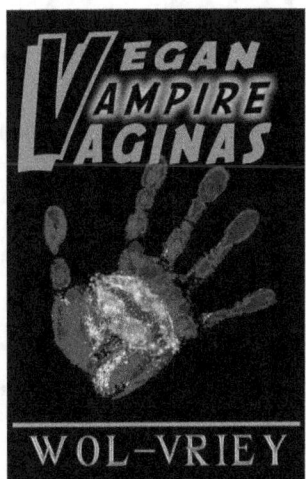

VEGAN VAMPIRE VAGINAS

The biggest bank heist in US history. And Tom Palmer can't remember pulling it off. And no, this isn't your standard case of amnesia. After a one-night-stand gone horribly wrong, Boston salesman Tom Palmer wakes up with a vagina implanted in his left hand. Then his day gets worse.

Tom is transported across space-time to a nightmare version of Boston, one where the Bizarro virus has transformed half the population into cannibals. Worst of all, Tom discovers that in this new Boston, he's the infamous gangster Pussypalm, wanted for robbing the Federal Reserve Bank of Boston a year ago. He also learns that the vagina in his hand is prophetic, i.e. it talks . . . after sex.

With 130 people left dead during his bank heist and six billion dollars missing, Tom knows he's living on borrowed time. It is in his best interests not to remember anything. Because once he does . . .

Burning Bulb
PUBLISHING

WOL-VRIEY
BIZARRO AND TRANSGRESSIVE FICTION

VEGAN ZOMBIE APOCALYPSE

In the post-apocalypse worlderness, zombies rule the earth. They're allergic to meat, and brains literally make them explode. Zombies now eat blood potatoes, parasitic tubers grown in the flesh of humancows corralled in maximum security farms. Two fugitives meet in the ancient ruins of Texas. The first is Soil 15-f, a womancow who's escaped her farm a week before she's due to be killed and her blood potato crop harvested. The second fugitive is Able Kane, former head necros food technician, now sentenced to death for heresy. But Soil is no ordinary humancow.

Unknown to herself, she's the vegan zombie agricultural revolution, and the zombies desperately want her back. And the necros equally desperately want Able Kane dead. He's fled with a forbidden discovery which will reshape the world for the worse if used. And Able is just hardheaded/misguided enough to use it.

MELANIE NEMESIS CATCHPOLE

In Springfield, Massachusetts, Melanie Catchpole is hired to fetch back a magic teddy bear worth millions of dollars from a warehouse across town. Problem is, the warehouse is down in Springfield' O-Zone—that totally weird sector of the city where Bizarro fell to Earth. The 'O' is a fairytale land, a place where dreams and nightmares literally live and breathe..

Worse still, the gingers—mutant cannibals—prowl the O. The gingers have already eaten everyone else Melanie's employers sent to get back the magic teddy bear.

Accompanied by the handsome but ruthless Doug Fisher (who she finds sexy but doesn't dare entrust her heart to), Melanie enters the O-Zone. Melanie and Doug are instantly caught up in an adventure they'd never have believed credible even if written as fiction . . . and Melanie's used to experiencing the very weird as the norm.

And now, additionally, there's a mystery to unravel: What does the dark, freezing-cold being called The Fixer want with Mary, the barkeep's daughter?

Burning Bulb
PUBLISHING

WOL-VRIEY
BIZARRO AND TRANSGRESSIVE FICTION

BIG TROUBLE IN LITTLE ASS

From Bizarro master storyteller Wol-vriey comes a truly weird western tale that will leave you awe-struck and on the edge of your seat...

In the town named Little Ass, tight-assed prostitute Rosa overhears a gunslinger's plans to assassinate rancher Edison Bennett. Once the badass Bennett learns of the plot, he ensures there'll be hell to pay for any attempt on his life!

Yes, it's going to take all of gunslinger Jude's shooting prowess, his eclectic collection of strange firearms, a trusty horse that requires an owners' manual, and the help of the lovely and invigorating Nell (who's EXTREMELY odd when the going gets weird), to survive the Bizarro hell that Edison Bennett unleashes in order to hold onto the land that he'd stolen from Madam Zizi.

BIZARRO 101 (A BASIC PRIMER)

Welcome to the strange place:

A collection of 37 flash fiction stories designed to introduce one to the Bizarro/New Weird Genre.

Weird, dreamy, nightmarish, absurd, sad, surreal, humorous . . . this collection of tales is all this and more.

***

"This primer is the very essence of any and all styles and types of Bizarro writing. Wol-vriey collects, distills, and bottles up these 37 tiny stories for your sensory enjoyment. This is an absolute must-read for anyone new to the genre, because it demonstrates the scope of what Bizarro is, and what it can be."
        –Teresa Pollack, Bizarro commentator and blogger

Burning Bulb
PUBLISHING

WOL-VRIEY
BIZARRO AND TRANSGRESSIVE FICTION

Dr. Orgasm

Courtney Taylor is young, intelligent, beautiful, and successful. She also has a boyfriend who loves her deeply. The problem is, no matter what Courtney does, she can't climax during sex.

When Florence Rigid's communist forces destroy the city of Metaphor, Courtney and her friends Teresa, Highball, Miki, and Heather are cast into the midst of a quest to find the only person able to save the land of Innuendo—Dr. Carol Orgasm, wanted by the communists for developing the O-Pill, a wonder drug that grants women sexual ecstasy on demand.

The communists will do anything to get their hands on the O-Pill and prevent its reaching the millions of Innuendo's women. But Courtney desperately wants that pill too. And so it's now a race between Courtney and the communists to find Dr. Orgasm first.

And Courtney has no choice but to win this race. She must win it: For her own orgasm . . . and for the freedom of female sexuality everywhere.

PUSSY TRANSMISSION

Pussy Transmission were the most decadent Pop Art ensemble of the 90's. Led by the beautiful painter Isis Lynch the trio revolutionized the art world. Then suddenly, without explanation, Pussy Transmission vanished into historical obscurity. Now, twenty years later, three women come to Lynch Place. Lily and Nina are journalists desperate to interview Isis Lynch. Raven, on the other hand, wants to find her boyfriend, who's gone missing inside Isis's house. Raven's worried—she's heard that Pussy Transmission broke up because Isis began dabbling in black magic . . . with devastating results. All three women will shortly wish they'd never left home. Particularly once the rats in Lynch Place start warning them that they're going to die . . . and Raven meets Betty Butcher, the bouncy supernatural psycho who's intent on chopping her into bits. Pussy Transmission, Baby! Just because . . .

Burning Bulb
PUBLISHING

WOL-VRIEY
BIZARRO AND TRANSGRESSIVE FICTION

GIRLS ARE NOT SMILING

Welcome To The Road Trip From Hell

Pagan is demon-possessed.

Lori is suicidal.

Britt is just terminally pissed off.

Meet three young Boston women on the run from the law, each with problems that will fuse into more than the sum of their individual parts, becoming a holocaust of sex and violence and terror, a literal rain of blood and horror and gore and evil.

And if that wasn't already bad enough, Pagan's pet demon is slowly transforming her into something both unspeakable and unholy. Truly, these girls aren't smiling.

BLUE NIGHTMARES

Consummate EVIL is coming. It is relentless and unavoidable. It is Blue.

Jessica Schreiber is seeing things. Very horrible things. Since arriving in Raynham for what should have been a relaxing vacation, she's been seeing *The Big Blue*.

Jessica is smelling things too—dead and rotting things that she can't see. She is sure those dead and rotting things are dead people. Lots of dead people.

Jessica's worst nightmares will soon become her reality. Her reality will soon become a terrifying nightmare.

The tentacled residents of the House of Death have a lot that they wish to show Jessica Schreiber. They have a lot that they wish to tell her. But will she survive long enough to learn their lessons?

Burning Bulb
PUBLISHING

WOL-VRIEY
BIZARRO AND TRANSGRESSIVE FICTION

BRAINCHEW

It was supposed to be a simple jewel heist, but it went badly wrong. Chuck got shot and died.

Lance hid his friend's corpse in the Pleasant Street Cemetery. But that was a big mistake—there was something undead, something extremely hungry . . . something eXXXtremely horrible, buried in the Pleasant Street Cemetery.

And Lance had just woken it up.

They called the monster Brainchew because it ate brains. Human brains. And it preferred those brains fresh from the heads . . . of the living.

And now it was awake again, Brainchew planned on feeding big-time tonight. Oh hell yes, it did.

BRAINCHEW 2: OUT OF THEIR HEADS

After Tiff Hooper recognizes Josh Penham, the man who abducted her and kept her in his basement and abused her, she brings her three friends to Raynham for a night of well-deserved revenge on him.

Only things don't go according to plan.

It is never a good idea to leave a corpse in Raynham's Pleasant Street Cemetery. You run the very real risk of awakening what lies underground there. And that thing—Brainchew—more horrible and more evil than anything the average mind conceives of even in its worst nightmares.

Brainchew is back! And this time the monster extra-hungry. But there are plenty of delicious human brains about tonight, and Brainchew intends to eat them all before dawn.

Burning Bulb
PUBLISHING

WOL-VRIEY
BIZARRO AND TRANSGRESSIVE FICTION

DARIA: AN EROTIC NIGHTMARE

Even the best laid women can go wrong.

Daria Simpson is HUNGRY. She's HUNGRY for sex and bloodshed and death.

Shelly Parker just wanted to have a threesome with her boyfriend Craig and her best friend Erica. Everything was shaping up nicely for their weekend of sexual fun and games, until they stopped at the creepy Crossway Diner and met Daria.

From the moment they met Daria, EVERYTHING went wrong for them; and it went wrong in the most horrific and terrifying of ways!

Daria: Paranormal service has been resumed.

WET BONES

Greg is about learning the hard way that you don't mess with Aunt Grace.

Nine completely fleshless skeletons recovered in the Massachusetts woods. Two detectives on the trail of a horrible, hungry monster.

Broken-hearted Allie Jackson has a date with a creature from Hell.

Things are about to get well out of hand for everyone, and in horrifying, terrifying ways they don't expect.

Burning Bulb
PUBLISHING

WOL-VRIEY
BIZARRO AND TRANSGRESSIVE FICTION

MR. UGLY

When a rotting corpse appears and starts butchering Raynham's youths, there's really only one question that needs answering:

Is this faceless and rotting monster Peter Howard, or isn't it?

Problem is, Peter Howard died 15 years ago. So how can he possibly be back from the dead and murdering people with such relentless and incredible brutality?

Peter's mother Malicia, who's just been released from the lunatic asylum may have the answers to the crazy puzzle, but the two detectives investigating the deaths don't even know the right questions to ask her yet.

BRUTAL

Jane Winters is 28 years old.

She works as a checkout cashier in a department store. She's an attractive woman with a winning personality. She has both a photographic memory and an I.Q. of 189.

She's met the man of her dreams.

But she's also a cannibal with a unique and very scary mode of operation.

The group known as TULIP (The Urban Legend Investigation People) are out to either prove or disprove the legend of Insane Jane.

But have TULIP bitten off more than they can chew?

Burning Bulb
PUBLISHING

WOL-VRIEY
BIZARRO AND TRANSGRESSIVE FICTION

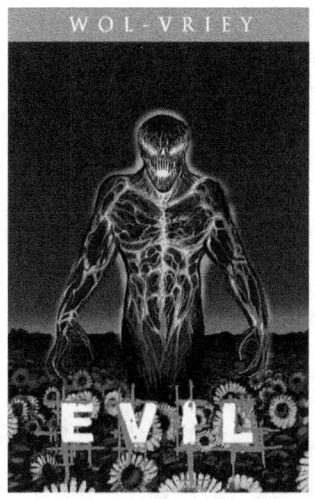

EVIL

The Evil began the week before Sylvia Stewart's 30th birthday.

Cathy Higgins died.

The Bargainer resurrected Cathy . . . for a price.

The price? Cathy's father Ronan had to plant some seeds for him.

But these were no ordinary seeds the Bargainer gave to Ronan Higgins. These were seeds from Hell: seeds which required human flesh as both soil and fertilizer.

And meanwhile, the unsuspecting Sylvia Stewart went ahead with the plans for her birthday party, which was to be held on Ronan Higgins' sunflower farm . . .

666

Ohio's State Route 666 stretches 14.7 miles between Zanesville and Dresden.

Most days, it's just a normal road with a funny name.

But for six minutes on the 6th of June each year, Route 666 becomes a gateway to somewhere else . . . a gateway to Hell.

Each year 13 unfortunates get trapped in the 666 underworld, with no way to get back home.

This year though, things are going to be very different. For one thing, there are currently a whole lot of turbulent human emotions at play in the underworld. And also . . . the psycho Al Gore is just about completing his collection of human heads.

And . . . what the hell is a church doing in Hell, of all places?

Burning Bulb
PUBLISHING

WOL-VRIEY
BIZARRO AND TRANSGRESSIVE FICTION

THE CLEAVERMAN

It began as a joke, a gag to pass the time that turned deadly. One rainy August night in Raynham, MA, nine friends jokingly invoke the evil phantom butcher called the Cleaverman.

These nine friends get a whole lot more than they ever bargained for. Because there's only one way to return the deadly Cleaverman back to the darkness he came from, and that is to solve his riddle, which starts: "Tell me the name of John Cleaverman's wife . . ."

And human beings being what we are, even with the Cleaverman out to butcher them all, our nine friends still manage to stir A WHOLE LOT of human misbehavior into the deadly mix.

At the rate they're going, it'll be a wonder if anyone survives THE CLEAVERMAN at all.

PERVERSE

When 21-year-old Heather Forrest accompanies three of her friends on a weekend trip up to Vermont, she has no idea what she's getting into.

Because, during a brief stop in the western Massachusetts woods, the girls get kidnapped and things go rapidly downhill from there. Soon Heather and her friends are fighting for their lives, fighting to survive the most perverted and impossible situation imaginable. And meanwhile, Hank Rollins is also in the woods, hunting the unholy monster that killed his wife and son . . . and he's hunting it with live human bait.

Oh yes, there will be blood. And there will be terror and buckets of gore also. And truly horrible atrocities will happen. Most definitely so.

Burning Bulb
PUBLISHING

WOL-VRIEY
BIZARRO AND TRANSGRESSIVE FICTION

THE VIRGIN

10 million dollars in prize money. 1000+ video cameras, lots of deadly weapons, 10 Suitors, 5 Virgins & 3 Hours . . . to keep your hymen intact.

Hailey Osborne wants to sell her virginity for a hundred thousand dollars. But then she's made an offer she really can't refuse: how about competing to win ten million dollars in a no-holds-barred underground game show, where all she has to do is remain a virgin?

There's just two problems:
1. Four other women also want that prize money.
2. There's ten suitors all contesting to take Hailey and the other virgins' precious hymens . . . by any means necessary . . .

But hey, it's just for 3 hours, right? How hard can it possibly be ? Hailey Osborne is about to find out.

THE BOOK OF ATROCITIES

Bestselling author Drake Melville has been missing for three years now. Drake vanished after publishing The Bleeding Oysters, an epic novel that set new standards for depictions of sleaze and depravity and human monstrosity in popular fiction. On vanishing, however, Drake Melville left a message for everyone, saying he'd 'left town' to go work on his follow-up novel The Book of Atrocities. The problem was, no one could find Drake. It seemed like he'd vanished off the face of the Earth. And now, three years later, Drake has just sent messages to his ex-wife Liz, his current (and abandoned) wife Melody; and his younger sister Chloe . . . asking them to meet him in Raynham, MA. Drake says he's now completed The Book of Atrocities and is ready to present it to the world. But there's a whole lot that Liz, Melody, and Chloe Melville don't know about Drake's Book of Atrocities. And unfortunately they're on their way to find out those excruciatingly painful truths. Because, see, Drake Melville is a VERY EVIL man with a VERY EVIL plan . . .

Burning Bulb
PUBLISHING

www.ingramcontent.com/pod-product-compliance
Lightning Source LLC
Chambersburg PA
CBHW070010260626
47159CB00005B/1743